# Swinging On A Star

## HOLLYWOOD REBELS AND ROMEOS
### BOOK TWO

## OLIVIA JAYMES

SWINGING ON A STAR

# Swinging On A Star

**It's all make-believe. Smoke and mirrors for the press and paparazzi.**

Carrie Johnson, an ordinary businesswoman, has agreed to a fake romance with mega movie star Maxwell Hayes. He needs to show he's not heartbroken after his nasty and public divorce. She wants her family and friends to believe she's not devastated after being dumped by her fiancé. It's a mutually beneficial arrangement.

Carrie's not the type for designer gowns and expensive jewelry, but she finds herself getting dressed up, walking red carpets, and posing for the cameras. With Max at her side, she's dancing the night away and having a ball. Life with the gorgeous actor is better than she'd ever dreamed.

Max may play the handsome and charming prince for the tabloids, but Carrie's no princess. This relationship has an expiration date, and there will be no happily ever after. It would be crazy to let her heart get involved. Wouldn't it?

# *Prologue*

TWO DAYS AGO...

Max wanted to bang his phone repeatedly onto the bar until it was smashed into a million tiny pieces. Then maybe his soon to be ex-wife wouldn't be able to get a hold of him. She'd randomly called him this evening to let him know she had a truck backed up to the house they'd shared in London and was loading it full of their belongings.

The house she'd abandoned months ago, along with him.

Instead of losing his temper, he'd coolly responded that he was glad to see all the rubbish go that would have reminded him of her. Now he could start fresh and she could have the castoffs from their marriage and think of him every day.

However, when he'd hung up it was all he could do not

to sling his mobile into the nearest brick wall. He didn't give a shit about the furnishings. It was only things and he could buy more. It was the feeling that he would never be free of Alana. If it wasn't her calling him to brag about something shitty she was doing to him, it was the press taking sides in their divorce. He supposed he should be happy that most were on "Team Max" but it was small comfort that so many people felt sorry for him. Like he was a stray dog without a home or a family. A mutt nobody wanted.

He'd thought about going out to the London clubs and picking up some lovely young thing but that wasn't what he wanted. He'd long grown tired of the single life. He wanted to settle down, have a family. Sleeping with a woman he barely knew wouldn't bring him the satisfaction he was seeking.

He shouldn't have even come to Nate and Paige's party tonight but he was the best man. Max had to make sure that his friends actually tied the knot. Knowing one or both of them, there was a very real possibility that someone might get a case of cold feet. If they needed a push down the aisle, Max would be there to do it.

Stepping outside the back door of the restaurant for a cigarette he shouldn't be smoking, the warm breeze tousled his hair and he pushed it out of his eyes. It was longer than he liked it but he needed it for his next role.

He lit his cigarette and looked out at the water, realizing he wasn't alone. Soft crying was coming from the end of the small dock that overlooked the water. At first, he thought to turn around and leave whomever it was in peace but then he recognized the sapphire-colored dress as belonging to Paige's assistant Carrie. A sweet and efficient young woman with expressive light brown eyes that contrasted with her fiery red hair. Paige swore up and down Carrie was a miracle in human form and kept her organized and on time.

"Are you okay?" Max approached the woman carefully, not wanting to pry but not feeling comfortable just leaving her here by herself. "Do you want me to get Paige for you?"

Carrie's head jerked up and she shook her head. "No, please don't. I don't want her to know that I'm out here crying. I don't want to ruin her wedding."

"I'm sure she wouldn't think you were ruining her wedding. Are you sad that Paige is moving to London?"

Max was aware that their future domicile had been a bone of contention between the happy couple and he was glad they'd come to some sort of compromise.

"I'm happy for her," Carrie said quietly. "This doesn't have anything to do with her."

He knew enough about women to guess. "Is it some bloke? Your fiancé? I'll go inside and tell him he doesn't deserve you."

He'd thought he might get a chuckle but instead she burst into a fresh spate of tears, her shoulders shaking with sobs. Startled and worried, he placed his arm around her shoulders and tried to say something soothing although that wasn't something he was good at.

"It's okay. It's going to be alright. Do you want to tell me about it?"

Sniffling, she dabbed at her cheeks with a tissue but there were already tracks of mascara under her eyes. "I don't have a fiancé. Not anymore."

He glanced at her left hand which was still wearing a ring. "You two probably just had a little row. It will be okay in the morning."

She snorted rather indelicately. "It won't. He's left me for the ex-wife he divorced five years ago but now they're back together. I've suspected something was going on with him for awhile. He told me last week but tonight he called me." She held up her phone. "He wants his ring back so he can exchange it for another one. You know, for her."

Clearly this fiancé was an idiot. Plus, the infidelity was a personal pet peeve with Max. If a person wanted to be with someone else, they needed to man up and just say so instead of sneaking around. If Alana had just told him that she didn't want him a year ago, they could have gotten a civil divorce and moved on with their separate lives.

"What a horse's arse," Max growled. "That's a man that doesn't deserve to have a good woman. You're well rid of him."

"I know that. I really do. But now everyone–"

She broke off and turned back toward the water.

"Let me guess, you think everyone feels sorry for you," Max said. "I know exactly how you feel."

Looking over her shoulder, she frowned. "You think people feel sorry for you?"

He shoved his hands in the pockets of his trousers. "Are you Team Max or Team Alana? Jesus, I hate that shit. I've seen the way people look at me, like I'm a big fucking loser because I couldn't keep my wife happy."

He'd made her smile although he wasn't sure what she found so entertaining. "Max, I'm not sure that people feel sorry for you. I think they feel sorry for her." She held up her hand when he started to protest. "In that, they think she's been an idiot for leaving you and going to him. That relationship has trouble written all over it, let me tell you. Personally, I think you've escaped and should be celebrating. Whatever the divorce is costing you, it's worth it."

He straightened at her words. It was Alana's loss. He'd treated her like a queen and she'd never appreciated it. "It's not so bad. We had a prenuptial but as we speak she's loading up all our belongings from our home and taking them away in a truck."

"You could sic your lawyers on her."

"I could...but frankly I just want to be done with it. I never wanted this war in the press. That was all her. She wanted to humiliate me."

Carrie looked at him curiously. "Why?"

Lifting his chin, he shook his head. "From what I can tell she hates me, although I don't know the reason. I tried to be a good husband but maybe I failed spectacularly. Everything seemed good until after the wedding. Then we started arguing like cats and dogs over the littlest things. She did say I drove her to cheat. That I was a boring husband, in bed and out."

"Ouch," Carrie replied, her brows pulling down. "That's a shitty thing to say. You know, I never liked her acting and this publicity can't be good for her career."

It was through his friends that Alana had landed her last two movie parts. "You might be right, although she's of the opinion that all press is good for her career."

"Then she should be winning an Oscar this year," Carrie said sarcastically. "She's all over TMZ with that skeevy guy. If that was her type, what was she doing with you?"

Max highly suspected marrying him had been a savvy career move. "Availing herself of my moviemaking contacts. Good luck to her."

Carrie stepped toward him. "I'm sorry you're going through this. It makes my problem seem kind of small."

Rubbing his chin, Max shook his head. "Hardly. Your problem is important to you. Besides, this isn't a competition. Who's the most miserable tonight? That's not a contest you want to win."

She laughed and blew her nose with a fresh tissue from her purse. "True. So we both are trying to hide something from Nate and Paige. Neither one of us want them to know how unhappy we are. Well, your secret is safe with me."

Max inclined his head. "And yours with me. We make quite the pair, don't we?"

As soon as the words came out of his mouth, a light-bulb went off in his head.

An idea.

Maybe a terrible idea.

But it would benefit them both greatly.

Did he dare?

Would she even agree?

He was tired of being the object of pity, and she didn't want that either.

He could help her. She could help him.

He liked the idea more with every passing moment.

"Carrie, I'd like to talk to you about something. You're familiar with the word showmance, right?"

# CHAPTER
## *One*

PRESENT DAY...

On shaking, stiff legs Carrie Johnson accepted her passport back from the unsmiling man behind the passport control counter and shoved it back into her handbag. After an eleven-hour flight from Tampa, Florida, she had finally arrived in London, a city that was much colder than the one she'd left. She didn't have many cold weather clothes so a shopping trip was high on her to-do list unless she wanted to spend the next several weeks and months freezing her ass off. The man who had been sitting next to her on the plane sure wasn't going to keep her warm. His demeanor the entire flight had been decidedly chilly. He was put out that she had turned down his offer of a showmance.

Seriously, of course she'd said no. No one in their right mind was going to believe it. An ordinary girl with an ordinary life wasn't going to be the next girlfriend of one of the biggest stars in Hollywood. He'd have to deal with his own problems, just as she'd have to deal with her own.

Since Carrie hadn't had much to pack, she'd carried on her bag so she breezed by the baggage claim and went straight to customs. It took only minutes to walk through the Green line that indicated she had nothing to declare. It was on the other side he would be waiting.

Him. Max.

The world knew him as Maxwell Hayes, star of stage, screen, and television. Or Haden from the *Thunder* movies as so many people referred to him.

Tall, dark, and handsome with crystal clear blue eyes, he was one of the most popular A-list actors in Hollywood at the moment. Coming off an Oscar nomination for some boring art film she'd fallen asleep in, he was in demand by everyone who was anyone. And Max Hayes was a big deal someone.

Two days ago, the night before Paige and Nate's wedding, he'd proposed a fake relationship - a show-mance, if you will - to keep people from feeling sorry for them because of his cheating soon to be ex-wife and Carrie's unfaithful fiancé. She'd said no and Max had taken the answer well outwardly but he'd spent most of the flight to London either glowering or sleeping. They'd shared the flight but little else. Paige and Nate had insisted that she fly back with Max but when she'd agreed she hadn't known this entirely sticky situation was going to come up. Now she was planning to share a taxi with a man who was pissy about being turned down. She was sure that was an unusual feeling for him. Everywhere he went women seemed to come out of the woodwork to throw themselves at him and the plane had been no exception.

Perhaps she had been a tiny bit rash to say no.

She'd been hurting that night at the dinner party, heart-broken and crying when he'd found her. He'd made it sound so simple and so seductive. Instead of friends and family patting her on the back and pitying her, they would be happy for her, or at least envious. She'd landed one of the most sought after men in show business. Of course it was all one big lie, but they didn't know that.

But she would know and she hated the thought of deceiving people, even strangers. Living a lie wasn't something she thought she could do.

"Are you ready?"

Max seemed to come out of nowhere, wearing shades and a hat to lessen the chance of being recognized. Her own gaze swept the arrivals lounge but everyone seemed immersed in their own reunions, not bothering with anyone else.

She hadn't known him long but when he wanted he could act like a pretty regular guy. He could also act like a pompous prick, looking down that patrician nose at her. She'd been sitting next to him for eleven hours and he'd said maybe a dozen words to her. He was making this more awkward than it needed to be. He should be thanking her. She was hardly his type and none of his friends were going to be impressed that he'd landed a slightly chubby personal assistant with great hair. That was her best feature. Her hair could star in a shampoo commercial if the rest of her wasn't so ordinary.

For now, she needed to make the best of things. Max

was a close friend of Nate's, who was now the husband of her employer and best friend, which was why she was here in London. She was planning to spend a lot more time here in this city and she didn't want it to be weird.

"Sorry I took so long." She shook her head when he reached out a hand for her bag. "It took awhile to get through passport control. I don't think the guy likes Americans very much."

Max had sailed through the line for British citizens with a promise to wait for her on the other side. "I'm sure that's not the case. Please let me get your bag."

Wrinkling her nose, Carrie shook her head. "You didn't see his face when he saw my American passport. Definitely not a fan of the colonies."

"Carrie, give me your bag." That deep voice he was so damn famous for. She looked up and his brows were raised in question and his hand was still out. Waiting. It didn't appear that they were planning to move until she handed it over.

Something else she was beginning to realize. He was bossy too. Those dozen words he'd spoken to her during the flight? All commands to do something. Close her eyes and sleep. Eat something. Have a drink. Use the blanket if she was cold.

"It's on wheels," she protested, looking down at the small suitcase. "And not very heavy. I only own two sweaters so there wasn't much to pack."

His full lips turned up at the corners. "It's not about how heavy it is. It's about how my mother raised me. Now please let me deal with the luggage."

Oh. That was different. Still bossy but different.

Relinquishing the handle, she followed him outside to the taxi stand where she quickly found herself in the back seat of a real black London cab heading to Hampstead where Max and Nate both owned homes. Carrie would be staying at Nate and Paige's until she found a flat for herself.

Carrie leaned forward in her seat to get a better vantage point. It was an early Monday morning in the UK and the streets were jammed with commuters, but it gave her a chance to see the sights.

"You said you've never been to London."

Carrie shrugged. "Never had the opportunity. Visited France and Greece though. Really enjoyed it. The food was out of this world good."

"We have excellent restaurants in London. I can recommend a few, if you'd like."

She had to give him credit, he was trying to make it less awkward. If he put forth the effort, she would as well.

"That's very kind of you but before I do much of anything I'm going to need to go shopping and get some warm clothes. Maybe a real coat too, although we're heading into the summer months. Paige told me a few stores to try."

Her friend and employer had no idea what was going on in Carrie's life. It wouldn't have been right to dump her broken engagement on Paige's wedding day, although she was going to have to come clean when the newlyweds finished their short honeymoon in Paris and settled in LA while Nate filmed a new movie.

"I hope they're having a good time," she said wistfully. "They looked so happy at the wedding."

"They're in love and on their honeymoon," Max chuckled. "They're having a good time. I'm sure of it. Speaking of a good time, since you've never been here I can get my assistant to take you around or she can book you on a proper tour."

That sounded like *proper* torture. People following along like cattle listening to someone drone on and on from a script. "Thank you but I'll probably just get a guidebook and putter around. See where inspiration takes me."

"Whatever makes you happy."

That was a loaded statement if she'd ever heard one. She hadn't been happy since Mark had so unceremoniously dumped her. She'd cried for days when she wasn't with Paige, constantly asking herself what was wrong with her. Why had Mark fallen out of love with her? Maybe he'd never really loved her at all. Maybe she wasn't lovable.

Max pointed out some of the famous landmarks and Carrie made a mental note to hit the London Eye right away, preferably both during the day and after dark. She wanted to see this city from a high perch.

"I know you didn't tell Paige about your engagement," Max said, his gaze still on his phone. "Did you tell your parents? Are they concerned about you coming here to London all alone?"

It was at that moment that Carrie realized they didn't know each other well at all. She knew a few things because she'd looked him up on the Internet but he knew nothing at all about her except that she worked for Paige. Hardly enough to base a relationship on. The whole idea had been ludicrous.

"My parents have passed away so I don't have to worry

about what they think. I have an older brother who's married with two kids. When he finds out about Mark I'm going to have to talk him out of burying my ex in a shallow grave."

Max cleared his throat. "This Mark fellow deserves it."

Truer words and all that...

"Damn skippy he does but it's illegal. And morally wrong," she added as an afterthought.

The tension between them was lessened to a degree so she was feeling more comfortable with him when they arrived in front of his home on a lovely residential street. High black iron gates kept the riffraff out but they swung open when Max tapped out a code on his phone. Technology. Nice. She loved anything that made life easier and more organized.

Max told the cabbie to wait for Carrie. "Why don't you come inside and get that spare key to Nate's home? I can't believe they took off and forgot to give you one."

Smiling, Carrie remembered the blissful expressions of Paige and her new husband. "I can. They had a lot on their minds that day and the next morning too. I'll have a copy made and get it back to you as soon as possible."

"Good plan," he said, leading the way up the front steps. "I can point out just the shop to have one made."

Unlocking the door, he pushed it open with his shoulder and they stepped into the foyer where he placed the bags. She walked a few feet into the living room with Max right beside her and that nasty tension was back but this time it wasn't her fault. Not at all.

His home looked like a war zone. What Alana hadn't taken and loaded into that truck the other night, she'd destroyed. It looked like some crazed person had taken a sledgehammer to every mirror, photo, chair, and dish in the house. There was glass scattered across the floor as far as the eye could see, shredded throw rugs and pillows, and the masterpiece - the biggest damn flat screen television she'd ever seen with a hammer lodged in the face.

"Bloody hell," Max groaned, scraping his fingers through his hair as he walked forward cautiously, the sound of glass crunching under his shoes. "What in the ever-loving fuck?"

If the rest of the house looked as bad as the kitchen and living room there was no way he'd be spending the night here. Her business instincts came to the fore, and Carrie pulled out her cell phone and began looking for a hotel. Then she'd find a cleanup crew for this mess. After that? A home furnishings store. He'd need everything new right down to the forks. Thank God he could afford it, although that didn't make this any better.

*Note to self. Max's ex-wife is a total bitch.*

"This is criminal, Max. You could call the police on her."

He didn't turn around but simply shook his head. "I don't want or need that kind of publicity. It would play right into her hands."

"Maybe she's counting on you staying quiet."

He glanced over his shoulder, his expression a mask of fury.

*Another note to self. Max has a temper and he was currently hanging on to it by a thread.*

"I know how to handle this," he growled, his jaw set. "She thinks she's got me by the balls. She's mistaken."

They walked through the rest of the house and every room was no better than the last.

"She broke every mirror in your home," Carrie observed. "That's like...thirty-five years of bad luck. She's screwed."

"She'll have more bad luck than that." Max looked around his master bedroom, the mattress ripped to shreds. "I can't stay here. I'll need to find somewhere else while I replace all of this."

Carrie smiled and held up her phone. She might not be able to be the girlfriend of his dreams but dammit, she was good to have around in a crisis. "Way ahead of you, Hamlet. The Ritz, The Four Seasons, or The Savoy?"

That famous eyebrow quirked up and his forehead wrinkled as if he was puzzled.

"The Ritz, I suppose."

"I'm on it. Now I've found a possible cleaning company but we might do better to call your regular service. Do you have their number?"

"I do here in my phone. I'll call them."

She shook her head as she typed into her phone. "I can do that. Then we need to go shopping to replace all of this. Did you pick it out yourself or did you have a designer do it?"

"Myself."

"Are you going to want to do that again? I can probably arrange for a few designers to talk to you."

His large hand came into her view and gently tugged her phone away from her. "Carrie, you don't have to do this. I have an assistant and she can handle this."

"But I'm here and we can get on top of this right now."

He stepped into her personal space, looming over her. She caught a whiff of his aftershave along with a few other scents - soap, mint, and maybe cigarettes too.

"Carrie." He'd bent his head so their faces were close, inches apart, and her heart accelerated, banging against her ribs. Fear? No, this was something else. Attraction? He was handsome with a voice to die for. No, she couldn't be attracted to him. He wasn't her type. She didn't do assholes. "This isn't your problem to solve."

Her fingers gripped her cellphone and she slowly exhaled a breath she didn't know she'd been holding. "I'm happy to help you."

"No need. I'll call my assistant to take care of all of this, but I do thank you for offering. Not many people would have."

"Not many people have their entire home destroyed by a vengeful ex-wife."

He grimaced, his mouth turned down. "Soon to be ex. The divorce isn't final yet but it shouldn't be long now. It can't come soon enough."

"Clearly."

That had him chuckling but then he turned serious again. "Carrie, I don't want to push this but I'd like to extend the offer one more time. I think we can help each other out. I need you and I think you need me too."

There was tension in the way he held himself, showing that he wasn't altogether comfortable having to ask. Again. For a moment she wavered, wondering if she'd done the right thing. He was a handsome, sexy movie star and this would be her only chance of ever dating someone like him, even if it was fake.

But then she remembered that they'd have to walk down red carpets and she'd have to wear designer clothes and jewels. She simply wasn't the type and if he'd been thinking straight, he'd know that. He was a desperate man and right now she looked like a viable option. She didn't have a stylish bone in her body and she sure as hell didn't want to see his face when he eventually realized it.

"I'm sorry, Max." She tried to keep her voice cool but she could hear it shake slightly. "I just don't think I'm the right person for this. I'm sure you won't have a hard time finding a woman who will."

One call to his publicist and he'd have a whole list of actresses and models beating down his door to pretend to be his girlfriend. All prettier and more talented.

His expression looked to be carved from granite and his eyes had gone ice blue. He could turn the charm on and off like a faucet. "You're right. No problem at all. Let me lock up. I hope you don't mind if I share your taxi to a hotel."

Oh goody, more time with Pompous Max. Lucky her.

He might be angry now but tomorrow when things didn't look so dark he'd be relieved, wondering what in the hell he'd been thinking. Carrie was many things - organized, practical, business-minded, predictable, even boring, but she wasn't glamour material. The only red carpet she'd be walking down was if she bought a scarlet throw rug and placed it in her foyer. Maxwell Hayes, on the other hand, had been born to walk down a red carpet and be photographed.

Just not with her.

# CHAPTER

*Two*

MAX HAD SUGGESTED lunch in a cafe not far from Nate and Paige's home and Carrie found herself agreeing, despite knowing he was only being polite. The handsome actor fascinated her with the way he could change his personality at will. One minute he was friendly and sweet, the next icy and remote. She couldn't help the curiosity that kept her in his company, trying to see beneath the facade he wore. The mystery? Which was real and which was fake? Perhaps they both weren't true.

Carrie and Max were wrapping up a quiet lunch when her phone rang. One look at the screen and she groaned. It was her brother Greg and since he rarely called her now that his second child had been born, nothing good could come from this conversation. She almost hit the Decline button but thought better of it. It was going to happen sooner or later so it might as well be now.

"It's my brother. I have to get this."

Max nodded and pulled out his own phone to check his

messages, effectively giving her as much privacy as their proximity would allow.

"Hi, Greg. What's going on?"

"Hey, Sis, is there anything you want to tell me?"

Hmmm...it sounded like he knew something was up.

"Frankly, brother dear, I never want to tell you anything. You're like a worried old woman most of the time. What's on your agenda today?"

"I talked to Mark."

The words came out as a snarl and Carrie's heart fell to her feet. She hadn't been given much time to come up with a really good explanation. Maybe the truth wasn't the worst idea.

"Then you know the engagement is off."

Her statement caused Max to pull his attention from his phone and to her call, listening intently. No pressure there.

"I do now but I'm wondering why I didn't hear if from you."

"Because I didn't want to discuss it with you. I thought you might do something stupid and beat him up. Why did you even talk to him anyway?"

"He had a few things of yours that he wanted to give back - well, actually he said he wanted to get rid of them - but you didn't answer your door so he stopped by here and left the box. As for punching him, should I? Has he done something that deserves a smackdown? Because I'm just the guy to do it. I never liked him in the first place."

"I know," she sighed, checking out Max who appeared to be pretending that he wasn't listening. He might be staring at his phone but he hadn't changed the screen in way too long. "You told me so repeatedly."

"So what happened?" Greg demanded. "Did you guys have a fight?"

Several of them. None that made a damn's worth of difference.

"Not a fight," she finally said. "Things have been going south for quite awhile and we've been growing apart. Eventually he decided he wanted to get back with his ex-wife and I've moved on as well. No hard feelings. I'm just thankful we realized that we weren't suited before we got married."

She'd been practicing her explanation and she thought it sounded damn good to her own ears.

"His ex-wife?" Greg exploded and she had to hold the phone far away from her still ringing eardrum. "That sniveling little shit went back to Tina? What an asshole. What a fucking asshole. I am going to beat the shit out of him. He deserves it, breaking your heart like that."

She couldn't let that happen. Greg was a husband and a father that didn't need an assault and battery charge to complicate his life. She had no doubt that Mark would press charges, the prick.

"He didn't break my heart. I told you, we'd been growing apart. I was actually relieved when he left and I truly have moved on."

There was silence on the other end of the line.

"Greg? Are you there?"

"I'm here. What do you mean by moving on?"

Smiling widely, Carrie hoped that old saying was true. That people on the phone really could tell if you had a smile on your face.

"I haven't had a chance to tell you but I'm in London."

She took a deep breath. "Paige is moving here, you know, and they've offered to rent me a flat. I was thinking I would see the sights and have some fun. Go see Paris, Berlin, Dublin, Edinburgh, Rome, or even Venice. It's the chance of a lifetime."

"London...as in London, England? You're on another fucking continent? Jesus, Carrie, what are you thinking? You don't even speak the language."

Giving up the pretense of not eavesdropping, Max was scowling at the phone as if he'd never heard someone say something stupid before. Carrie loved her brother but sometimes he made her want to smack her own forehead. Greg was a sweetheart but he was far too protective. "Greg, I'm in England. They speak English here. I know that language just fine."

"Yeah, but that's Europe and they speak French and German and other languages. You took high school French, Carrie. You only know how to ask where the bathroom is."

She knew slightly more than that but not much. "They have an app for that on my smartphone. I'll be fine. I'll take pictures and send them to you."

"And Paige is okay with this?"

Greg worshipped Paige as if she were a goddess on Mount Olympus. "She does and she wholeheartedly approves. She wouldn't steer me wrong, now would she?"

"No, she's a smart one."

Christ on a crutch, was he saying Carrie was dumb?

"Everything is going to be fine," she assured Greg in her most soothing voice. "I'm here to do a job and on my off-time I'll see Europe."

She couldn't see her brother's face but she could almost

hear his frown through the cell phone. "I think you should come home, Sis. I don't like the idea of you wandering around a foreign country by yourself."

Time to get tough with him, otherwise he'd talk to her until she was worn down to a nub.

"Greg, I think we both know that I am more than capable of taking care of myself. Of the two of us, who is the more organized person?"

"You are," he grunted.

"That's right. I am. I'll be fine."

"But you need your family with you at a time like this," Greg protested. "Jeannie said that her yoga instructor has a brother who teaches high school math. Real handsome and about your age. Just got a divorce. We could invite you both over for dinner–"

Yikes. Not a blind date with a brother of an acquaintance who was looking for a rebound. She hadn't sunk that low. It was time to end this call before she agreed to something she would later regret.

With her fingernails she lightly scratched the surface of her phone while blowing puffs of air loudly into the microphone. "I think I'm losing you, Greg. You know how these international connections are. I really do need to go. Love you. Kiss Jeannie and the kids for me, okay?"

She hung up and Carrie heaved a huge sigh. "I think he bought the explanation. I'm assuming you could hear all of that."

Max nodded. "I did and you were good. Very convincing, especially that international connection part. I never thought about scratching at my mobile but I think it added a realistic touch. Although I have to say I might have let your brother kick Mark's arse. He deserves it."

"No," Carrie shook her head. "I want people to think I'm fine and the breakup doesn't bother me. Besides, Greg doesn't need an assault and battery charge. He'll get kicked out of the state bar."

It did give her a fun-filled preview of what the future was going to be like whenever she spoke with anyone who didn't know about the breakup. She'd be fake smiling and pretending not to be heartbroken. It wasn't going to be easy. She was a lousy actress.

Stroking his chin, Max didn't look convinced. "I suppose so but I still think Mark is getting off lightly. Sometimes karma is too slow."

Chuckling, she tucked her phone back into her bag. "You haven't met Mark's ex. If even half the crap he told me about her is true, she's a psycho. A real crazy lady just like Alana. I think a lifetime with her is punishment enough."

Frowning, Max signaled for the check. "If he knows that's what she's like, why would he go back? It doesn't make any sense."

It made complete sense to her.

"I think it's like my friend Auggie used to say. Auggie was a real womanizer. He went through them like Kleenex so of course every now and then he'd get the crazy ones. He'd still date them and when I asked why he said the crazy chicks were exciting. They had no inhibitions and were completely unpredictable. So if I were to venture a guess? Mark wants a little insanity between the sheets."

It hurt to think he hadn't been happy with her and their

sex life but if the truth be told, she hadn't been thrilled either. He'd been rather staid and formulaic from the first time. She and Paige had had a drunken talk one night and decided he had a Madonna-whore issue.

Carrie was a *nice* girl, so she couldn't want dirty sex.

Except that she totally did.

Mark wouldn't even curse in front of her. She would bet cash money that he swore like a sailor in front of his ex. Carrie had tried bringing a sex toy into their relationship but he'd flipped, accusing her of thinking he wasn't enough. After that, she'd stopped trying. Sex had never been that important to her, and she'd assumed things would improve as they became more comfortable with each other. That hadn't happened either.

Max fidgeted in his seat, his face tinged red. Her statement must have hit close to home. His ex was a psychopathic bitch too.

"Sorry. I just realized how that probably came out. I'm sure Alana has some wonderful qualities and it wasn't the wild sex that drew you to her. You wouldn't be that shallow."

He looked out the window, then at the bar, then back to her.

"Sadly, Carrie, you would be wrong."

# CHAPTER
## *Three*

THE FIRST DAY of rehearsals for a new play was always hectic. Most of the people he already knew but there had been a few new faces. One blonde actress who was playing a small part had stared at him for most of the day, making him wonder if she was planning to seduce him or stalk him. He was becoming rather cynical when it came to females but then he had good reason.

"Here's your mobile, boss. You have a message from Nate Mason."

So he wouldn't be disturbed, Max's assistant Gemma had been holding his phone for him while they were doing the table read. Constantly at his elbow and anticipating his needs, she was one of the better assistants he'd had. Most didn't last long in the position. The long hours, bountiful travel, and lack of personal life took a toll and the average span of employment was about six months.

Quiet and efficient, Gemma had lasted seven and appeared to be happy in her job although Max had been fooled before. He remembered one named Candace who had written her resignation on the Do Not Disturb sign that he'd hung on the hotel room door. He'd gone to sleep employing an assistant and woke up without one. She'd called him an asshole. She was probably right.

"Thank you. I'll give him a call back." He accepted the bottle of water she held out. "I think we're done for the day. I'm heading home and you should too."

"Should I order you some dinner and have it delivered? Also, what should I pick you up for breakfast tomorrow? The usual?"

He'd been thinking about that. Her day had consisted of watching him work and fetching him water bottles. There were more important tasks that needed to be done.

"Actually, I'm glad you mentioned tomorrow. The new furnishings for the house are going to be delivered in the morning about ten. I'd like you there to meet them and the designer. She'll show up about nine-thirty. She said she'd be there most of the day so you should plan to be also. I'll stop by after rehearsals and see the progress. I'm hoping to move back next week."

The walls had been painted, the floors scrubbed, and the decor ordered. All that was left was to put it all into place. It was amazing what money and fame could buy him. What would have taken anyone else months had only taken him a week, as long as he wasn't too fussy about the decor. Luckily his favorite color was blue and that made designing around it easy.

Gemma tapped a note onto her tablet, her thick glasses sliding down her snub nose. "Sure, absolutely. I'm on it. Anything else?"

"That will be all. Have a good evening."

The assistant nodded, still glued to the screen. Max shrugged into his coat and headed out into the chilly rain. When he was in London he tried to keep a low profile and live as ordinary a life as possible. That meant there was no private car to whisk him out of the dreary weather and back to the hotel. He had to hoof it to the nearest Tube station just like everyone else. He always marveled at how he blended into the crowd when he wasn't dressed in a tuxedo. Nobody expected him to be wearing faded denims and a t-shirt but just in case, he wore his hat low so half of his face was obscured. Waiting for his train, he checked his phone and found Nate's cryptic message.

*Call me when you can.*

Max waited until he was back inside the hotel room, shedding his outer warmth and dialing the number at the same time. Nate answered on the second ring.

"How was the first day?"

Max settled onto the settee and stretched out his long legs, propping them on the coffee table. "Good. Long. Like they always are. I want a hot shower, room service, and bed. How's Los Angeles?"

Nate was starring in a new movie and his bride Paige had traveled with him. They'd be out of the country for at least two months, maybe more.

"Sunny and dry."

"How's married life?"

"Fucking fantastic. I highly recommend it, mate."

Max was just getting out of a marriage and wasn't looking to dive back in any time soon.

"Good for you. So, did you call just to hear about my first day?"

"Hardly," Nate chuckled. "I called to ask you to check on Carrie for us. Invite her out to dinner or something. Take her to a movie and get her out of the house. When Paige talks to her she says she's fine but she doesn't sound it. My beautiful wife is beginning to get concerned that Carrie isn't happy in London. You know I offered to buy her a flat so she and Paige can work closely together but if she misses Florida that entire plan isn't going to work."

It was hard to keep secrets from his best friend. Max was well aware of why Carrie sounded out of sorts but she'd made it clear she wasn't going to ruin the first few weeks of her friend's married life by telling them her fiancé had run off with another woman.

"I'm sure she's fine. She's only been here a week. It takes time to make the transition."

"You were on a plane with her for eleven hours. How did she act? Did she seem sad or upset?"

He didn't know Carrie well but she seemed like the type who didn't wear her heart on her sleeve. Except for the night before the wedding. She'd been crying and upset then but she hadn't expected Max to find her out there. She'd been quite mortified at being found but her reaction to her faithless fiancé had been natural. He still was of the opinion she should let her brother beat on him until he learned his lesson.

"She was quiet. She read and slept mostly. So did I," Max replied. "We were both knackered after all the wedding festivities. We had lunch together when we got to

London and she seemed fine. She even talked to her brother."

Max could hear Nate talking to Paige in the background. "You had lunch with her? That's great. So you wouldn't mind taking her out again? It would put Paige's mind at ease."

He wasn't going to get out of this. Nate and Paige were his best friends and this was what friends did for each other.

"Of course I will. I'll call her today and set something up."

"We owe you one. Paige says to tell you that she really appreciates this. She just wants to make sure that Carrie sees how great London can be."

For Carrie, the best thing about London probably was that her ex wasn't here.

"I'll do my best to sell its charms and report back."

He and Nate chatted a few more minutes before hanging up. Max scrolled through the contacts until he found the one he was looking for. Might as well get this over and done. Spending the evening with a woman who was privy to his greatest failure - and then turned him down when he'd proposed a business relationship - wasn't an activity he was anxious to do but he'd promised.

He'd take her to a movie. They wouldn't have to talk.

# CHAPTER
## *Four*

TO CARRIE'S SHOCK, Max had asked her to have dinner and go to a movie with him. She hadn't expected to hear from her favorite pompous actor but here she was knocking on the door to his hotel suite. They were meeting here to decide where they were going to eat. She was hoping for Italian but he'd mentioned steak.

The door swung open and a scowling Max beckoned her in. "I just need to put on my shoes."

"No hurry."

She stepped into the hotel room but stayed by the door as he searched in the closet, tossing a few random things out as he went. So far, Max had rejected a pair of tennis shoes and brown boots. Organization must not be a thing for him and she found herself itching to get ahold of his clothes and possessions to bring order to chaos.

Shifting restlessly on her feet, she tried to make conversation. "So I was surprised to hear from you."

He took so long to reply she didn't think he was going

to but he finally did, his voice muffled by the closet. "I talked to Paige and Nate. Apparently she's worried about you. You're not doing a very good job of acting like nothing's wrong. They asked me to take you out and show you how great London is."

*Loser. I'm a fucking loser.*

The breath whooshed out of Carrie's body and she had to grab hold of the doorjamb to keep her knees from giving out. Her best friend was so concerned about her she'd asked Max to take Carrie out. It was deja vu all over again. Just like Greg had thought she was too pathetic to find herself another man, Paige thought Carrie was too pitiful to find friends.

To add insult to injury, Max didn't look or sound like he was relishing this task. He had the job of taking the plain girl to dinner. Someone give the man a medal for altruism.

He crawled out of the closet holding a pair of ugly black shoes that were only slightly better than the awful gray ones Nate used to wear before Paige threw them away. What was it with these two and their godawful shoes?

She didn't intend to stick around and find out. She was no one's pity date.

"I had no idea she was worried. You know, you don't really need to do this. I'm fine and I'll make sure she knows that next time I talk to her."

Looking up from tying his shoes, Max shot her an irritated look. "You're here so we might as well go. Are you hungry?"

"Of course I'm hungry. I'm always hungry, but I'm sure you have better things to do than squire me around. We both know why I've been down and an evening out isn't going to cure this."

Max stood and shoved his hands in the pockets of his black trousers. "If you'd seen your way to accept my business proposal, Paige wouldn't be worried about you at all."

Really? He was going to whine about that again? He didn't know when to let things go.

"Possibly, but then she'd be worried about me spending the rest of my life in jail."

"Jail?" he asked, frowning as he picked up his keys and cell phone.

Carrie smiled brightly. "For murdering you, probably in your sleep, although I'm not sure a jury of my peers would find me guilty."

Those icy blue eyes settled on her, making her inwardly shiver. "Funny. Now are you ready to go? I promised Nate and Paige I would take you out."

Shaking her head, she edged toward the door. "I'm no one's mercy date but thank you anyway. I'd rather eat a Lean Cuisine for one in front of bad reality television than have you take me to dinner and remind me every five minutes why you had to be pushed into this evening. And thank you for that, by the way—a real gentleman would never have let me know that this wasn't his idea. But not you. Not the famous Maxwell Hayes. You made sure I knew right off the bat. I wasn't even here two minutes before you ensured that I knew how pathetic and sad I was. Classy move."

For a moment, she almost thought she saw regret flicker across his features but if it did it was quickly hidden beneath that frosty, patrician demeanor. He'd missed his calling. He should have been the headmaster at a snotty boarding school.

"I do apologize. I didn't realize you were sensitive about the subject. As I said, if you had accepted–"

"For the love of all that's good and holy," Carrie broke in, not letting him finish again. "Let it go. You don't take the word 'no' very well, but then I guess you don't hear it much. As for dinner, I'd rather starve."

How could Maxwell Hayes look that good and be so unpleasant? Paige had said he was a difficult man to get to know but this was ridiculous. Truly the only thing that kept Carrie from losing her cool with him was that he was a friend of Paige's. There had to be more to him than what she was seeing if her boss liked him so much.

Hidden depths. Way down. Buried like Atlantis, more like it.

He shoved his keys and phone into his pocket. "Stop acting like a child. Paige and Nate want us to spend time together so that's what we'll do. We'll have dinner and then I'll call her and tell her you're doing wonderfully. You love London and everything about it. You've made lots of friends and barely think about Florida at all. Then we never have to see one another again except to make polite conversation at social engagements."

"I am not a child," Carrie said through gritted teeth. "Just tell her we went to dinner. She'll never know whether we did or not."

That impeccable eyebrow quirked up. "Do you lie to your employer regularly? Perhaps this is something I should let Paige know about."

Letting her mouth drop open, she widened her eyes in

mock surprise. "Please don't tell her I've absconded with the family silver. Little Tommy needs an operation."

He almost smiled. Almost. "Your secret is safe with me. If you go to dinner. We'll call them from the table and they'll be thrilled that we're out together."

They could have eaten already in the time it took to argue about it.

"Fine, but do you mind if I freshen up in your bathroom before we go? I'm still getting used to this wet weather."

Giving her a small bow, his arm swept toward the back of the suite. "Please be my guest."

Everything was a drama with this guy. "I'll only be a moment."

Hurriedly she ran a comb through her long hair, damp from the London rain, pulling it back into a ponytail. She swiped a fresh coat of lipstick on her mouth and made a face into the mirror. This was as good as she was going to get. She was a businesswoman, not a model or actress shot up with collagen and Botox.

Slinging her purse over her shoulder, Carrie headed out to the main area of the suite but she paused outside the bathroom as she heard two voices. *Unhappy voices.* Max had company and since he'd planned to go out with her, they were probably a surprise to the handsome thespian.

"Max, we need to talk. It's important," a husky, feminine voice said.

She knew that voice, had heard it in a few movies. Alana Crenshaw had tracked Max down and was now standing out there hoping to speak with him about heaven knows what.

"For fuck's sake, the divorce will be final soon. Anything you have to say can go through our representatives."

Carrie's first instinct was to hurry to his side, a show of solidarity in the face of the enemy, but that little voice in her ear gave her pause. They'd just had a nasty exchange and there was no love lost between them. There wasn't even a mutual respect. He disliked her and she wasn't all that enamored of him at the moment, although she knew there was something redeemable inside of him. Paige was rarely wrong when it came to people.

"This is personal," Alana said in her upper-crust British accent. "I need to speak with you right away."

Carrie could only see the back of Max but his shoulders had stiffened immediately. He was not amused by Alana's sudden appearance at the hotel.

"It's not a good idea." Max's words were clipped and colder than usual. Even chillier than when he spoke to Carrie. But she could hear the underlying panic in his tone. He hadn't been prepared for this especially after just fighting with her moments before. "You should go."

"I'm not leaving until you listen to me."

Carrie had seen divorce before. She'd had friends who had split up and it was an ugly, hurtful thing, especially if the two parties were at odds with one another. That there was more vitriol than normal between these two was clear after what Carrie had witnessed at Max's home. Alana was a destroyer.

Carrie had seen the type quite well during her college days. When something didn't go their way, they made sure that no one else was happy either. As much as Max got on

Carrie's nerves, she felt for him in this situation. Living with Alana had to have been a nightmare.

"Alana, go home. We have nothing to say to one another."

Carrie thought she heard the woman snarl. "I can make your life a living hell, Max. You'll wish you were never born."

"I already do."

There was no good reason for it. Later Carrie would probably question why she was doing it but dammit, she hated to see someone who was hurting so badly be emotionally wrung out like a sponge. Gliding to his side, she wrapped an arm around his lean waist and gazed adoringly - or as close as she could get to that - up into his face. Whether he would play along was the question of the day. After the words they'd flung at each other there was a good chance he'd openly question what the hell she was doing.

But he didn't. He placed his arm around her shoulders and dropped a kiss on her forehead. "Darling, I thought you were on the phone."

"All done." She looked from Alana to Max and then back again. His ex was a few years older than herself but she had a brittle, hard look to her that aged her even more in Carrie's opinion. Innocent ingénue roles were out of the question. She wasn't going to play someone's best friend either. Alana was perfectly suited to the bad bitch roles, right down to her icy blue eyes and her sharp but elegant features. She was certainly a beautiful woman but she didn't radiate any warmth or caring.

Put another way...if Alana was walking down a busy

London street no tourist was going to stop her and ask for directions.

*But I might be biased.*

Alana scowled at Carrie. "Who is this?"

*Nah, I'm right.*

Max pulled her closer to his large frame and Carrie could feel the heat from his body alongside hers. Not unpleasant. "Not that it's any of your business but this is Carrie, my new girlfriend. Now I think you should leave. If you have any message for me, send it through my attorney."

His ex's eyes turned to slits and her lips pursed, her total attention back to Max. She'd effectively dismissed Carrie as too insignificant to worry about. Lovely. "I want to talk to you. We need to discuss the money situation. I can't live like this."

"Like this," Max repeated slowly. "I'm not sure what you mean. You took everything that wasn't nailed down in our home so I would imagine you are living quite well. As for the money, the prenup was very clear. You get a lump sum at settlement."

"You owe me," she hissed, two red flags appearing on her cheeks. "Don't think I won't play dirty."

"I have no doubt that you will try. Now please leave. How did you find me in the first place?"

She smiled, checking her manicure. "I have my sources. Now write me a check," she demanded. "Or I'll go to the press and tell them that you were cheating on me with this little vanilla miss when we were married."

"You'll do nothing," Max replied, his tone hard and cold. "And do you know why? You've already damaged what little career you have left. If you get into a tabloid war with me, you won't be able to get a job taking tickets at the local theatre. You're difficult to work with, Alana, and you've pissed off a lot of people that would love to get their revenge. Don't make it easy for them."

Whirling on her stiletto heel, Alana marched down the hallway. "This isn't over, Max."

Carrie didn't say anything as his ex disappeared into the elevator. They simply stood there for a moment not speaking, not even looking at each other. Just standing as if trying to absorb what just happened.

"I think I need a drink," Max finally said. "Fancy a whiskey?"

"Make it a double, Hamlet, and you've got a deal."

# CHAPTER
## *Five*

MAX HAD BEEN surprised many times in his life. But the most recent event was when the woman that hated his guts put her arm around him and pretended to be his adoring girlfriend for the benefit of his evil soon-to-be ex-wife. He hadn't expected that at all.

He was, however, so grateful he could kiss her feet.

Back in his hotel room, he poured them both a generous whiskey, an excellent brand that the hotel manager had brought up personally along with a basket of chocolates. Sipping it slowly, Max savored the burn in his belly while he also enjoyed the quiet. That was one of the nice traits of Carrie. She wasn't one of those women who felt the need to fill every silence with meaningless babble. She was comfortable with not saying a word. In the end, it was him that finally spoke.

"Why did you do that?"

She didn't answer, instead asking him a question of her own.

"Are you angry that I did?"

"No. I'm glad actually, but I'm surprised. We haven't exactly been friends."

A smile played on her pink lips. "Let's just say you're lucky these windows don't actually open."

The thought of a little thing like her tossing him out on his arse was amusing. "I'm not sure you could get me out the window. I'm a few pounds heavier than you."

"Maybe I was planning to drive you so crazy you'd jump out voluntarily."

"Even Alana hasn't managed that. So I'll ask again. Why did you do it?"

She stared at the amber liquid in the highball glass. "Because I know she hurt you and I hate to think of her doing it again. I wasn't too sure if you'd play along. I was waiting for you to ask me what the hell I was doing."

Tentatively, he sat next to Carrie on the couch. So many things in their short relationship had gone awry and it was mostly his fault. His issues kept him from connecting to people and she was paying the price.

"I'm grateful," he confessed. "I didn't expect you to try and help me, but I'm glad you did. Although now that I've announced you as my girlfriend it makes it hard for you to pretend otherwise, never seeing me again."

"I thought about that but I still couldn't let her hurt you again."

A big, soft heart. He should have known. Carrie's ex-fiance was a damn idiot. This care and tenderness could have been all his but he'd treated her shabbily. With any luck, karma had taken note.

"It's not that I'm really hurting anymore. She doesn't have the power to hurt me now. She's killed any love I may have had for her with her actions. It's that I'm completely humiliated. I was such an idiot when it came to her. I wanted to believe everything she said and why? Because I wanted my marriage to succeed even when the signs were there from day one that it was doomed. Sometimes I wonder if I loved her at all. Maybe I loved the idea of being a husband and having a family. Does that sound awful to you?"

Carrie took a sip of her whiskey before answering. "I think that's probably more common than you think. In love with love. You wanted to be in love, you wanted to be married, so you found an attractive, desirable woman and put a ring on her finger. But happily ever after has to be earned. Look at Nate and Paige."

They'd been through hell to get where there were now. Little had come to them easily except love and passion. But making room for each other, making compromises, that had been a hard road.

"Bloody Christ, is that what I did? Just picked a woman and married her. No wonder I'm divorced. Or soon to be, anyway."

"I've seen men do that, even my brother before he married Jeannie. Men want a woman that other men want but can't get, right? You chose a female that men found desirable but hey, she chose you too. But there's more to marriage than other males wanting your wife."

Max nodded. "Hmmm...like what?"

She gaped at him in surprise. "You don't know? You're

forty and you don't know what's important to you in a life-time mate? You haven't given it any thought whatsoever? And don't say great sex. You won't care about that when you're ninety."

"I care about it now," he retorted. "I'm tired of women saying sex isn't important. Sex *is* important. And I'm thirty-nine, not forty."

"Excuse the hell out of me. Thirty-nine," Carrie shot back. " And I'm not saying it isn't important but it can't be the only criteria for selecting a woman, Max. You should make a list of the traits you desire in a wife and mother. Be sure to list sex because as you say that is important. But I can't believe, especially now that you've been married, that you think that's all it takes to make it work."

Holy Christ, she was taking this organization stuff too far. "You want me to make a list? Should I prioritize it as well? Color code it? Laminate it?"

Huffing out a breath, she rolled her eyes. "Stop making fun of me. I simply think it would be helpful for you if you had some idea as to what you're truly looking for in a woman. There's a school of thought that talks about writing things down as a way to manifest them in reality. Just don't limit yourself to that list if you meet someone in real life that doesn't meet every single criteria."

Max frowned and drained his glass. "Have you done this?"

"I've done this exercise a few times in my life. Even if you don't use the list, it's an interesting exercise. What do you truly value in a mate? What are deal breakers? What could you live with?"

"What are your deal breakers?"

He didn't know why he wanted to know. But he did.

"Physical violence, of course. Verbal assault."

"Those are a given."

She nodded. "They are. Addictions are out too. Gambling, alcohol, drugs. He should be gainfully employed. He doesn't have to be rich but he should be hard working, but I don't want a workaholic either. He should know how to balance work and life."

"A regular paragon," Max drawled.

She elbowed him in the ribs. "You asked."

"You're right. Anything else?"

Tapping her chin, she chewed on her lips. "Hmmm...smoking. I'm not fond of cigarette smoke."

He was a reformed smoker. He only did it for roles now. Or when he was incredibly stressed.

"I quit a few years ago."

"That's good. You'll live longer. Now what do we do?"

He refilled their glasses. "We iron out a deal. One we can both live with. Will you do that for me, Carrie? Will you help me? I can help you too. We can do this if we stick together."

Several emotions flickered across her expressive features. She didn't like him much and that was his fault. He wasn't the warmest of men when meeting new people and she was a prickly one. But she was also smart and she had to be able to see he could help her too. With no false modestly, he knew that being his girlfriend would ensure no one felt sorry for her now that her ex had broken the engagement. In fact, Max made a mental note to have his PR people put out the story that she broke it off.

For him, of course.

"The chances are high that we'll end up at each other's throats but I can hardly say no now that we've told Alana that I'm your girlfriend. So against my common sense, I will." She lifted her glass. "Here's to fake love and devotion."

The best kind. The only kind he'd ever known.

# CHAPTER
## *Six*

MAX HAD SENT her a text inviting her to lunch at a neighborhood pub the next day to talk about the agreement. After saying yes to his business proposal last night, her brain had been busily thinking of everything that could go wrong.

It was a long list.

At the top was the fact she wasn't sure anyone was going to buy this.

The pub wasn't all that busy and she easily found Max in a booth near the back. He was staring at his phone - again - and she had the most evil urge to toss it into the Thames. She loved her phone and iPad but even she didn't lose herself in them as often as this guy did.

Clearing her throat, she slid into the booth. "Hello. Thanks for inviting me to lunch."

He looked up and didn't smile. He didn't scowl or frown either though, so this was progress. "Thank you for coming on such short notice. My PR people brought by a sample contract and I thought it best if we discussed it as soon as possible."

She picked up the menu. "You don't have rehearsals today?"

"Not today, although I do have costume fittings this afternoon."

They always seemed to run out of conversation quickly. Last night's dinner had been excruciatingly quiet with both of them trying to be polite. By dessert, she was longing for when they'd just snipe at each other. At least they were talking.

The waitress came and took their order before Max pulled some rolled-up papers from his jacket pocket. "I've read through it and it seems straightforward. You, of course, can get an attorney if you like."

She paged through the contract, nothing ringing any alarm bells. In her business she looked at contracts quite a bit. "Pap walks. That I expected. Public appearances. Normal. Clothes and jewels? No way. You are not buying me anything."

"This I won't budge on. You're here to help me. You wouldn't need any new clothes or jewels if you weren't. This is a business expense as far as I'm concerned."

"Then I'll return everything when we're through."

Chuckling, he casually stretched out his legs. "And what will I do with the clothes? I can't return them. You might as well keep them, Carrie. Consider it a parting gift, one that you will have more than earned at the end of this four-month contract."

She'd give them back and he could donate them to charity. However, she didn't bother wasting her breath to argue the point. He was in bossy Brit mode at the moment, so it was best to simply let him think he'd won.

"Here's a gem. There will be no sex." She looked up at him with a smirk. "I know I can go without it but can you?"

She was half-relieved he didn't want to have sex with her and half-insulted. Did he only date great beauties? She'd Googled him and his ex-girlfriends and every one of them had been drop-dead gorgeous.

His ruddy cheeks answered her own question without his having said a word.

"You weren't planning to go without sex." She took a big gulp of the soda the waitress had set in front of her. "Man, I am so naive."

"I wouldn't do anything to embarrass you," he said, shifting in his seat. "I'd be discreet as I would expect of you also should you find someone you're interested in. Just because we don't have sex..."

Hollywood from this angle looked sleazy.

"Ah, I get it. It's all on the down low. Daytime friends and nighttime lovers."

"Something like that," he mumbled, studying his phone again while she turned her attention back to the contract. Reading further, it all looked standard. If there was such a thing when it came to a relationship. There were out-clauses at certain milestones if either of them felt it wasn't working out in the first few months, which she was relieved to see.

"I don't see any red flags here. Do you want me to sign now?"

He looked surprised but she had no issues with it. She

dug a pen out of her purse and held it up. "Looks like I just have this one place to sign. Correct?"

"Yes, then I'll sign it. My PR team will get you an executed copy in a day or two."

They'd finished just in time as their meals were delivered to the table. Carrie's stomach growled as the scent of fried fish wafted around her nose. She loved junk food. From the way Max was digging into his lunch, it looked like they finally had something in common. Maybe she could find a few more things they both liked. Puppies and rainbows, for instance.

The contract was signed. She had to make this work.

———

Max and Carrie were halfway through their lunch when her question came out of left field. For some reason that he couldn't understand now, he'd thought they could glide through this showmance without really getting personal. Frankly it was an insane thought but he'd been holding on to it since the moment the idea had come to him.

"Why don't you tell me a little about yourself," she suggested. "People are going to assume that I know quite a bit but I don't, except for the few things I found on your Wikipedia page."

It was like being interviewed, a task he hated. They asked the same questions over and over until he wanted to scream with frustration.

"What do you want to know?"

"What do you think I should know? What will your friends and family expect me to know?"

Drumming his fingers on the scarred wood surface of the table, he pondered her question. "I'm not sure. They'll probably assume you know that I snore and hog the blankets. I like to read and I can only cook a few things. I do a nice baked chicken and also a pasta with red sauce. If you want anything other than that, we'll need to call for takeout."

*Was that enough?*

"Okay, that's a start. How about you tell me about your childhood. Was it a happy one?"

"If you read my Wikipedia, you already know the answer to that."

He'd never get used to people knowing personal things about him. It was...creepy.

"I know what you tell interviewers. But I'm asking for the real story. Did you have a happy childhood?"

"Yes, actually I did. Because I was an only child my parents doted on me and took me everywhere with them. They treated me like an adult from quite a young age. They were very encouraging about my career."

"Your mother and father are in the business."

"They made it seem like the greatest profession in the entire world. I never thought to be anything else. Except maybe a cowboy. I watched a lot of American westerns when I was a boy." He took a sip of his beer. "What about you? Happy childhood?"

Carrie wrinkled her nose, a sign he was beginning to recognize. It meant she was thinking about her answer. He had to admit that he liked that about her. She didn't just blurt out the first words that popped into her head. She tended to ponder over things before she spoke.

"I did have a happy childhood although, unlike you, I had to share my parents with Greg. He was three years older and a star athlete. I was the geeky, book smart little sister who trailed after him and had crushes on his friends."

"I think geeky and book smart is a good thing."

He could see her sitting in class with her red hair down her back and a pair of glasses perched on her nose. Wearing a schoolgirl uniform. Max knew enough about the States to know that wasn't the norm but a man could dream, right?

"My parents thought it was too when I got a full-ride scholarship to college. Higher education is expensive in the States and we didn't have tons of money growing up. My mom was a teacher and my dad worked for the power company."

"Having a teacher for a mother must have been helpful when it came to your schoolwork."

She rolled her eyes and bit into a chip. "What it really meant is that I could never, ever miss a day of school unless I was on death's door. I hated that. Plus, she knew all my teachers in grade school so I couldn't get away with anything. Nothing. If I so much as chewed a piece of gum my mother would hear about it. I was never so happy to go to middle school where I was anonymous."

He'd bet his new Jaguar that she was the smartest kid in her class.

"So what university did you go to? What did you study?"

Popping a piece of fried fish into her mouth, she hummed in appreciation. "I did my undergrad in business and then went on to grad school and got my MBA. Oh, and I went to Stanford. That's in California."

Schools were different in the UK than the States, but an MBA was an MBA, and he'd heard of Stanford.

"Are you telling me that you have an MBA from Stanford? What in the bloody hell are you doing being a personal assistant?"

Her cheeks turned pink and she took her time chewing and swallowing the food in her mouth before answering. "First of all, I am not a personal assistant, not that there's anything wrong with that. That's just the way Paige and I describe it but my official title is Chief Operating Officer of her corporation. It's a multimillion dollar business, by the way. I'm in charge of pretty much her whole life or anything that isn't personal. I run her day to day business, I keep her marketing on track, I watch her sales trends, and lately I've begun to deal with the studio that is going to be making the Flynn movie. We employ several people that report directly to me including an accountant, an attorney, a research assistant, two virtual assistants for me, and a financial advisor. The reason I'm involved in her life is because she and I are friends, actually more like sisters. She gets buried in her writing and forgets to take care of herself. I'm organized and can help her with that." She popped a fry into her mouth and grinned. "And she pays me a small fortune too. But after my childhood, I've always believed in living below your means. I could buy designer gowns but where would I wear them? It's a little formal for the beach."

This he hadn't expected at all. He'd thought Carrie was...well... Dammit, he was ashamed to even think it.

He'd thought she was sort of...unsuccessful. She certainly wasn't one to flaunt her achievements.

"I apologize and stand corrected. I had no idea that you had all that responsibility. It must be a great deal of work."

She nodded. "It means that I won't be bored while you're working but I do have my systems down at this point so everything should run like clockwork. My assistants are also well-trained and can deal with things in my absence if need be, although if a major decision needs to be made then I have to do it. This is Paige's career and I take it very seriously."

The iron-clad bond between the two women was apparent to anyone who saw them together.

"How did you two meet anyway? You've known her a long time, yes?"

"Noah's mother was a friend of my mother. When I was nearing graduation I came home for spring break and they had cooked up a meeting between myself and Paige. She had just hit the New York Times then and Noah was sick. I could tell she needed someone to take control of the business side of things and to be frank, I wasn't thrilled about the idea of putting on a suit and heels every day and working on Wall Street. She and I had an instant connection and I trusted my gut. I've never regretted it for a moment. I get to do all types of work and I get to do most of it in my pajamas. Of course, my parents were thrilled because it meant that I would be local."

He wasn't sure whether it was a good subject or not but he was curious. "So your parents haven't been gone all that long?"

Sadness flickered across her features and her gaze skittered away, her full lips trembling. "Five years ago. They went out to see a movie and a drunk driver crossed the center line, hitting them head on at seventy miles an hour."

He couldn't even imagine not having his parents in his life, didn't want to contemplate the day they passed on. She'd had to have been amazingly strong to have gone through something that tragic.

He wanted to reach for her hand but wasn't sure she would invite physical contact. He wasn't sure she even liked him as a person. "I'm so sorry. No one should have to deal with that."

She turned back, her eyes bright with unshed tears. "I wouldn't have made it through without Paige. With all the shit she had going on in her own life, she dropped everything for me."

"Was Noah..."

"He died a few months later. We sort of grieved together. It was good to have someone around that felt the way I did."

Slapping the table, Carrie shook her finger at him. "Clever, very clever, Hamlet. I try to get to know you and we end up talking about me. I'm on to you. Now, tell me something your girlfriend would know. Like...boxers or briefs?'

He wasn't sure why but he kind of liked it when she called him Hamlet. "Boxers."

"Favorite book."

"*The Picture of Dorian Gray*. What's yours?"

"*Scruples* by Judith Krantz. Never heard of it, have you?"

"I have to admit that I have not. What's it about?"

"Sex, mostly. It's about a woman who becomes a rich widow and fashion icon in the seventies. My mother used to read Judith Krantz and as soon as I was old enough to sneak them into my room, so did I. I suppose you don't approve since it's not great literature."

She said "literature" with a bad British accent.

"I'll tell you what. You read *Dorian Gray* and I'll read *Scruples*. What do you think?"

By her mischievous smile he could tell he had her. She was going to play.

"Deal, Hamlet." She reached for her phone. "I'll download it right now."

Shaking his head, he tsk-tsk'd her choice. "I like real books. Books you can hold in your hand."

Her expression turned scandalized. "Are you one of those people that sniffs your books?"

"I like the smell of old books."

She shuddered and continued pressing buttons on her phone. "The last time I had a musty book I got an allergic reaction and had to take a Benadryl for the itching. You should think about switching to electronic books. You can carry like five-thousand books with you all in your pocket. The way you travel all the time it would be more convenient."

He regarded her closely, perhaps for the first time, taking a close look at the woman sitting across from him. Not just her flame red hair and light brown eyes or her curvy figure and easy smile. No, he looked at *her*. The way her gaze darted here, there, and everywhere as if taking in every detail of her new surroundings. The way her sweater was buttoned all the way, rather prim and proper but then this was a woman who liked order and control.

Would she be like that in the bedroom?

*Hold on just a minute. No way am I going to ever find that out.*

A sexual relationship with Carrie was out of the question. He wanted to keep this on an even keel, no complications. Sex was a huge complication. Somebody's feelings were bound to become involved and it would probably be Carrie's. Women seemed to fall easier than men. They couldn't do the casual thing very well and he doubted seriously if Carrie was a friends with benefits type. No, she was the kind that fell deeply in love and planned a future. He'd had enough of love to last him a lifetime.

"I'll take that under advisement," he finally said to her recommendation. "Now is there anything else you want to know?"

She placed her phone on the table and looked him straight in the eye. "I think I should know about your marriage and breakup. A girlfriend would know these things."

She spoke the truth but that was one topic he wasn't ready to discuss. Not now. Maybe not ever.

"Not if I don't discuss it. Next topic."

Sighing, she picked up a chip and dipped it in ketchup. "Fine. How about your favorite food?"

That was a question he could handle.

# CHAPTER
## *Seven*

AFTER THAT MORE THAN interesting lunch with Max, Carrie was glad to have some time to herself to go shopping. One thing she was beginning to realize, Max was an intense man, whether it was intentional or not, and the time she spent with him one on one was intense as well. She needed a breather.

When it came to clothes Carrie wasn't a picky woman. At home in Florida she wore shorts and t-shirts most of the year. When it turned chilly she had a pair of blue jeans and a few hoodies. June in London, however, wasn't anything like the Sunshine State. It was wet and chilly, the kind that sunk down into her beach bum bones. Or maybe she was simply a wuss after spending a lifetime growing up where it was warm. Either way, she needed to find sensible clothes that didn't look like she was wearing a potato sack. Where Max went, photographers were sure to follow. She needed to remember she couldn't leave go outside wearing no makeup, a scraggly ponytail, and baggy shorts. That was no way to end up in *People.*

Not being stick thin and six feet tall, shopping was always a challenge. She had hips, she had boobs, and dammit, she had a caboose too. Her belly wasn't flat from a thousand crunches a day. It was soft and when she bent over, it folded onto itself. Her bras had three hooks on the back for support and she could never buy those delicate little lace ones that couldn't hold up a balloon. She needed a feat of engineering with underwire and elastic.

So it was with extreme trepidation that she walked into one of the stores Paige had recommended. Her friend and boss wouldn't send her anywhere that didn't have something to fit her but she'd learned that the salespeople could be downright snotty in certain circumstances. Because she didn't dress up much, they assumed she couldn't afford what they sold.

*Hah!*

Max had learned a valuable lesson as well today. Don't assume from appearances.

"Can I help you?"

Excellent. An older woman with a little cushion of her own. She'd understand.

"Thank you, yes, you can. I'm visiting from a much warmer climate and basically have nothing for this weather. I need jeans, pants, sweaters, skirts, a few dresses, probably some boots and shoes. And a raincoat too."

Lay out on the line. If the woman worked on commission, all the better. Carrie would get great service.

The woman's face lit up. "A whole wardrobe. We better get to work then. My name is Alice, by the way."

"Carrie, and I'll follow you."

Alice led her through a maze of clothing racks, asking questions here and there about favorite colors and styles. By the time they'd traversed the labyrinth to the fitting rooms, Alice had selected a huge armload of clothing.

"This should get you started. While you try these on I'll go grab some more. If you don't like something, place it on this hook. If you like something but it's not the right size, place it here. If you like it and you think you might want it, hang it there."

An organized woman. No wonder Paige had sent Carrie here. It was shopping nirvana.

"Got it and thank you."

Alice smiled. "Actually, I should be thanking you. This is the most fun I've had all week. Can I get you anything to drink?"

Carrie shook her head. "I'm good. I just came from lunch."

"I'll be back in a few then."

Shopping was actually enjoyable. Alice was easy to talk to and seemed to understand Carrie's concerns about showing too much cleavage but at the same time accentuating what her momma gave her. It was a thin line and she wanted to make sure she stayed on the correct side of it. Alice totally got it and brought her tasteful, classy clothes that showed off her curves without being obvious. Her buy pile was growing at an alarming rate but she always followed the motto that when she found clothes that looked good on her, she would buy them. Season be damned. She might not be able to wear them much in Florida but Paige traveled and Carrie would get a chance then.

Frowning, she checked the tag on a particularly lovely peach lace blouse. She needed a size up. It went perfectly with the white wool skirt she had on.

"Alice," she called through the door. "Do you have this in a larger size?"

At this point, it was like doctor and patient so the saleswoman stuck her head in the door and reached for the blouse. "Hmmm...I'll have to check in the back. It's so new only one was unpacked for the display mannequin."

"You stripped a mannequin for me? That's dedication, Alice."

The woman laughed as she bustled away. "I took the skirt too so she's naked as the day she was made in the factory. Shocking, just shocking."

"You're a wild woman, Alice," Carrie called after her, slipping her feet into a gorgeous pair of black stiletto Mary Janes that made her average legs look inches longer and much leaner. It did wonders for her ass and Carrie took a moment to admire what expensive, well-cut clothes could do for a regular woman such as herself when she heard a crash on the other side of the fitting room door. Alice was quick. And apparently a little clumsy. She'd probably grabbed another armload of clothes to try on in addition to the blouse.

*I should give her a hand.*

Without even thinking about her state of undress, she opened it and froze, her entire body stiffening even as she felt a blush rise from her toes all the way up her chest and ending at the roots of her hair.

It wasn't Alice. It was a man. A very handsome, dark-haired man who was currently wearing a wide but familiar smile.

Tyler fucking Gaylord. One of Nate's - and Max's - costars in the *Thunder* movies along with several other roles that had brought him fame, fortune, and women.

He was standing there. Right in front of Carrie. *London must be filled with movie stars.*

Glancing down at herself, she could only feel relief that at least she was wearing a bra and a skirt. All the bits and bobbles were covered up at least and for that she would be forever grateful. At some point she didn't remember, her hands had flown up to her boobs, covering them just above where the satin edge ended. It was a futile effort but the only option appeared to be to try and brazen this out.

"Um, hello?"

That wide smile turned to a predatory grin that would have had most women's panties on the floor. He didn't immediately turn away, his gaze traveling leisurely from her head to where her feet were encased in fuck-me black heels. From the warm look in his amazingly blue eyes, he was enjoying the view.

Blushing all the way to her breasts, she reached back with one hand and grabbed a sweater hanging from the fitting room door and held it in front of her.

The handsome actor took a step closer. "I'm Tyler Gaylord. And you are?"

"Mortified, mostly," she said curtly. His charm wasn't going to work on her. "What are you doing in the ladies' fitting area, Tyler? Is this how you spend your down time between movies? Does TMZ know about this?"

This was why she didn't shop.

He shrugged those wide shoulders. "Some people knit..."

"Others creep around half-naked women. Got it."

Laughing, he shook his head. "It's nice to meet you, ma'am. Seriously, I'm not a pervert. I think I got turned around. The salesperson out there told me to go have a seat for a moment and then she could help me." He held up in his hands in surrender. "I swear I'm only here to buy my girlfriend a gift."

"Monica Batfort," Carrie replied knowingly. She'd seen a picture of the two of them while in line at the grocery store. "You really did take a wrong turn."

He leaned over and picked up the naked mannequin he'd knocked over. "I guess I got a little flustered and next thing I knew this little lady was hitting the floor. I hope she forgives me."

"I heard you were backstage at a lingerie fashion show so I'm having a hard time picturing you flustered by an undressed mannequin."

He leaned forward and gave her a wink. "Don't believe a fraction of what you read."

Carrie of all people should know how bogus it all was.

"A fraction is more than enough. I don't think you'll find anything for Monica back here. She and I don't wear the same size."

Monica was tall and thin with no boobs.

His gaze caressed her curves. "Clearly you don't. But it's not Monica I'm buying for. It's Angie."

"Angie," Carrie echoed, trying to place the name with a face. "I doubt she's my size either."

He stuck his hands in the pockets of his tight jeans.

"The fact is I don't know what to get her. This place was recommended by the wife of one of my costars. She said it had everything and the service was top-notch."

That was exactly what Paige had told Carrie. It couldn't be?

"Did Paige tell you that?"

His brows shot up and then he threw his head back and laughed. "You know Paige? How do you know Paige?"

Of course.

"She's my boss."

Something in Tyler Gaylord's demeanor changed. Just like that, he'd gone from arrogant womanizer to regular guy-next-door. These actors really did turn it on and off.

"You're Carrie," he said warmly. "We would have met at the wedding but I couldn't get away. Paige and Nate talk about you all the time. They say you're a miracle."

It was always nice to hear good things about oneself.

Except when one was half-naked.

"I am a miracle. I am also a little chilly."

At first, he looked at her blankly but then he got what she was saying.

"Clearly, I need to find out where I'm actually supposed to be waiting. I want you to know that I don't normally do this."

Maybe. She'd believe that half-naked women dragged him *into* the dressing rooms. Then had their wicked way with his fine self.

"That would be more believable if you weren't still standing here. Off you go, Mr. Gaylord. I'm sure you're a busy man."

Whirling around, he presented his back to her, but she

could tell he was laughing by the way his shoulders shook. He looked as good from this angle as he did the front.

"Do pardon me, Carrie. I'll just be on my way. It was lovely meeting you. We should do this again sometime."

Of course he got in the last word as Alice bustled back in, an alarmed expression on her face.

"Oh my goodness, I'm afraid to ask what happened but I think I already know. Constance should have escorted him to a chair instead of just sending him in this direction."

The entire situation was funny and absurd. Carrie couldn't help but burst into laughter at the older woman's fearful expression. Was she afraid that Carrie was going to scream and complain? Call the cops? Walk out without buying anything?

"Thankfully he didn't see anything of importance."

Carrie was sure he'd seen it all before. And much better. He'd dated a long list of glamorous beauties.

Alice glanced over her shoulder to where he'd been standing. "A man like that could get me to show him anything he wanted. No questions asked. This will make a funny story at the next office Christmas party."

It was going to make a funny story sooner than that. Carrie would tell Paige the next time they talked. They would both get a king-sized laugh out of it. It was such a small world.

"Glad I could help, Alice. Now that Tyler Gaylord has found the exit, did you find that blouse in my size?" she asked hopefully.

The woman beamed and held it up. "I certainly did."

Carrie would chalk the afternoon up to one of those strange moments that you giggle about years later. It might even make Max laugh. Or maybe not. That stick up his butt probably made it difficult to laugh or have fun. When she'd seen him in interviews he didn't seem that stodgy.

It might just be her that brought out the pompous ass in him.

# CHAPTER
## *Eight*

MAX HAD INSISTED on taking her out the next night for dinner. To be seen together in a casual way. Walking arm and arm down the street or coming out of a movie theatre. He explained it was the best way to introduce a new relationship to the public. Float a balloon and see how it goes over. Since she'd never fake-dated anyone she had to take his word for it.

He didn't get out of rehearsals until late and she'd wanted to see The Eye at night so she sent him a text that he could meet her there. By the time she'd taken the thirty-minute ride and returned, he was waiting for her on the ground.

Looking around like he was casing the joint and checking his watch.

"You're late."

*Nice to see you too.*

*He's a nice man. He's a nice man. Paige says he's a nice man.*

If she repeated it enough, would her wish come true?

"I'm sorry. I waited in line longer than I thought. It was amazing up there though. The city is beautiful at night."

That seemed to soften him up slightly. "It is, isn't it? It's been years since I rode The Eye at night. I should have gone with you."

She glanced over her shoulder at the long line and smirked. "I'm game if you are."

The look he gave the queue could only be described as longing. He wanted to do it but he was already shaking his head no. "We'd better not. My luck has held this long and I'd be pushing it if I tried to stay longer."

"Your luck?"

His gaze darted around nervously and he hunched his shoulders. "I'll tell you what. I'll book us a private ride for one day next week. A whole car just to ourselves. Doesn't that sound better?"

Not really. Carrie liked meeting new people and she'd talked to several during her own ride but it was clear Max didn't feel the same. His loss.

"Sure, whatever you want. Are you ready for dinner?"

"I am. Do you trust me to pick the restaurant?"

If she didn't like it she could always order a pizza later. "That's fine. Where are we going?"

Max smiled. "A little place not far from here. I think you'll like it. We can have our privacy there."

More of that privacy stuff. He had quite the fetish.

Carrie figured out why when they stepped out onto the sidewalk. There were blinding flashes of light and his arm went around her immediately, pulling her into his side protectively.

"Don't look at them. Don't give them the money shot they're looking for. One of the Eye employees must have called the paps or maybe one of the people in line tweeted I was here. Just stay close and I'll get us out of this."

*This* turned out to be a crush of photographers that all seemed to be yelling at once. It didn't take a genius to see why Max didn't like crowds and why he'd asked for some privacy. She ought to smack her forehead, she'd been so stupid. Tonight explained quite a bit about this man she'd tied herself to.

To his credit, he didn't leave her side for a millisecond, keeping her close while he flagged down a taxi and bundled her in. The paps seemed to take that as a challenge and actually followed them, shooting pictures as their cars pulled up alongside, like a Formula One race through the streets of London. It was incredibly dangerous and she was more than relieved when they went through an almost red light that caught the rest of them. Max directed the driver to pull over and she stumbled out of the vehicle, still shaken by what she'd experienced.

"Are you okay?"

The taxi drove away and they were standing on a street corner but apparently Max had thought ahead. They were right next to a Tube station.

She nodded, breathing slowly to get her beating heart under control. "I am just surprised they'd go to those lengths to get a photo."

His brows pinched together. "That was actually rather tame. Shall we go before they catch up?"

They quickly caught a train but she didn't know enough about the city to know what direction they were going in. He was seated next to her but he'd hardly spoken since they'd boarded, simply making sure she was comfortable. Nudging his elbow, she moved closer so he could hear her without everyone else being privy to their conversation.

"Thanks."

"What for? Getting you out of there? It's my job to take care of you."

She didn't take offense at being referred to as someone's *job*. If she'd learned anything about Max in the short time she'd known him was that he took his responsibilities very seriously. It would be just like him to call many things in his life a job or work.

"I'm still grateful. I've seen Paige and Nate with the paparazzi but they were never chased around London in the dark."

The car stopped and Max stood, helping her to her feet. A cheery automated voice told her to mind the gap as she exited the tube and she followed him to the street.

"Where to next?" she asked, looking around. She had literally no clue where they were.

"You mentioned once that you like Italian food. We're close to some of the best Italian food in London, maybe the world—except for Italy, of course."

She glanced down at her casual attire. "Am I dressed for this palace of culinary delight?"

He gifted her with one of his true rare smiles. "It's very come as you are." Offering her his arm, he led her down the street, slowly enough that she could take in the little shops and restaurants. "I hope you like this place. It's owned by an old friend from school. He's always willing to get me a table on short notice."

"Where are we? I mean, in relation to where we were?"

It might help in learning her way around.

"Close by. We're in a section called the South Bank." He stopped and held up his palm, pointing just above his wrist. "The South Bank is down here. Here is the Thames. Here is the city of London. Now up here is my home in Hampstead. We'll get you a map for the Tube. You can get pretty much anywhere you want to go on it. If I remember correctly, you don't have much public transit where you're from."

Taking in the buildings so close together, she nodded. "We're too spread out. Americans love their elbow room."

"I've learned that. I've always said that I'd like to take a car ride from one coast to another. See those wide-open spaces that I've heard so much about."

She couldn't stop the laughter that bubbled up and he gave her a strange look. "Sorry, it's just that when we were kids my mom and dad would take us on road trips for our summer vacation. Pack us all in the minivan and see how many states we could hit in two weeks while Greg and I argued about where we would stop and whether the other had encroached on our personal space. It wasn't all that glamorous."

"It's sounds like good fun," he said kindly. "I still think I'd like a trip like that."

If he kept acting human like this, the next four months weren't going to be so bad. She might even enjoy herself.

They'd resumed walking and now he was opening the door of a small restaurant, the delicious smells hitting her straight in the olfactory senses. Her stomach gurgled in approval and she could have kissed him at that moment. Everything smelled like perfection. The place looked bigger inside, all done in earth tones with splashes of blue and green here and there.

A portly man with a thinning hairline came to greet them, a big smile on his face and his arms opened wide. "Maxwell, I was wondering if you were going to make it. It's good to see you, my friend."

They hugged and then Max stepped back, placing his arm around her waist. "We ran into a spot of trouble but we're here now. Carrie, I'd like you to meet Albert Whittaker. Albert, this is Carrie Johnson."

The man beamed and heartily shook her hand. "Any friend of Max's is a friend of mine."

"It's nice to meet you, Mr. Whittaker. Your restaurant is beautiful and everything smells amazing."

"Call me Albert. You must be starving. Max said that you were visiting the Eye before you came here. Did you like it?" Albert kept up a steady stream of conversation as he showed them to their table. "Now make sure Max shows you his impressions. He does the best I've ever seen."

Max's cheeks were red and he was trying to hide behind his menu but Albert was having none of it. He slapped his old friend on the back and launched into a tale about the time they snuck out of boarding school to go do a voodoo ritual one of them had read about out on the grounds. Now this was a Max she could hang out with.

"A voodoo ritual?" Carrie teased, accepting the glass of wine the waitress slid in front of her. "What kind?"

Propping his head in his palm, Max groaned. "We were cursing our mathematics professor because we had an exam coming up."

Both men looked surprisingly boyish, their sly grins lighting up their faces. There was more to this story than they'd revealed so far.

"And did you succeed?"

"Hardly," Max said dryly. "We almost set fire to ourselves melting some wax and did manage to scorch the grass rather badly. Part of the ritual was to sacrifice a chicken and of course we couldn't do that. So instead we brought our baked chicken from dinner out there and sort of went through the motions. Pathetic, really."

Laughing so hard that tears were flowing down her face, Carrie held her stomach as she hiccuped once or twice. For his part, Max was laughing as well as he and Albert bantered about who had run faster when they thought they'd been caught. This was pure gold. "Awesome. Just awesome. How did you do on the test? It sounds like it would have been easier to just study."

"Poorly. My mum grounded me during break."

Albert slapped Max on the back again and headed to the kitchen. "I've got a million of these stories, Carrie, but I'll leave you to have dinner. Anything you need, you let me know."

Carrie studied the menu. She wanted to hear more stories but her hunger needed to take precedence. "Remind me to tell you some stories from a few slumber parties I attended. Teenage girls are just as silly as teenage boys. Have you ever heard of 'light as a feather, stiff as a board'?"

Frowning, Max shook his head and placed his menu on

the table. He probably knew all the really good things to order. "I don't think so. Should I have?"

"It may be an American thing. I'll tell you about it...if you want me to. It's not all that interesting, actually."

What grown man wanted to hear about the day to day lives of young girls? Especially this man. She had the distinct impression he barely tolerated her when she spoke.

Then he smiled. A real, genuine smile that changed his entire face from forbidding to kind. Even his ice blue eyes were in on the action, becoming a softer shade, like a blanket for a newborn boy.

Her heart fluttered and for a moment she forgot to breathe. The veneer, the mask, he'd been wearing was gone and this was...him. All it had taken was an old friend to rip away that protective layer.

"I'd love to hear about it."

# CHAPTER
## *Nine*

HAVING no siblings Max didn't realize the life of an American teenager was quite that colorful. He'd had no idea that if he bit a wintergreen Lifesaver in the dark it would spark. That was actually a little frightening, but he was definitely going to try it.

He'd also learned about games girls played at slumber parties and he certainly wished he'd been a teenage boy crashing that party. He'd missed out on girls practicing kissing. He would have been happy to volunteer as a test subject rather than their bed pillows or stuffed animals.

"You braided each other's hair and experimented with makeup?"

They were currently consuming a huge slab of tiramisu after filling up on spaghetti, lasagna, and garlic bread. He liked that Carrie wasn't afraid to eat. So many women around him ordered a salad and complained about having to watch their figure. Food was meant to be savored and enjoyed and it was even better in good company.

Carrie was definitely good company. He'd chosen well.

"We did," she confirmed, her pink tongue snaking out to catch a morsel falling off her fork. His breath caught in his throat at the sight of her licking at the fluffy marscapone. "Don't even ask to see the photos because I've hidden them under lock and key. Thank God this was before Facebook and Instagram were much of a thing."

"Do you embarrass easily? As an actor I don't have much sense of shame, I'm afraid."

Laughing, she waved her fork in the air. "I can't embarrass too easily because it feels like I'm always doing stupid things. Somehow I get myself into situations that are deeply humiliating. You're lucky you don't care about those things. I could have used you earlier today when I went shopping for clothes and Tyler Gaylord saw me half-naked in the changing room."

*What the...?*

Almost choking on his water, Max slapped the glass down on the table. "Tyler was in your changing room? He barged in while you were changing? What in the hell was he doing there?"

Her brows went up and her mouth twisted. "He was looking to buy a gift for his girlfriend. Someone named Angie. Anyway, I heard a crash and I thought it was the saleslady, so I opened the fitting room door to see him leaning over a naked mannequin he'd knocked down. Luckily, I was wearing a skirt, high heels, and a bra so everything important was covered but I think he and I were both pretty mortified."

Carrie...in nothing but a skirt, high heels, and bra... Were the heels red? Damn, he loved red high heels on a female. Every nerve in his body had woken up and was now paying close attention. His filthy teenage boy mind had already conjured up an image of her in a tight, short skirt and a black lace bra. All the blood in his brain had migrated in a southerly direction and he'd lost track of what she'd been saying.

"...so he apologized and left after explaining that it was Paige who recommended the shop. It's all okay, really. It's not like he really saw much. I've shown more skin in a bathing suit."

Fuck, now he was thinking about her in a bikini. This was going from bad to worse. He needed to change the subject right away or his mind would stop functioning completely and he'd simply be a drooling mess babbling incoherently.

"So we have a party to attend on Saturday night," Max said, feeling a trickle of sweat at his hairline. "I can have my publicist call a few designers and see if they are willing to dress you for it."

Wrinkling her nose, she seemed to take the switch in topics in stride. "Honestly, I'd rather not unless it's some big event. It's a fundraiser, right?"

"For the children's hospital. Black tie and there will be a red carpet."

She was scrolling through her phone. "Paige gave me the name of a London stylist. Yes, here it is. Why don't I call her in the morning and see what she says?"

"Excellent idea."

With a smile and a sigh, Carrie set down her fork and patted her stomach. "That was great. Good choice on the restaurant. Albert seems like a terrific guy too."

Albert was one in a million, along with his wife and kids. They treated Max the same way today as they had before anyone had known his name.

"I can assure he is one of my oldest and dearest friends. A truly good person."

Playing with her fork, Carrie fidgeted in her seat. "Listen, I want to apologize about earlier. I'm sorry about the way I acted."

It was sweet of her to say she was sorry but he had no idea what she was talking about.

"That's thoughtful of you but I don't think you have anything to be sorry for actually. Unless you've done something I don't know about."

She tilted her head, their gazes colliding. Every time he looked into her amber-colored eyes he saw something he hadn't seen before. This time it was the flecks of gold around the iris.

"I was acting bitchy at the Eye. It's just...I thought you were being difficult about me doing touristy stuff and being a little late. But after the whole paparazzi thing and then seeing you with your friend Albert, I get it. That's why I'm sorry. I judged too quickly."

He should let this go but some little voice was egging him on. "What is it that you think you know, Carrie?"

"I get why you have the protective veneer with people. Why sometimes you act like a pompous, arrogant asshole. You don't know who you can trust or what they want from you so you keep them at arms' length. You're totally different with Albert than you are with most people. I can see who you really are."

That was a truly disturbing thought. Max wasn't even

sure he liked who he was. Certainly Alana hadn't liked many facets of his personality and had complained about them on multiple occasions. He'd driven her into another man's arms because of his neediness. He liked to cuddle, talk, say *I love you* every day. When he was in a relationship he wanted to spend as much time with that person as possible. Alana had hated that, said she felt suffocated and that any woman who had her own life and career would feel the same.

"I see," he said, stalling for time. He wasn't sure how to respond. Clearly she thought it was a good thing and she seemed to like what he'd revealed but that was a small part of who he was. Showing her all of himself wasn't something he was eager to do. "I do have to keep up somewhat of a mask for the public. You're correct when you say that I don't know who to trust or what others want from me. It's not easy to become close to new people in my life. I tend to depend on my old friends or those who are also in the business and in the same position I am. They...understand."

She gave him a lopsided smile. "And I'm not in either of those categories. I get that. I just want you to know that you can trust me. I don't want anything from you, Max. We're here to help each other and it's a mutual agreement. I'm not looking for money or fame. I just want to be able to hold my head up high, that's all."

In his experience, everyone wanted money and fame.

Okay, maybe not everyone but almost everyone. The only difference was what people were willing to do to get it. Alana, for example, had been willing to not only fuck him but marry him to get what she wanted.

What was Carrie willing to do? She might not even realize that she wanted more, but when it was offered to her she'd grab it with both hands.

"I want you to be able to do that," he finally said. "That's what we both want. If we work together we can get through these next few months."

Smile faltering, she took a sip from her water glass. If she'd hoped for some deeply personal revelation from him she was probably quite disappointed. "That's good then. You know...that we understand each other."

Max didn't need for her to understand him. He needed her to do what he was contracting her to do. They didn't have to get all emotionally sloppy here. He liked Carrie, she seemed like a sweet woman but he wasn't looking for a relationship. He'd had one of those already and it hadn't turned out well. He bloody well wasn't ready for another one, not yet. His heart was still in shreds from the chaos Alana had wrought.

If he'd been anyone else but who he was, he would have gone off for several months and licked his wounds. But he was a famous actor and in the spotlight, and he wasn't allowed to be heartbroken.

The show must go on, and he with it.

# CHAPTER
## *Ten*

THE NEXT MORNING over coffee and a Danish Carrie called the stylist, a friendly girl named Lisa, and set up an appointment for the next day but made sure to warn her about her measurements. Lisa wasn't getting a supermodel to style but she seemed fine with it. If she wasn't, she was too polite to say so.

She'd just hung when her phone buzzed again. Greg. This was unusual. Their normal call pattern was once every few weeks or when something major happened. Her stomach clenched with fear as she thought about her niece and nephew. Had something happened or had he butt dialed her just to give her a heart attack?

"Hey big brother, didn't I just talk to you? Is everything okay?"

"You're in the news."

No *hello*. No *how are you*. Just *you're in the news*.

"Did I win that Nobel Prize I've been campaigning for? I assumed I was a shoo-in."

She was playing with Greg but she had a feeling she knew what he was talking about. Those paparazzi last night had taken their picture and one or more of them had probably ended up in some tabloid rag.

"Funny, Carrie. I'm being serious here. You're on the internet."

Already tapping the keys of her laptop, the photos were incredibly easy to find once she typed in the search phrase *Maxwell Hayes's new girlfriend*.

Bingo. Time to drop the bomb on poor brother Greg.

"I guess I didn't mention that I've met someone."

"You've met Maxwell Hayes? Funny you should say that because I'm having a secret affair with Angelina Jolie."

Inwardly sighing, Carrie tried to remember the rehearsed explanation but it had fled her brain when she'd seen the tabloid photos.

"Funny, big brother. I'm serious. I'm...dating Maxwell Hayes. He's a friend of Nate Mason, Paige's husband."

Lightning didn't strike her down for telling that huge fib. Interesting. Her parents had lied about that.

"So...wow...okay. I saw the photos and figured something was up but I just assumed you were doing work for him or something."

"Work?"

"You know, like assistant work. The stuff you do for Paige."

Like most people in her life, Greg thought she was pulling down minimum wage fetching lattes for Paige. He didn't seem to get her job responsibilities and frankly she'd been too busy to educate him.

"Well, we're dating."

Silence.

"Greg? I said we're dating."

"So I guess that's good then? You must be over Mark."

Actually, now that he'd brought her ex up, she realized she hadn't thought about idiot Mark in quite awhile.

"I am," she said firmly. "Max is a great guy."

Sometimes.

"So you were out on a date with this movie star?"

"Max and I were chased by some photographers last night when we visited the Eye. It's no big deal, Greg."

It wasn't a small deal either. Her likeness was splashed all over a couple of UK tabloids with some pretty lurid headlines.

*Hayes rebounding with mystery redhead*

*Has Max given up on Alana?*

*Is that a baby bump? Why Max gave up on Alana*

*Mystery redhead soothes Max's broken heart*

Baby bump? As if. The way her life had been going lately it would have had to have been an immaculate conception. But she could see why the headline read that way. At the angle they'd caught her, and in that particular jacket, she did look slightly pregnant. Or chubby. Maybe she should be happy no one called her fat. Or plain. They just called her a mystery which for now was fine.

"They think you're pregnant, Carrie. I'd call that a big deal. I mean...you're not, are you? It's okay if you are."

Christ on a pogo stick.

"I know it would be okay but rest easy, Greg, I'm not. Not even a little bit. It's just the press trying to sell papers. When I don't give birth in a few months, they'll realize they're wrong. Of course by then they will have made up a dozen or so other stories. You need to not react every time they write something because I'm guessing it's going to get worse."

Carrie didn't trust Max's ex not to try and win in the court of public opinion if she couldn't win in court. Smearing Max, and maybe Carrie as well, might be the way to go about that.

"Seems like a tough kind of relationship to be in, Sis. In the public eye all the time. I hope he's worth it."

Interesting question. The glimpses of the real Max? Yes, he was worth it. The snotty guy who often showed up here? Not in the least. She'd thought she was getting some-where last night when they'd talked but he'd closed himself off completely, the mask coming down. She'd watched as he'd transformed himself in seconds from a friendly, open guy to a stiff, cold asshole.

"He is," she said instead. Greg must never know the lengths she'd gone to keep her family and friends from feeling sorry for her. "He's a good man. You'd like him if you met him."

"Me and some British actor guy?" Greg laughed. "Sure, I bet we have a lot in common. Has he ever hunted gator?"

*Really, Greg?*

"No, and neither have you," she shot back. "Stop acting like you're some kind of redneck. You're an attorney, for heaven's sake. You live in a gated community. You play golf on the weekends."

"I could hunt gator if I wanted to. In fact, I've been thinking about it."

Snorting, Carrie almost dropped her phone laughing. "Jeannie would never let you go in a million-trillion years.

Now I really do need to go and I'm sure you have to take someone's deposition or bill hours to some poor shmuck. Thanks for letting me know about the pictures. There may be more so you need to get used to it."

"I'll never get used to seeing my sister in the gossip columns," Greg grumbled. "Next time they try and take your picture, duck or something."

"Now why didn't I think of that? Say goodbye, Greg."

"Goodbye, Greg."

That was an old joke between them and she was chuckling as they hung up, but her attention was quickly back on the photos. She didn't look too bad in them. None of them were all that great, a little blurry as she and Max rushed in the opposite direction. It had been dark so their faces were illuminated by the flash and she didn't like how pasty white she looked but Max was the same so it didn't have anything to do with her. The only thing that could have made it any better was if she was five inches taller and twenty pounds thinner.

Ahhh, wishful thinking.

A knock on the front door pulled her from the pictures and she slapped the lid down on the laptop. It was probably Max. He'd sent her a text earlier that he would be by today with the executed contract.

Pulling open the door, her mouth fell open when she saw who it was, standing at the door with an armload of pink roses in a delicate crystal vase. She'd never thought to see him again and just how did he find her?

Tyler Gaylord, perverted changing room guy and Hollywood heartthrob. What in the hell did he want?

Flowers. Smiling. *Wait.* Did he want...her?

# CHAPTER

## *Eleven*

MAX TUCKED the executed copy of the contract into his messenger bag. His publicist had delivered it this morning during play rehearsals and Max wanted to give it to Carrie personally. If only because he was worried she'd changed her mind after her face appeared in those rags. It was one thing to agree to do this, but it was something quite different to have her face splashed across a supermarket tabloid. She might be having second thoughts.

He needed her desperately and the tabloids' coverage of their evening out only underlined that fact. Every single story had mentioned how Alana had another man, and a few of them out and out stated she'd cheated. Alana had indeed been unfaithful but Max's people had been trying to smother that little nugget whenever it cropped up. It was bad enough that she'd left him; he didn't need to be seen as not able to keep a woman happy.

Then there was Carrie.

He couldn't tell if she was happy or not. She seemed so

last night when she'd thought she had *figured him out*. Being around his old friend Albert, Max couldn't help but be himself. But when it was just him and Carrie, that was an entirely different scenario. He needed to keep control of the situation at all times. If she gained the upper hand, he'd be at her mercy and he didn't want to feel that way with a woman. Again.

In a way, he already did. He needed her more than she needed him. His humiliation would be for the world to see while hers would encompass a much smaller circle. Frankly, she was doing him a favor. Maybe he should buy her a present to show his appreciation. In his experience women liked gifts. Flowers. Candy. Jewelry.

Entering Nate's key code for the gate, he bounded up the front steps of the house. Laughter drifted through the door and he hesitated, his hand raised to knock, as he heard the soft murmur of voices and the melodious tinkling of Carrie's full-throated chuckle. She had company but who? He wasn't aware that she knew anyone in London. It must be the stylist she was going to call.

It only took her moments to answer after he rapped lightly on the door, dressed in a pair of faded denims and a bright blue sweater, her feet stuffed in fluffy white socks. Her cheeks were pink, probably from laughing and he had to admit - at least to himself - that he wished she looked that happy and carefree all the time. She always acted rather tense around him but then he did the same with her.

"I have your copy of the contract." Frowning, he peered around the doorway but couldn't see who was in her sitting area. "Is this a bad time?"

She waved him in. "No, come on in."

His friend Tyler Gaylord stood up from the love seat. A dozen pink roses in a vase were sitting on the coffee table in front of him.

What in the hell was going on here?

"Tyler, I thought you were in Milan."

His friend grinned, knowing full well what he was doing. Arsehole. "I was in Milan. Now I'm in London. Did Carrie tell you about our rather...unusual meeting?"

Still eyeing the bouquet of flowers, Max cleared his throat before he inched over to Carrie and placed an arm around her waist, hoping Tyler took the hint. "She did and we had quite the laugh. You were buying something for your *girlfriend*?"

Wincing, Tyler shook his head. "That didn't work out. I'm back on the market. A free man."

Gaylord certainly went through the ladies at breakneck speed. "Too bad. Can't seem to keep a woman can you, mate?"

"I'll worry about that when I find the right one."

*It's not Carrie, you randy goat.*

She must have seen Max's increasingly unhappy expression.

"We were just talking about good restaurants in the area."

*I'll just bet he was. Then he'll ask you to go out to dinner with him.*

"There are several," Max said, keeping his eye on Tyler who had his eye on Carrie. "If there is someplace in particular you want to try, Carrie, all you have to do is ask. I'd be more than happy to take you anywhere you want to go."

Maybe Max was laying it on a bit thick but he knew

Tyler Gaylord and how he was with women. A total player who never looked back after he broke a heart. Max wouldn't allow his friend to treat Carrie like that.

His too pretty face wreathed in smiles, Tyler moved toward the door. "I guess I should be going. I have an early photo shoot in the morning. Carrie, it was lovely seeing you again."

"Yes, you should be going," Max opened the front door. "You don't want to be in makeup for hours tomorrow because you didn't get enough rest."

Carrie elbowed him as she and Tyler hugged. They must have become close quite quickly.

"Thank you so much for stopping by to check on me, and also for the flowers. They're gorgeous."

She sounded way too enthusiastic. They were just roses, for fuck's sake. It's not like he gave her a handful of diamonds or a ticket to Bora Bora. She bid Tyler a goodbye before shutting it behind her with a firm click. Rounding on him, she leaned back against the oak slab and gave Max a disgusted look.

"You were very rude."

"I thought I was quite restrained. What was he doing here?"

She brushed past him and went to the refrigerator to retrieve a water bottle, holding it up in offering but he shook his head. "He was checking to see how I was settling in to London. It was very thoughtful of him to stop by."

Arching a brow, Max stalked forward to the coffee table and reached out a fingertip, tracing a velvety petal. He could hear the blood rushing in his ears, acid rising in his throat. Carrie shouldn't be entertaining strange men. It wouldn't look right. What if the paps had caught her?

"You know that Tyler Gaylord is one of the biggest playboys on earth? Possibly *the* biggest?"

"I did know that," she answered breezily, a smile on her face. "But I'm not the type to fall for a dozen roses and a smooth line. Give me a little credit."

He plucked a petal off a bud and let it fall to the table. "He was here to chat you up."

Snorting, she settled in a chair. "No shit. Listen, I may be dumb about men but I'm not stupid. Besides, if I hadn't figured it out his asking me to dinner would have tipped his hand."

A haze of red passed in front of his eyes. He was going to have a little talk with his friend.

"He asked you out? He's a fast worker, isn't he? But I can see you didn't tell him you had a boyfriend. You didn't even introduce me as such."

"I didn't need to," she sputtered, her cheeks going red with laughter. "You did everything but pee on me to mark your territory. No words or descriptions were necessary. He got the not-so-subtle hint, Max."

"I simply greeted my girlfriend."

Her lips turned down and she shook her head. "You really believe that, don't you? You don't think you did anything wrong."

He straightened up to every inch of his six-one height. "I know I didn't do anything wrong. He was in the wrong, coming here and bringing you flowers."

"He was very sweet to do that. He didn't have any idea that I was seeing anyone." She held up her hand. "I'm not wearing any rings, after all. He seems like a nice man and you could have been kinder. He's your friend."

Astonished, Max barked with laughter. "Kind? To the man trying to steal away my girl? I think not. If anything I should have kicked his arse out of this house. You belong to me and only me."

The minute the words came out he regretted them. It was the exact wrong thing to say to Carrie and the fury in her expression was clear for anyone to see. Her eyes were bright with tears and her lips trembled, but not with fear or sadness. Carrie was beside herself with anger, and the way she kept fisting her hands and then relaxing them told him she wanted to smack him hard across the face.

"Well, then...Thank you for bringing by the contract but I think it's time for you to go."

Her tone was dangerously soft. He was walking on razor thin ice here. "Please let me apologize. That did not come out the way I intended it."

"Then tell me what you intended to say."

He opened his mouth and then snapped it shut. Whatever he said was only going to get him into more trouble. Better to be silent and ride this out.

He cleared his throat. "I don't think either one of us is in the right state to discuss this any further."

Her brows shot up. Damn, he'd fucked up again. He began easing toward the exit. She might blow at any minute and he wanted to be out of the blast zone.

"I think that what you really wanted to say to Tyler Gaylord was that you owned me and he needed to stay away from your property. Is that about right?"

*Don't answer. Don't answer. Don't answer.*

"Of course not. I don't think I own you, but you are my girlfriend and I'm your boyfriend. You're spoken for and so am I. You're being ridiculous."

*Dumbass. I told you to shut up. This is why you're divorced. You always take the bait.*

Hopping up from the sofa, she got in his face - or as close as she could at her height - and poked at his chest with her finger. "I'm being ridiculous? I cannot believe you said that. I am not being ridiculous."

Those words were spat out between gritted teeth and he stood there helpless, not sure what to say or do. He could remain motionless and wait out the storm or try and talk her down. Usually when the woman in his life got like this he swept her into his arms and kissed her. It worked more times than it didn't, so it was his go-to strategy but she wasn't his to kiss and there would be no "sweeping" of anything in this fake-lationship.

More pokes into his chest. "Are you listening to me?"

"Yes, I am and as I said I do want to apologize. My behavior was uncalled for."

Her eyes narrowed and she regarded him suspiciously. "Which behavior would that be?"

"All of it," he answered promptly, not really meaning it but knowing she expected it. "I am sorry and I hope you can forgive me."

She fell back onto the love seat and rolled her eyes. "For an Academy Award-winning actor, you suck at lying. You're not sorry at all."

Now it was his turn to grit his teeth. "I was simply nominated. I did not win."

"Well, now you know why."

No one in Max's life had ever had the gall to say something like that to him. Ever. People told him what a great actor he was and that he should have won. They didn't tell him why he didn't. It was staggering.

He threw the contract he'd been holding in his hand, already crumpled from his unrelenting grip onto the table between them. "I came to bring you your copy of the contract but honestly I cannot imagine why I signed an agreement with someone like you. You're rude and unpleasant. What Paige sees in you as a friend I have no idea."

"Same to you, fella. I think her first evaluation of you was correct. Stiff, cold, arrogant, superior, and pompous. She called you a judgmental asshole and I concur."

Paige's opinion of him hurt, more than a little. Max did take time to warm up and get to know people but he didn't like to think he wasn't a good person until he did. He just kept to himself.

"I do not judge people."

"Really? You judged me. Guilty as charged, officer. Some poor bastard came by here with flowers and asked me out. Somehow this became my fault. It was completely innocent - at least on my part - and you blew it out of proportion. You know, it's just as well you're calling all of this off because I couldn't pretend to be your girlfriend, Max. Just for your edification, I'm not an actress. If I'm going to act like a girlfriend, I actually have to know you a little bit. I have to like you as a person. To do that we have to spend time together and do more than stare blankly at each other. You've been so busy protecting yourself, you haven't noticed that you've been pushing me away. So here

I am. Ready to leave and go back home. I'd rather face my friends and family than have to deal with your sourpuss day in and day out. For a fucking millionaire sex symbol movie star, you sure as hell don't have much to smile about." She pointed to the door. "You can show yourself out."

For a moment he couldn't move, frozen to that spot on the carpet. But then he realized she was serious, her lips pressed together and her light brown eyes dark with emotion. Fury. She was absolutely furious with him.

He wasn't all that calm either and that was just fine with him. He wasn't the one at fault here. She was the problem. She had the issues.

Good riddance.

# CHAPTER
## Twelve

AFTER THE UGLY scene with Max, Carrie had managed to lose herself in her work so it was a shock when she received a text from Paige. She wanted to talk to Carrie as soon as possible.

It was a dreary evening outside, cold and rainy but the gas fireplace in the living room was warm and cheery and Carrie sat down on the overstuffed chair, her legs curled under her as she brought up Skype on her laptop. In less than a minute she was seeing Paige's glowing face. Marriage agreed with her.

"Where's Nate?" Carrie asked, blowing on her hot chocolate. "Did he have to work today?"

It was still afternoon in Los Angeles.

"No, but he had a meeting with the director and producer but he should be home any time now. What I want is for you to tell me what's going on in London. According to the tabloids I'm going to be an auntie. I have to say I'm kind of surprised you're carrying Max's baby. You two didn't waste any time."

Rolling her eyes, Carrie sipped her cocoa. She had told Paige about her broken engagement a few days ago, albeit a sanitized version designed to not upset her newlywed friend. She and Max had planned to tell Nate and Paige together about their relationship, but the moment was upon her and she didn't think she could pretend with her best friend in the whole world.

"There's something I need to tell you about me and Max."

"Are you going to tell me that you and Max are fake?"

Almost dropping her mug, Carrie carefully set it on the table next to the chair. "How on earth did you know?"

Paige nodded. "I didn't know for sure until you just confirmed it but I know you. You don't hop from being engaged to one man to dating another without a care in the world. You're more deliberate than that. You'd think it through, although if you agreed to a fake romance with him I'd say you might not have thought that through either. Want to tell me what happened? And don't leave out any details."

It was then that Carrie began to explain the real truth - about Mark, his ex-wife, seeing Max outside when he went for a cigarette that he shouldn't have been smoking, and then lastly how crappy the last few days had been. She and Max at each other's throats, his ex-wife, and Tyler Gaylord. By the time she finished, Carrie needed a tissue to wipe the tears from her eyes and blow her nose.

"That sniveling little rat-faced git," Paige fumed, her lips tight. "I'll punch him right where it counts just for being a jerk. He should have known if he was getting involved with you that meant he was getting involved with me too. Asshole."

Carrie waved her tissue. "There's no need. It's over. He called it off and I'm okay with it."

Paige scowled at her friend. "I'm going to put my foot up his ass."

She didn't need that kind of help. Max had been a jerk but not enough to warrant corporal punishment. "It's not a big deal. He and I just don't get on well. He's got...issues. And then there's what I said."

"What did you say?"

"I kind of said that I could see why he didn't win an Oscar."

Paige hissed as she exhaled slowly. "Ouch, that had to hurt. But still, so what? Doesn't give him permission to be a jerk."

It did, though. But all the other times? That was on him.

"Um...didn't Nate act a little arrogant when you first met him? I think it's this movie star thing. People fawn over them and they start to believe their own press."

"Max is tough to get to know. He doesn't open up easily but when he does he's a nice man. Very protective too."

"I'm not sure I have that kind of time."

She was in her thirties now. How old would she be when he warmed up to her?

"You've been photographed with him, my friend. Plus, that wicked witch of an ex-wife has seen you together. Running away may not be a valid option anymore. Besides, you'd have to face everyone at home. You agreed to this for a reason and my guess is that reason hasn't suddenly vanished."

Wrapping her cold hands around the warm mug, Carrie contemplated her less than stellar options. "They haven't but I'm not sure I can pull this off. I thought Max and I would at least become friends, if not friendly. I wasn't thinking we'd fall into bed like you and Nate but I kind of hoped we could have fun and laugh. You know, enjoy ourselves. I mean...what does that man do for fun? He hardly ever smiles."

Paige's brows pinched together. "You know, I don't know what he does for fun. I do know that he and Nate go play darts and have a few beers down at the pub. But as for how else he spends his free time, I don't know. He once told me he likes to read."

"We have that in common then but I'm not sure that's enough to base a relationship on, even a make-believe one."

Heavy footsteps sounded and then Nate breezed in, kissing Paige soundly and giving Carrie a smug grin. This was a happily married man before her. She'd been worried about whether he could do this but clearly marriage looked good on him. He snuggled next to Paige, wrapping an arm around her shoulders while she rested her head on his chest.

"Carrie, it's lovely to see you my friend." He frowned and leaned closer to the camera on the laptop. "Have you been crying?"

Paige nodded. "She most certainly has and it's all Max's fault."

Frowning, Nate looked from his wife to Carrie. "What's going on here?"

"Max is an asshole," Paige growled before Carrie could answer. "You should hear how your best friend has treated my best friend. He ought to be ashamed of himself."

Nate settled next to Paige, his elbows on his knees. "I think I need to hear about this."

"It's not a big deal," Carrie protested, already seeing this was going to be trouble. Nate was over the top protective of the females in his life, even her. "We'll get it worked out."

"The relationship is fake," Paige declared smugly. "Just as we thought but Max has been a total arrogant jerk. Let her tell you about what he said when she was talking to Tyler Gaylord. He's lost his mind."

"Tyler? How did he get involved with this? Carrie," Nate said softly. "Talk."

"I've got it handled. Everything is under control."

He smiled that smile. The one that made women swoon on several continents. "Talk. Don't make me do something drastic."

"It's not a big deal," she tried again. "I just don't think he and I are compatible, that's all. No harm, no foul. Let's move on."

Nate and Paige just sat there staring at her, not saying a word.

"I'm not going to say anything."

More staring.

"Seriously, I've said too much already. Let's change the subject. How's the traffic in LA?"

Silence.

Fuck. This wasn't going to go well.

---

Max wasn't a man that sat around feeling badly about himself but he found himself doing exactly that. He'd always known he had a few issues but he hadn't thought they were all that serious.

Clearly he'd been deluding himself.

According to Carrie - and he had no reason to disbelieve her - he was cold, remote, arrogant, and spoiled.

He'd also seen his need to win rear its ugly head. He was a competitive arse and he hated to lose, even when the stakes didn't matter. It was the reason he wasn't allowed to play checkers with Mike and Amy's kids anymore. He had to win the game even if his opponent was only five years old. He hadn't been all that proud of his behavior that day and he wasn't today either. His words had been cruel and unnecessarily so. The last word, the one-upmanship, had been the goal, not being a decent human being.

He'd been hurt when she'd made the remark about why he didn't win. To be honest, he'd known he wasn't going to win from the moment he'd been nominated. Two of the actors in his category were older and had been passed over several times. It was going to be the year for one of them. Since it was Max's first nomination it was his job to attend the awards, smile at the cameras, and say what an honor it was to be nominated.

It *was* an honor and he'd totally *wanted* to win. He'd hoped for a miracle, and it hadn't come.

Twisting open a bottle of beer, he lounged back on his

bed, the television on in the background but it was just noise. The entire situation had to be settled, one way or another. They had been photographed together plus Alana knew about Carrie. Breaking up at this stage wasn't a good option but sniping at each other constantly wasn't either. He was going to have to let down his guard and be himself. If she didn't like him then, he couldn't say he hadn't tried.

What would show her he truly wanted to work this out?

Like a lightbulb over his head, the idea came to him. A smile on his face, he reached for his laptop on the side table, opened up his word processing program and began to type.

# CHAPTER
## *Thirteen*

TWO HOURS later Max was questioning the wisdom of his decision. What had sounded like a perfectly easy task had turned into an ugly monster. He was thrilled for the break when he heard pounding on his hotel room door loudly enough to wake the dead.

"Christ, I'm coming," Max called before swinging the door open. His good friend Mike stood there, pulling his right arm back and then throwing it forward. His fist made a horrible thud against Max's jaw, knocking him off his feet and onto his arse.

Shutting the door behind him, Mike entered the hotel room and skirted around the still sprawled Max and headed straight for the wet bar, shedding his coat and gloves on the way. Max had no idea what had gotten into one of his best friends in the world but he wasn't averse to throwing a punch or two of his own.

"What the bloody hell?"

Slapping two glasses down on the bar, Mike poured a generous measure of whiskey into both glasses.

"I just talked to Nate who asked me to come over here. I think you know why I hit you and I also think you know that you deserve it. Now come have a drink." Levering off the floor, Max took the other glass as Mike held up his own. "A toast. To Amy, myself, love, and happiness. Something you'll never find unless you get your head out of your arse."

Irritation twisted in Max's stomach but he clinked his glass with Mike's before taking a large gulp. "I assume Nate has spoken to Carrie."

"You would assume correctly, although it wasn't easy to get her to spill her story from what I heard. She was trying to protect you, but why I have no idea. It's not as if you earned that right."

Mike pulled his phone from his pocket and dialed. Before Max could even ask who it was Nate's voice was coming through the speaker.

"Paige is beside herself, mate, and I don't blame her. I had to pry the story out of Carrie and I was appalled. Now what else do you have to confess? Get it all off your chest and you'll feel better."

Max relayed his side of the story, trying not to gloss over the parts he'd screwed up. He could be fussy, arrogant, and generally pompous when he first met a person. It hadn't been all that bad before but since his breakup with Alana it was terrible. He found it hard to trust anyone.

"How do you intend to fix this?" Nate asked through the phone.

"I'm not sure I even can. Did Carrie say whether she was staying or leaving? When I left her she wasn't sure."

"She's still not sure. In her head she knows you're not that bad but you've hurt her, Max. Carrie may come off all strong and capable but she has a soft heart, just like Paige."

Scratching his head, Max sighed. "I tried something that I thought she might like but it probably won't work."

Mike nodded encouragement. "At least you're trying. What is it? A surprise dinner? Jewelry?"

Grimacing, Max shifted on his feet. Nate and Mike were never going to let him hear the end of this. "A list."

"A list," Mike repeated, blinking in confusion. "Just how would a list make Carrie like you again?"

"She mentioned something about how she made certain lists and I kind of made fun of her about it. So I decided I would show her that I was open to it and I worked on the list."

There was silence until it was broken by Nate. "Is this the list about desirable traits in a significant other? Carrie told us how you made fun of her for that."

"It is," Max exhaled, his gaze darting around the room, not wanting to make eye contact with Mike.

His smile widening, Mike chuckled and came down to sit next to Max on the sofa, propping his feet on the table and setting the phone between them on a cushion. "Show it to us."

"Fuck both of you. I'm not showing you something so personal."

"Show it to me or we won't believe you. Maybe if we can see it we can put in a good word for you with Carrie.

Otherwise, I'm thinking that she might as well end this farce with you right now," warned Nate.

"Blackmail," Max hissed through gritted teeth. "You're devious little shits."

"Guilty," Mike said cheerfully. "Now show me the list. I might even be able to help you with it so you can impress Carrie. I've dug myself out of a few doghouses with Amy."

"That's true."

"Gentlemen," Nate's crisp voice came through the line. "I'm going to hang up and let Mike handle this. Mate, hit him again if you think he needs it."

"Will do," Mike said cheerfully as he hung up. "Now let's see this list."

Standing, Max went in to the bedroom and came back out with his laptop, handing it to Mike. A quick perusal of the document had him tapping at the keyboard.

"Are you crazy? You make your dream woman sound like Betty Crocker in black leather. That's not going to get you any points with a woman like Carrie."

Frowning, Max pulled the laptop from Mike's grasp. "It doesn't say that."

"Sure it does. Your dream woman can make a Baked Alaska and you also want her to play games in the bedroom. You're a sick man. Baked Alaska? Really? How about a nice cheesecake?"

"What's wrong with Baked Alaska? It's an elegant dessert."

"Is this truly what you're looking for in a woman? It's rather an anemic list. Vague crap about optimism and enjoying good books. It's complete and utter bullshit."

Max didn't like his friend's tone. "It's not bullshit, and I've been working on this all evening."

Mike rolled his eyes like a thirteen-year-old girl. "You need to completely redo this list. It's superficial at best, laughable at worst, although I now completely understand how you ended up with Alana. Don't you ever think about what happens when you get out of bed with a woman? I've heard the rumor that you have to talk to them when you're not fucking them."

"I talk to them," Max growled, wrestling for control of the laptop. "Give that to me."

Mike managed to gain control and stood up with the computer, walking over to the bar. "Enlighten me. What did you and Alana talk about after a lively romp in the sheets? Politics? Football? Climate change? No? Let me guess. Baked Alaska."

Rubbing his jaw where Mike had hit him, Max groaned in frustration. "I see what you're trying to get at. I'm simply not in the habit of revealing my innermost soul to the women I sleep with."

"You can once you marry them, mate," Mike shot back. "In fact, it's kind of a requirement. Do you think that you chose Alana because you wouldn't have to show her who you were inside? She's not the type to care."

"You've been in therapy too long. Everything doesn't have underlying meanings. Sometimes a banana is just a banana."

"Or as Amy would say, sometimes a chicken shit is just a chicken shit. Who or what scared the hell out of you and made you hide who you are?"

"Fuck you."

"That's lovely. Really nice. I'm trying to help you." He opened a new document. "Now let's work on this goddamn list again and this time try to think about something other than her boobs and whether she can whip up a gourmet meal in the kitchen for you wearing nothing but a sheer apron. For once, stop thinking with your dick and think about the kind of person you want to grow old with. The kind of woman that you'd want to mother your children. In fact, let's start there. Do you want kids?"

"I'm not doing this." Max stood and came to the bar, smacking the lid closed on the laptop. "I'll be sorry to see Carrie leave but if I have to bare my soul to keep her here then I don't think this was meant to be. I'll get her a lovely gift for her trouble. I do appreciate what she's tried to do even if it doesn't show. I hope she can find it in her heart to forgive my behavior but I'll understand if she cannot."

Mike looked like he wanted to say quite a bit but simply shook his head. "Fine. I'll let her know that you'll be forwarding an expensive gift that you'll have your assistant pick out and your thanks. I'm sure she'll be relieved to face all her family and friends now that you've pulled her into all your troubles and had her picture in the tabloids. It's only made things ten times worse for her but what do you care? You're a fucking movie star and she's just a regular person. No one cares about her life or problems. Certainly you don't if your actions are any indication. You'll have to live with the fact that she tried to help you with Alana but you're too much of a bastard to help her in return."

Turning on his heel, Mike strode toward the door but he didn't get all the way before Max finally spoke.

"It's not like that. I really do want to help her but I don't think I know how."

Mike didn't bother to look back. "Then you shouldn't have started all of this. It was your idea and this one is on you."

His responsibility. His fault. Just like everything else.

# CHAPTER

## *Fourteen*

**THE NEXT DAY** Carrie tried to shake off her argument with Max. She'd said a few things she regretted and he probably did as well. He was difficult to get to know and she wasn't a woman that took much crap so it was a recipe for a rocky road.

She needed to apologize. The crack about his Oscar nomination had been completely uncalled for and more than that, it had been cruel. Winning that golden statue was probably his dream and she'd kicked him when he was down. Not a kind move.

She'd spent most of the morning pretending to work so when her phone rang and it was Tyler Gaylord of all people, she'd jumped at the chance to meet him for lunch. Anything that extricated her from these four walls was a godsend in her book. He'd chosen a back booth in a quiet cafe off the beaten path.

"You must know every place in this city to eat where you won't be recognized," she said as she sat down across from him. He was handsome as usual in a pair of faded denims, a simple blue t-shirt, and a brown leather jacket that was a nod to the cooler than normal temperatures.

"I know this one place in London and there's no guarantee that we won't end up on a fan's Instagram. But I've had decent luck here slipping under the radar and the burgers are fantastic." He leaned forward, his gaze heated. "Might I say you look very fetching today, Red."

"I accept all compliments," she laughed, looking down at her clothes. They were some of the new ones she'd purchased the day she met him. "And it's just jeans and a blouse."

"You make it look special."

He was full of it but why not enjoy the ride? She'd had precious little flirting and compliments these last few months. They quickly ordered and she settled back into the booth.

"So how did you get my number?"

His brow quirked and he gave her a secretive smile. "I bet you can guess."

Of course. "Paige."

"Technically it was Nate but they're sort of one and the same these days, aren't they? In the matrimonial sense."

"The matrimonial sense," she repeated with a giggle. "Have you ever been married, Tyler?"

He shook his head. "Oh hell, no. I'm not the marrying kind."

The waitress placed their drinks on the table and bustled back to the kitchen, appearing not to notice she had a real-live sex god movie star at her table.

SWINGING ON A STAR   109

Carrie stuck out her lower lip in a pout. "Did some mean woman do you wrong? Break your heart?"

He grinned, showing off all his dazzling white teeth. "Not at all. I've never had a broken heart. I just don't see the allure of marriage."

"I've never met anyone who hasn't experienced at least some heartbreak. How old are you?"

Laughing, he shrugged out of his jacket. "Thirty-eight. And a half. You've met someone now and I don't think I've missed anything. It looks awful and sad."

That's when it hit her. "You've never been in love."

"I don't think I'm the type. I'm too into my career. Maybe someday I'll find the right woman and settle down."

Tyler Gaylord didn't look like the absence of love in his life bothered him all that much. If anything, he looked joyous, as if he didn't have a care in the world.

"I should take a leaf out of your book," she said, envious of his carefree attitude. "All love has ever brought me was pain and heartache. How do you do it?"

He shrugged. "It's easy. I keep busy and concentrate on my work. I tend to date women who either feel the same way I do about love or that fulfill a need in my career."

Ahhh. "A showmance?"

His eyes widened and then a grin broke out onto his face. "What do you know about the big bad world of Hollywood public relations, Red?"

It was her turn to shrug. "Not much but I've heard of it. Have you been in a lot of fake relationships?"

She wouldn't mind some advice without actually

revealing that she was in one herself. Or maybe she wasn't. At this point it could go either way.

"About half a dozen or so. Sometimes the lines get blurred and it's hard to tell."

The number made Carrie gasp in surprise. She'd never have guessed so many.

"What do you mean by blurred?"

He leaned forward and rested his elbows on the table. "Sometimes it just starts out as a friendship on the set and then we'll decide to hang out together. For publicity, not because we're into each other or anything. It's casual and there's no romance but the public and the tabloids don't know that."

Her finger traced a figure-eight on the table top as she avoided his eyes. "What if you didn't get along with someone you were supposed to be pretending to be with? Has that ever happened?"

"Once. But it was only because what we really wanted to do was have sex with each other."

*No, no, no.*

Her head popped up. "And did you?"

"Repeatedly," he announced, his brows waggling wickedly. "Once the sexual tension was resolved we got along quite well. Ended the relationship as friends once the affair ran its course. We still hook up now and then when we're both between significant others because the sex was so damn good."

Her cheeks felt hot. Sleeping with Max would be a gigantic blunder. He was gorgeous. And sexy, that was no doubt, but sex? No way. She didn't sleep with people she didn't like and respect. She wasn't about to start now. Their issues weren't sexual tension but Max being an asshole. They didn't have to get naked to have it resolved.

"Friends with benefits, huh?" she said, wanting to act casual. "I bet you have one of those in every major city all over the world."

His blue eyes twinkled. "You're absolutely right."

Tyler Gaylord was fun, outrageous, and he made her laugh. She was glad she'd accepted his invitation to lunch. Which then brought up the question...

"So why did you invite me today?"

His middle finger rubbed against his full lower lip, an affectation Carrie was sure he'd learned as an actor. It was probably quite effective with the ladies, reminding them of what that mouth might be able to do.

"Maybe I have an opening in London."

At first she didn't know what he was talking about and then his meaning seeped into her muddled brain. Friends with benefits. London. She was getting slow on the uptake.

"I'm afraid to ask about the application process."

His hand over his mouth, Tyler laughed quietly, trying not to garner any extra attention.

"Carrie, I really like you."

This entire conversation was strange. A hot movie star was flirting with her. Was this something Paige and Nate had asked him to do? Like when they'd asked Max to take her to dinner. Everyone felt sorry for poor loser Carrie.

"I'm a lovely person," she replied lightly as the waitress slid their burgers in front of them. Carrie had ordered a classic cheeseburger and Tyler had ordered cheese and mushrooms. They ate in silence for awhile but eventually came back to the conversation.

"Carrie, can I ask you a question?"

It was polite to say yes but there was a part of her that wanted to say no based solely on the expression on Tyler's face.

"Depends on what you're asking."

He set his burger back on the plate and wiped his hands with the paper napkin. "How long have you been dating Maxwell Hayes?"

She and Max had never actually discussed the details of their dating relationship should others ask questions. She would have to go it alone, assuming that they had any sort of relationship after their falling out.

"I met him last fall at Thanksgiving dinner at Paige's. We sort of became friends then. I'm not sure I'd characterize what we're doing as dating. I'd say that we spend time together."

*I could be a politician. I just gave a great non-answer answer.*

"I'm sticking my nose where it doesn't belong, but I think you're a nice person. Just be careful, okay? Max is a great guy and one of my best friends but he has a terrible track record with women."

She took a drink of her soda before answering. "The obvious reply to that statement is that you do too."

Chuckling, he nodded in agreement. "That's true but the difference is that I know I'm a lousy boyfriend but Max thinks he's a good one. The truth is he's not much better than I am. He has major trust issues and they've only gotten worse since he broke up with Alana."

Something she'd experienced up close and personal but it was kind of nice to know it wasn't her. This was just how he was. "Perhaps he has good reason not to trust women."

Tyler appeared to be struggling for the right words. "There is some truth to that. In this crazy business and with our level of fame, it's hard to know who you can trust, but this goes deeper than that. Max always wonders what people want from him, whether man or woman, and everyone is guilty until proven innocent. He was like this even before he became super famous."

"And yet he married a woman that wanted him for his money and connections," she found herself saying. "That doesn't make any sense."

"That's another of Max's issues. He lets his...male anatomy do a lot of the thinking for him."

That's basically what Max had said to her that first day at the pub. He'd been attracted to Alana because of the great sex.

But this was becoming increasingly uncomfortable. She barely knew Tyler although he seemed like a nice man, and she didn't like talking about Max behind his back.

"I appreciate your concern and I'll take what you said under advisement."

"In other words, you're going to ignore every word that came out of my mouth."

He had no idea how much he'd confirmed all of what she'd been thinking.

"Not at all, I simply do not feel comfortable discussing Max when he's not here. It doesn't feel fair to him."

Tyler signaled to the waitress, seeming to take her rebuke well. "The world has been more than fair to our buddy Max but I get what you're saying. I just ask one thing. Please think about what I've said here today. Max is a complicated guy. If you get involved with him, it won't be easy. He'll fight you all the way."

Then it was better that he'd ended things. If Tyler was right, she and Max would have ended up right where they were now at some point no matter what. If Max couldn't be honest with her, she didn't see how any relationship between them was going to work out. She wouldn't be walking any red carpets with Maxwell Hayes.

# CHAPTER
## Fifteen

AFTER LUNCH CARRIE wandered around Regent's Park for awhile before heading back to Paige and Nate's house. She had plenty of work to get done but her mind was still busy working on the puzzle that was Maxwell Hayes. Sometimes nice, sometimes rude. She'd seen the happy, boyish side of him when they'd went to his friend Albert's restaurant and she'd liked it. That slightly silly young man was definitely someone she could easily spend time with. Did he still exist or had he been obliterated by Max Hayes - mega movie star and all-around tight ass?

Digging into her purse for the house keys, she didn't see Max until she was only a few feet away. He'd come through the gates - he knew Nate's key code - and was lounging against a pillar on the front porch, looking more handsome than should be allowed. His dark hair was tousled by the wind and his off-white sweater was the perfect backdrop for his gorgeous blue eyes.

Those eyes were currently watching her every move as

she approached him, perhaps worried she might chuck a potted plant at his head. Lucky for him she wasn't the violent type.

"It's chilly out here. How long have you been waiting?"

He straightened and shoved his hands in the pockets of his jeans. Not as tight as Tyler's but they still looked good. "Not long. Carrie, I'd like to apologize to you and I hope we can talk about things."

It sounded rehearsed but then he was an actor and that's what he did. There was no getting out of this, and it was better if they faced it head on anyway. She wasn't a huge fan of letting this fester until they hissed at each other whenever Paige and Nate had a big gathering and Carrie happened to see Max. Somehow they had to come out of this at least civil to one another.

"Come in and have a glass of wine or something. Does it ever warm up here? It's supposed to be summer."

She didn't expect an answer but he surprised her. "It is unseasonably cold but it's supposed to get better in a few days."

"That's...good."

He followed her in after she unlocked the door, settling into the cushions of the brown leather couch. Carrie kept herself busy in the kitchen pouring them some wine and trying to pretend her hands weren't trembling. She wasn't nervous and she wasn't angry anymore so she wasn't sure why she was this emotional. Perhaps it was simply that Max brought out strong feelings in her, good and bad.

Returning to the living room, she handed him a glass and noticed for the first time that he had brought a laptop with him. He must have come straight from a cafe or coffee shop. He sat up and smoothed down his sweater, clearing his throat. It looked like he wanted to talk first.

"Carrie, I'd like to apologize to you for my behavior yesterday. It was completely out of line then and before. You're absolutely right about me. I'm difficult and stubborn, not to mention touchy when it comes to personal subjects. But none of that is an adequate excuse for how I've treated you. You've agreed to do this incredibly generous thing for me and I have not shown my immense gratitude, something I intend to rectify if you'll let me. I hope that you will accept this apology and that we can start again. I can assure you that I am determined to show you that I can be more than a pompous, self-centered actor."

Blown away, Carrie sat heavily into a chair next to the sofa. She'd expected an apology but this one was so...fucking eloquent.

"You rehearsed that, didn't you?"

His cheeks turned slightly red. "I did. For once with you, I didn't want to fuck things up. It thought if I delivered a prepared speech our meeting might start out well."

"I think your apology was wonderful. Quite moving. I don't think mine will be nearly as good."

He began to speak but she shook her head and held up a hand. "No, I owe you one as well. What I said about the award thing...unnecessarily nasty. When I'm hurt I can hit out with the best of them. I'm really sorry about that crack and all the other snarky crap I've thrown at you."

She'd barely finished and taken a breath when he replied. "I wholeheartedly deserved it. You have every right to defend yourself."

"Defense is one thing, but offense is something else."

He swallowed, his Adam's apple bobbing in his throat. "I brought something of a peace offering. To show that I'm sincere about trying again and being more open."

Okay, this wasn't foreseen. "That's very thoughtful but I've accepted your apology."

He moved to the end of the couch near her chair, fumbling with the laptop and finally getting it open. "I need to show you something. I know that I haven't exactly been boyfriend material, or even fake-boyfriend material, but I want to prove to you that I'm not as spoiled and narcissistic as you may believe. I do have a few good qualities."

If Page was to be believed, he had several. He'd pulled up a document and for a moment she thought he might have convinced some females to give him some sort of testimonial.

*Max was a great boyfriend. He always opened my car door.*

*Max is a great cook and he always made me breakfast in the morning.*

*Max is a considerate lover and always let me come first.*

This was why she didn't have a man. She was too sarcastic, too outspoken.

"I wanted to show you this."

He turned the laptop around so the screen was facing her and then set it in her lap. At first she frowned and stared at it, not sure what she was seeing. It was a list and as she realized what kind of list it was she began to smile.

"You made the list."

He nodded, clearly wanting her approval. "I did. At

first I put stupid things on it but later I really tried to make it serious."

*He made the list.*

Carrie was so overwhelmed she almost couldn't speak. This was no small feat. Even if he hadn't thought about it all that hard...he'd made the list.

She started at the top. "Baked Alaska and black lingerie. That sounds dangerous, what with a blowtorch and a lot of skin bared but this is your list."

"Mike gave me a hard time for that part."

"He shouldn't have. Feeling free to express yourself is part of the exercise. Don't hem yourself in with rules. Let's see what else you have here. She should like music, preferably classical. That sounds good."

"Bach would be preferable but Beethoven is fine too."

He wished his soulmate could sing because he couldn't. He wanted her to be a night owl because that's what he was. He didn't care what her favorite color was as long as it wasn't orange because he hated orange.

With each successive item he'd revealed himself a little more.

Whoa. This was getting a little personal. Maybe she should stop reading.

He wanted his soulmate to be a little kinky in the sheets but not all the time. He liked the idea of roleplaying in bed.

This wasn't what she'd had in mind when she said she wanted to get to know him but beggars couldn't be choosers. But now she was totally going to picture him as the pizza delivery guy.

"You've put a lot of thought into this, Max."

He wanted her to want lots of children. Shit, that one

got her right in the heart. He was a softie for kids. Then he gave her the one-two punch. He liked dogs too. He had to be a good person if he was a sucker for a cute canine. This day was certainly turning out differently than she'd planned.

"I wanted to show you I could do this." He paced nervously back and forth in front of the fireplace as she read through it. "What do you think?"

She didn't hold back. "I'm impressed. Very impressed. First, that you did it at all and then second, that you really took some time with this. You have a sense of who you are looking for."

He stopped and ran his fingers through his hair. "I doubt I'll ever find someone like that. A little kinky and wants several children? What are the odds?"

It was all Carrie could do not to raise her hand. She met those criteria but some of the others were non-starters. She couldn't sing and she was a morning person, although she wasn't all that fond of orange either. She didn't know diddly-squat about classical music but she bet he didn't know shit about Blake Shelton.

"You never know," she replied instead, perusing the second column of the list. "You may not get everything you write down but I like the fact that you even made a section for deal-breakers. That may be the most important thing to know when going into a new relationship. You don't want anyone addicted to alcohol and drugs. That's good. You want someone who has their own interests and friends. Wise. You don't want someone who just lives through you. And the last here, you don't want a woman who is with you to further her own career. Wow, I would hope so."

He dropped down on the couch. "In my business that isn't a given."

Alana. Tyler had warned Carrie that Max was deeply wounded by what his ex had done. He might not be in love with her anymore but she'd screwed him up for the next woman.

*Hold on, I'm the next woman.*

Placing the laptop on the coffee table between them, she lifted her wine glass to her lips, giving herself time to process what she'd seen. He'd certainly become more human in her eyes. She could be a friend to a man like this.

"What about your list?"

She froze, looking at him over the rim of her wine glass before slowly lowering it to the table. "I beg your pardon?"

"What about your list?" he repeated. "Shouldn't you share yours with me? Isn't that the point of this? To get to know one another?"

It was but mostly for her to get to know him.

She shrugged and gave him her best sorrowful look. "I don't have a recent one. The last one I made was like...five years ago."

He opened the laptop again. "Then let's make a new one. You talk and I'll type."

*Shit. Son of a bitch. Damn.*

She had no one to blame but herself for this. Making a fuss about getting to know one another and now look where she was - caught between the devil and the deep blue sea. She held up her half-empty wine glass.

"If I'm going to do this, I'm going to need to a refill. More than a few times."

# CHAPTER
## Sixteen

MAX'S HANDS were poised over the keyboard. "So start brainstorming and I'll just type everything down. You can go through the list later and decide if they stay."

This was real progress. Carrie had accepted his apology and they were getting to know one another. He couldn't wait to tell Mike and Nate that he'd opened up and it hadn't been that bad.

Carrie's fingers fiddled with the stem of the wine glass. "I guess...he should be kind."

"Kind to animals? Children? The elderly?"

Pressing her lips together, she rolled her eyes. "To everyone."

He began to type but then stopped. "Even people who aren't nice to you? Wouldn't that make him either a dolt or a jerk? Why would he be kind to someone who isn't kind to his soulmate? It doesn't make sense to me."

"I thought we were just brainstorming."

"It was just a question."

He wasn't sure why the answer was important to him.

"It was three questions, actually. Let's just say that I want him to be *kind* in the general sense and move on."

"Fine," he said shortly. "It's your list."

"I would want someone who takes care of himself."

She was so vague in her answers. Jesus, he'd been specific. Black lingerie and Baked Alaska. It didn't get much more definitive than that.

"Emotionally? Physically? Spiritually?"

"All three."

Of course, he should have known without asking. "Quite the paragon of virtue you've described so far. He pets dogs in the park whilst on his daily five-mile run, then helps little old ladies cross the street on the way to his therapist appointment, but before that he'll give a lollipop to a child after stopping to worship the deity of his choice."

Max had a wicked, sarcastic sense of humor and for the most part the women in his life either hadn't gotten the jokes or did and didn't like them. He really needed to tone it down if he and Carrie were going to get along. Christ, they'd only just made up and then he had to go off on a small rant.

*Great job, arsehole. She's getting to know you now.*

Only Carrie wasn't angry, she was laughing. Her cheeks had turned a most attractive shade of pink and she was holding her stomach, almost doubled over. She wiped at her eyes, still giggling, and then took a gulp of her wine.

"Oh my stars, you are so right." She hiccupped and tried to stifle her laughter. "When you say it like that this guy sounds like a real snore. Like the kind of guy that my mother would love but I would hate."

She was quite beautiful when she smiled like that, without a care in the world. She also looked much too young for him with her guileless whiskey-colored eyes and dimpled cheeks. Fresh and innocent, two things he didn't find much in Hollywood.

With a grin he erased everything he'd already typed. "How about we try again and be honest this time? Not that I don't think you want a kind man, I'm sure you do. But think out of the box a little. For example, how do you feel about black lingerie?"

Still laughing, she nudged him on the leg with her sock-covered foot. "You just can't let that go, can you? How do I feel about black lingerie? I think it goes well with my coloring. Can we move on from that subject now?"

He wouldn't rise to take the bait. "It's an important one. The fate of nations rest in the balance."

"God help them then. Now let's see. What do I really want in a man?" She tapped her lips and smiled. "I want him to be handsome. of course, with a great body. He doesn't have to be musclebound but firm abs would be lovely."

Max had a six-pack, a requirement in Hollywood, although his weren't quite as good as Nate's eight-pack. His friend had taken it to a whole different level for the last *Thunder* movie.

"Adonis body," Max typed. "What else?"

She grabbed his arm to look at the screen. "Hey, that isn't what I said. I said he should have a good body."

"You said great body."

Her eyes widened and she reached over him to get to the keyboard but he moved the laptop out of the way. "Are you going to remember every word I say because it's annoying. I just want a guy that looks good."

Did she think he looked good? Other women did. Casting directors did. But Carrie wasn't one to follow the herd. Maybe he wasn't her type. Maybe Tyler was.

"I'd like it if he slept in the nude," she stated with a sly smile. "I hate pajamas on men."

She lived in Florida where it was warm all year round so getting cold wasn't an issue.

He added to the list. "Starkers at bedtime. Okay, next."

Giggling, she covered her mouth with her hand. "Starkers. That sounds dirtier than nude."

He nodded in agreement. "Art is nude. Pole dancers are starkers."

"I don't want a pole dancing boyfriend." She elbowed him. "Type nude instead."

Backspacing, he fixed the entry. She was picky about this stuff.

She took another gulp of her wine. "He should be able to cook and clean. I shouldn't have to do it all. It's not fair."

That ex-fiancé really was a nightmare. "Did Mark make you do all the housework?"

"He said that because I was home all day I had more time to do it. I never could get him to realize that my home was also my office and I was working. Asshole."

"You're well rid of him. Did he have abs?"

"No, he didn't and I wouldn't have cared if he hadn't been a douchebag. But if I have a choice, I'm going with the abs next time."

Max added her latest request to the list. It was shaping up nicely. "That can't be all you want. What else?"

Slumping against the cushions, she seemed lost in thought. "I want him to be smart but not obnoxious. I want him to be funny, but not too funny."

Smart and funny. Good choices. Time to kick this game up a notch.

"How about good in bed? Do you want him to be a good lover?"

Carrie almost choked on her wine. "That goes without saying. He should be...knowledgeable about where every-thing is and what to do with it."

"He should know where the...doorbell is."

Frowning at him, she didn't seem to get the reference. He hadn't thought he was being ambiguous. "Doorbell?"

He waited and then finally her cheeks suffused with heat and she dropped her head into her hands. "I just got that. You are a sick puppy."

"I am," he agreed readily. "So he should be good in bed. A veritable stallion along with all those kind qualities from earlier. What else?"

She drained her glass and set it on the end table. "I just..."

When she didn't continue he tried to prompt her. "You just... what?"

She looked at him then, her lips turned down and her expression unutterably sad. A moment ago they'd been laughing.

"I just want a man that loves me more than anything else. Is that too much to ask?"

It shouldn't be. But in his experience, it was rare indeed.

# CHAPTER
## *Seventeen*

CARRIE HAD BEEN on red carpets before but this was the first time any of the cameras would be pointed at her. Not at her specifically, of course. Just in her general direction.

When she was standing next to Maxwell Hayes.

Always before she'd been with Paige and they hadn't had the laser focus on them that she could expect walking the carpet with Max. People were going to be looking at her, judging her, and they weren't going to be gentle about it. She would be held up next to Max's ex-girlfriends for comparison and chances were she would be found wanting, at least in the looks department.

Which is why she'd gone all out and seen a stylist about her dress and hair tonight. Lisa had been friendly but she'd also been a genius. The red dress Carrie ultimately chose wasn't anything she normally would have worn. First, it was red. Her mother had always told her redheads didn't wear that so she'd avoided that color like the plague her entire life. Then the first dress Lisa had pulled out had been this crimson number and Carrie had almost run from the building. The stylist had patiently explained it was all in the shade of red that made the difference, and she'd certainly been right.

The dress was deceptively simple, off the shoulder with a ruched skirt that ended a few inches above her knees. A fashion genius, Lisa had accessorized the outfit with gold heels and bold jewelry. A sleek ponytail swept her long, thick hair off her neck and kept it under control while artfully applied makeup accentuated her best features. Looking in the mirror it was like a stranger was staring back at her.

A woman that just might be able to hold her own at the charity event tonight. A spray of perfume in her cleavage and a tube of lipstick in her tiny clutch purse and she was ready to go.

Remembering Paige's exercises to make herself calm, Carrie listened to the thud of her heartbeat as she closed her eyes and pictured a sandy beach with the rhythmic waves rolling in, one after the other under the warm sun. Seagulls soared overhead, dipping and circling, finally diving down...and stealing her hot dog right out of her hand.

Okay, that didn't go so well. Puppies. She'd think about puppies. Cute little balls of fur that barked and rang doorbells.

*Puppies don't ring doorbells.*

But movie stars do. When she opened the door she almost couldn't catch her breath. Max looked devastatingly handsome in his tuxedo, his dark hair tamed into submission and combed back from his chiseled face. His light blue eyes looked even bluer tonight but that might also have to do with the fact that he wasn't angry or frustrated with her. For the past two days they'd gotten along quite well.

"Don't you look gorgeous," he said in that smooth as silk accent that could send her pulse into overdrive. "Twirl for me, love. Let me see that dress."

Of course, it was the dress. She dutifully turned in a circle, letting him see every side of the outfit. He whistled, his gaze warm and appreciative. Damn her fair skin, she couldn't help the blush that crawled its way up her chest all the way to her eyebrows. Now her hair, skin, and dress were a matched set.

"You look stunning. The paps are going to love you." He held open the door for her. "Are you ready to go?"

Taking a deep breath, she nodded. "As ready as I'll ever be. Let's do this."

She locked the door behind her and followed him to the car parked at the curb. It was a simple fundraiser tonight so he'd refused a limousine. A car service would do just as well. They could drink without worrying about driving themselves home later.

He helped her into the back seat and sat beside her as the vehicle smoothly pulled into traffic. It wouldn't take long to get to their destination - a posh hotel in the center of the city.

Carefully she focused on her breathing, hoping to slow her galloping heart. Breathe in for ten seconds, breathe out for ten. Repeat.

"You're going to do fine." His deep baritone brought her

out of her reverie. "I'll be right next to you the entire time and I won't leave your side all evening. I promise."

Fidgeting in the seat, her fingers tightened on her purse. "I've done this before with Paige. I know what to do, I swear. I'm just a little nervous."

His hand hovered over hers for a moment as if unsure but then he placed it on top of hers, warm and reassuring. "It's completely natural to be nervous. There will lots of attention on us tonight. I haven't walked a red carpet with anyone since Alana."

"We'll be in the papers tomorrow," she said more to herself than him. "They'll be speculating as to who I am."

"We're not keeping that a secret. If they ask me your name I'll tell them. My publicist has the bio you put together and can disseminate that information if needed. The idea tonight is to keep the frenzy to a minimum which means acting calm and matter of fact. We met last fall, which is the truth, and we've become closer as we've spent more time together. Also the truth. The less we embellish on the story the better. If we're not over the top, hopefully they won't be either."

She looked up at him. Really looked this time. "This doesn't bother you at all? All those people looking at you, yelling your name, the flashbulbs in your eyes?"

His smile was gentle and he squeezed her hand. "This is such a small part of my life, honestly. It's the work that truly matters, not the fame that comes with it." His smile widened into wicked grin. "The money isn't bad though. I quite like that part."

"It doesn't hurt, does it?" she laughed. Maybe tonight wouldn't be so bad after all. This Max was lovely to be around. "I do feel for you sometimes though. You wanted to ride The Eye with me that night but you couldn't. I think that's sad."

"Every vocation has its good and bad parts. As my mum and dad often say to me when I start complaining, someday all this will be gone and no one will give a rat's arse what I'm doing or who I'm dating. Fame is fickle and it can be gone tomorrow. Enjoy it while you can."

"Enjoy it," she echoed, wondering if that were possible. Max didn't seem to be reveling in it. On the contrary, he appeared to be tolerating it. "Is that what you're doing?"

He looked out the car window, the skyline of London glittering against the night sky.

"I'm trying to enjoy it."

"Because you love being an actor."

He nodded. "I do."

The vehicle came to a stop and that meant it was time for this showmance to really get started. Everything they'd done up to this point, the dinners, the walk in the park yesterday, had all been a rehearsal for this moment. The car door opened and she could see the red carpet, hear the crowd, and see the flash of cameras. For a moment her heart stuttered but she sucked air into her lungs and pasted a smile on her face. He got out of the car and held out his hand. She took it but didn't exit right away. When he bent down to see what was wrong, she only had a moment to tell him what was on her mind. The crowd was going nuts for him, screaming his name.

She leaned forward so she could whisper in his ear, words only for him.

"I'm going to do the very best I can for you, Max. Just tell me what you need me to do."

The brilliant smile she received in answer sealed their deal. His fingers closed around hers and she stepped from the car as a wall of shouts reached her ears. She didn't know what would happen tomorrow or next week but tonight they were a team.

———

The champagne flowed, the music played, and Carrie was a damn good dancer. He should have known she'd be able to move with the music, her dress swirling around her hips, a big smile on her beautiful face. She'd looked gorgeous tonight, glamorous and sexy, so different from the somewhat uptight, buttoned-up woman she could be at times. Tonight she was like a flame in that scarlet dress and he was the helpless moth who was destined to be consumed in the fire.

He grabbed two more flutes from a passing waiter and handed one to her. They'd worked up a thirst dancing and the chilled, golden liquid slid down his parched throat. She looked up at him from under her lashes as she sipped at her champagne.

"Thank you," she said huskily so only he could hear. "You made tonight easier than I thought it would be."

He inclined his head formally but a knot had taken up residence in his chest. Her simple words of thanks were in stark contrast to the effusive compliments - most undeserved - that he'd received from admirers tonight. Usually female. Carrie never felt the need to flatter him or stroke his ego, no matter how much he might want her to. She was too straightforward and honest for that.

"It was my pleasure," he replied instead. "You did an amazing job with the photographers, as if you'd been posing all your life. You're a natural."

Giggling, she shook her head. "Not in the least. I'm just glad I had you to hold my hand."

That hand was currently holding her glass, the nails short but manicured in the same shade of red as her dress. The fingers were delicate but capable. This was no woman-for-show. Carrie was a professional, the mighty engine behind Paige's literary career.

"I'll always be there to hold your hand," he said gallantly, taking the other in his and raising it to his lips. The guests would get an eyeful and that was the point, but it didn't hurt that her skin was like satin.

Other women might have swooned but not Carrie. She didn't roll her eyes but he could tell she wanted to. Clearly her ex hadn't played the suitor, courting and wooing her more tender affections.

"Someone kissed a blarney stone," she whispered with a smile, her gaze roving the room, probably gauging how many eyes were on them at the moment. "Do women usually fall for that?"

He kept his expression deadpan. "Always."

Laughter like music bubbled from her full lips. "Then you're overdue for someone who doesn't believe a word you say."

He set his champagne glass on the table next to them and then took hers from her unresisting fingers, setting it next to his own before taking her hand in his. "And you're overdue for another dance. Let's show them how it's done."

They might not be able to go more than a day or two without arguing but on the dance floor they were truly in tune. He whirled her around, her skirt lifting slightly, showing off the creamy soft skin of her thighs and making his mouth water. Reminding himself that this was a business arrangement and not a date did nothing to cool his admiration. Carrie was, after all, a beautiful woman and he was a man.

A man who had been without a woman for too long. He needed to remedy that but not with her. Business. Make believe. She barely tolerated him, so making love with him was out of the question. He almost snorted at his thoughts. When was the last time he'd made love to anyone? He couldn't even remember. He had sex. Raunchy, rowdy sex. Making love was what other couples did when they had actual feelings for each other.

The music changed to something slow and sultry, the lights dimming overhead. Max pulled her closer, their bodies brushing with each step, driving him calmly and deliberately out of his mind with desire. Everything about her tonight made him want her as more than a friend or business partner. He wanted to be her lover. To hear her say his name at a moment of passion. To see her face flushed with pure pleasure, her hair a fiery river of silk on his pillow.

Whoa. Not going to happen. The only thing sleeping with Carrie would bring were complications galore. He doubted she was the casual sex type and that's all he was. While the pleasure they could give one another was enough for him, it wouldn't be enough for her. She would want love and commitment.

"Are you okay?" she whispered, looking up at him with concern. She must have felt his body tense as thoughts of her calling him a jerk ran through his mind.

"I'm good but it's about time to leave, don't you think?"

She nodded. "Whatever you want to do. This is your show."

It was and he'd do well to remember it. If he stayed business-like he'd be in control of this romantic farce but if he gave in and let his baser instincts take over...she'd be in charge. He couldn't allow himself to be at her - or anyone's - mercy like that. Not again.

# CHAPTER
## *Eighteen*

"I DON'T THINK she likes me," Carrie whispered to Max as she set the bags of food on the table. "At all."

After his long day at rehearsals, Carrie had brought over dinner so he didn't have to cook which he thought was sweet. Gemma, his assistant, had offered to order in for him and even would have cooked although she was terrible at it, but he'd told her he already had plans. That hadn't gone over well from the looks of things. His normally amiable employee was sulking as she checked her tablet for the hundredth time that evening. Nothing had changed since the last time. She was avoiding him. No, make that them. He and Carrie were a couple for all the world to see. Their debut the other night had been nothing less than triumphant. Most of the fans and the tabloids had thought they looked beautiful together and the few that didn't weren't happy with anything, anywhere, at any time. Fuck 'em.

"I think I'm set for the evening, Gemma," he said loudly enough to get her attention back on him. They'd just finished going through his schedule and also Carrie's, looking for any conflicts that needed to be ironed out. So far there were only a few minor issues. "I'll see you in the morning."

As if she hadn't heard him she headed straight for the stairs to the second floor. Eyes wide, Carrie looked at the back of Gemma and then over at Max. "Does she fly home on a broom using the roof as a runway?"

Why did women have to be so infernally strange? He needed this issue with his assistant like he needed a hole in his head. All he asked of her was that she do her job. That's it.

Stomping up the stairs after her, he found Gemma in his closet, checking his suits and tuxedos. "Gemma, what are you doing? I said we were done for the night."

"You might be done but I'm not." Her voice was slightly muffled as she bent down and inspected his shoes. "I need to make sure your clothes are ready for any event that might come up."

He stepped into the opening of the closet. "Gemma, we know all the events that I have coming up and we're prepared. That's why you keep my schedule on that blasted tablet. Now, you'll be happy to know that your day is complete and you can go home and not worry about me for at least twelve hours."

She didn't even look up, instead restacking his shoe boxes. "What if something unexpected comes up? You need to be prepared."

"Then I'll wear jeans."

Now she was simply rearranging the boxes she'd already stacked. "Gemma, go home."

He didn't bother to be polite and reasonable this time. His dinner was getting cold downstairs and he and Carrie had things to discuss, mostly the upcoming opening night of his play. He wanted her to be in the front row.

Huffing, Gemma stood and held her tablet to her chest, her eyes cold. "There is plenty for me to do here."

"There is nothing for you to do here," he shot back impatiently. Shit like this was why he didn't trust people. "Gemma, if you have an issue with Carrie or me then spit it out."

"No issue."

He stepped back so she could exit the closet. "Then please go home and enjoy your life outside of work. I'll see you tomorrow."

Without another word she descended the stairs, picking up her purse that had been abandoned on the sofa on the way to the door. She paused for a moment before leaving, her gaze firmly on Max, not even sparing Carrie a glance.

"Let me know if you need anything. Anything at all. I'm here for you."

The air seemed calmer when Gemma was gone and even Carrie breathed a sigh of relief as they sat down at the table to eat. "Is she always that intense or was that little show for me?"

Rubbing his aching forehead, Max could only shrug. "For you, for me. I'm not sure it matters much. Most of my assistants don't last long. The ones that do, like Gemma, sometimes end up like this."

He bit into the spicy chicken Carrie had picked up. Heaven.

"When you say *like this*, what does that mean exactly?"

"Overly invested," he clarified. "They somehow feel they are responsible in part for my successes but they aren't anxious to take any blame for my failures, of course. I'm not a psychologist but I would guess that when a person has no discernible achievements of their own they naturally gravitate to those that do."

Her lips twitched as if trying not to laugh. "Are you saying that your assistants want to...bask in your glory?"

He stopped shoveling food in his mouth long enough to answer. "You make it sound like I'm an egomaniac, but in a word? Yes. This has happened before and no good can come from it. I'll have to let her go."

Carrie's eyes widened. "For basking? You'd fire her for that? Seems kind of harsh. Can't you just have a talk with her? She probably just needs to be more involved with her own life and friends."

Even the rice was good. He'd have to find out what restaurant this was from. It was some of the best food he'd eaten in a long while. Carrie hadn't been in London long and she already knew better restaurants than he did.

"You're not really understanding," he tried to explain. "I don't want to talk with Gemma about her hurt feelings. They're none of my concern, frankly. I pay her to do a job and I just want it done with a minimum of fuss and no drama. As for getting her more involved in her own life, once again I don't want to be personally involved with my employees. I understand that you and Paige have one of those touchy-feely relationships and it works for you. That's fine, but it wouldn't work for me."

Carrie regarded him closely, a smile playing on her lips. "What's Gemma's last name?"

He opened his mouth to answer and then snapped it shut. Minx. She was smart and crafty.

"I don't remember. It's not important to our working relationship. I call her Gemma and she calls me Max. She might have forgotten my last name as well."

"If it wasn't on thousands of movie marquees," Carrie teased, lifting her wine glass and taking a sip. "How do you pay her if you don't know her name?"

"I have an accountant who pays her. He knows her name, her address, and probably a lot more." He placed his fork down on the plate. "Why are you defending her? She wasn't nice to you."

Pressing her hands to her pink cheeks, Carrie laughed. "I'm not defending her so much as trying to get into your head about this. These assistants to you are rather interchangeable from what I've seen. It's all about what they can do for you."

"Now wait a minute." She didn't see this at all. "I pay them outrageously for what they do. But if you're asking if I get personal with them, the answer is no. It would be a disaster, Carrie, plain and simple. Because of the demands of the job assistants don't last much past six months, if that. Can you imagine me getting attached to someone every few months and then they move on? I'd be depressed all the time. No, I've learned that I need to keep my private life separate from my work, that's all."

"Okay."

It was never that easy with this woman. She challenged him at every turn. "Okay? You're not going to argue with me about this? How disappointing."

Giggling, she helped herself to more chicken. "I can see you're heartbroken about it. Seriously, you made a good argument. If you can't keep an assistant very long it's probably not a good idea to get too involved with them. It's just..."

There it was. She was going to argue this with him, but she was pretending not to.

"Just what?" he asked wearily. Better to get it over with now than have it drag on all evening.

"It's just that if you took a personal interest in them and their lives they might last more than a few months."

He almost replied but thought better of it. Let her win. Or let her think she won. It was better for the digestion when they weren't sparring.

"That's something for me to think about," he said finally. "But I want you to know that I'm not planning on letting her go right away."

A smile bloomed on her lovely face. "That's so sweet, Max. You're giving her another chance."

He shook his head. "Something like that. Besides, letting her go right now just as the play is starting would be crazy. I can't train anyone else while I'm immersed in this role. She'll just have to do until the run of the play is over."

Carrie was openly laughing at him now, almost spitting out her wine. "You keep telling yourself that's the reason, Hamlet, but I know better. You're a softie. Just how many of these assistants have you actually fired? I mean, for real?"

He concentrated on cutting into his chicken, not liking the way her all too perceptive eyes seemed to look right through him. He was used to women who didn't look past the outer facade.

"None."

"None," she repeated with a smile. "That's what I thought. You're a nice man, Maxwell Hayes."

It was his turn to smile. "You're nice so you think everyone is."

Just that quickly her happy expression turned sad. "I know better than that."

Now he wanted to kick himself. She was thinking about her useless ex-fiancé who didn't deserve one second of her time after what he'd done.

He wanted to get Carrie thinking about something else. "What restaurant is this food from? It's amazing."

"Eating out all the time isn't good for you. I cooked."

The fork paused halfway to his mouth. "You made this? It's delicious. I could live on this chicken."

"Easy there, Hamlet. No one is asking you to. It's just dinner."

He was glad she'd cooked for him but he felt an obligation to tell her she shouldn't have.

"You didn't need to go to all that trouble. Takeaway would have been fine."

She shrugged. "It was no imposition. I like cooking and it's nice to have someone to cook for. Cooking for one isn't all that fun."

He took another bite and savored the flavors that exploded on his tongue. "What's in it?"

As she answered his question her face lit up again and she launched into a story that he barely listened to. Instead he watched *her* as she spoke, the way her hands moved and how animated she became when she talked. She was passionate about the things and people she loved. What might it be like to be one of them?

# CHAPTER
## Nineteen

THERE WAS nothing like a girls-only lunch to put Carrie into a good mood. Yummy food, excellent wine, and fun conversation. Amy Watson, American actress, had taken Carrie under her wing since she'd moved to London and they'd become fast friends. She and her British husband Mike were good friends with Nate and Max which meant they all spent a great deal of their social time together, so it was fortunate that they got along so well.

"So the red carpet evening was a success?" Amy asked, pushing away her plate. The pizza Carrie had brought had been demolished, nothing but discarded crust in the cardboard box.

"Better than I ever dreamed to hope. Max was actually fun and supportive. I can truthfully say I had a great time."

Amy tut-tutted. "I hate to say I told you so but I did. Max is a wonderful man. He's simply tough to get to know. He has all sorts of defense mechanisms that you have to get past. It's like running a maze that's booby trapped along the way."

That was a perfect metaphor for what Carrie had experienced since the day she'd met the famous movie star. She had the singe marks from the explosions to prove it.

"Well, he was a perfect gentleman at the charity fundraiser. We danced and drank champagne, and most importantly of all, we didn't argue. It was one for the books."

"I saw the pictures. You looked gorgeous in that dress."

Carrie had *felt* gorgeous, which wasn't a usual state for her. It didn't hurt that she'd received compliments from total strangers.

"I never would have chosen it because of the color but the stylist was right. I'll definitely have her dress me for future events."

They continued chatting about parties and Max. Amy didn't know that the relationship wasn't real and she was keen to see two people she liked so much fall in love despite their rocky start. Carrie didn't want to be the bearer of bad news so she let Amy go on about what a good catch Max was and how he truly was a sweet man. It was only when Amy waggled her eyebrows and gave her a wink that Carrie thought things had gone too far.

"I am not going to talk about that."

Amy giggled and took another sip of wine. "Come on and help me out. I'm an old married woman who only gets to live vicariously through others these days. I fell asleep at eight-thirty last night. I love my life but I yearn to hear sexy stories about romance and passion."

"Read a book," Carrie retorted, blowing out a breath.

"Better yet, read one of Paige's books. I'm just not comfortable discussing that sort of thing."

Amy leaned forward even though there wasn't anyone around to hear them. "It's okay, you can tell me. Lord knows his other girlfriends weren't so discreet. I doubt you'd say anything that would shock me after all I've heard from them."

Uh, just what had his exes said about him in the sack? She couldn't ask without Amy figuring out that Carrie hadn't slept with him yet.

She then had to remind herself that she didn't want to know either. She wasn't interested in Max...that way. Even if he had looked incredibly delicious in his tux the other night.

Carrie shrugged as nonchalantly as possible. "Then you've heard it all. I doubt there is anything I could add."

Eyes narrowing, Amy looked Carrie up and down before her brows flew up and her mouth fell open. "Oh. My. God. You and Max haven't–"

"Okay," Carrie interrupted, holding up her hand. "I think this conversation has become way too personal. We need to lay off the wine this early in the day."

"Honey, it's okay," Amy said softly. "Are you...saving yourself?"

Carrie almost asked *from what*. A marauding band of dinosaurs? Shaking her head, she tried to find a middle ground of telling the truth but not too much of it. She hated lying to people she cared about.

"I am not saving myself. We are just..."

Just what? Not really dating? Definitely not sleeping together? Not attracted to one another?

That would be a humongous lie, at least on her part. Max was a handsome man and a large part of the population thought so as well.

"Taking things slowly?" Amy finished much to Carrie's relief. "That is so romantic. Max must really think you're the one to do that. He wants to do this right after the fiasco with Alana."

Carrie could go with the romantic angle. If this had been a real love match it would truly have been special and sweet for Max to take things slowly with her.

But it wasn't, so special was out the window. It was a great explanation though.

"Yes, we're trying not to rush into things. Let the relationship progress at its own pace and not push. He's been through hell with the divorce and I think we both need to be cautious."

Amy nodded. "I know you were engaged not long ago too. I think you two are so wise. It's going to make it really amazing when it finally happens. I bet Max will pull out all the stops when it's time. Candles, flowers, champagne, an expensive hotel in an exotic locale. He's such a hopeless romantic. You lucky girl. Mine and Mike's first time was on my couch while my roommate was at the movies."

Max a hopeless romantic? Was this one of the things his ex-girlfriends had told Amy? It didn't mesh with the often-times remote and cold facade that he wore but she knew that was a big put on. He had a soft heart and she'd seen glimpses of it. He kept it locked pretty deep though so gold-digging actresses like Alana wouldn't get to it.

"I have no idea what he has planned," Carrie replied honestly. "He's an enigma."

"You and Max are going to do great. I know you two have had your ups and downs but this shows great maturity on his part. Has he said I love you yet?"

The peal of the doorbell saved Carrie from having to answer. Amy slapped her forehead and groaned, levering out of her chair. "I completely forgot. Tyler's stopping by to pick up the key to our little flat in Paris. He's spending a few days there doing some movie promotion and he hates hotels. I'll just be a minute."

"Tyler Gaylord?"

Amy hurried toward the front door. "One and the same."

The man was everywhere, although Carrie shouldn't be shocked. He was close friends with her friends which meant she was going to see him now and then.

If Carrie had thought he would hang out on the porch or in the foyer, she was wrong. He followed Amy into the kitchen, leaning against the counter while she retrieved a set of keys from a drawer.

"Just remember that the water in the shower takes a few minutes to heat up."

Accepting the key ring from Amy, Tyler turned his attention to Carrie. "I didn't expect to see you here, Red. How have you been?"

Normally she hated when people called out her bright hair color but there was something about the way he said it that made it sound like a compliment instead of a way to get a cheap laugh at her expense.

"Busy. How about you?"

"The same. I've been doing some voiceover work and

can I tell you a secret? I'm sick of listening to myself. How can anyone stand to hear me speak?"

Amy sighed loudly. "I've been saying that for years."

Hands over his heart, he groaned dramatically. "Dear lady, you wound me."

Rolling her eyes, Amy held up the wine bottle in offering. "I couldn't dent that ego of yours with a magic sword so don't try that 'poor me' routine. Carrie doesn't buy it either. Now do you want a glass?"

He shook his head. "I'll have to pass. I have a meeting with an interviewer this afternoon. They want to ask me questions I've answered a hundred times before."

Amy pretended to choke. "Fame is so hard, you poor, put-upon sex symbol."

His grin widened. "When you put it like that..."

Carrie checked her watch. "Yikes, it is getting late. I have a conference call with the States in an hour that I need to prepare for."

"You're both leaving me? I'll have to drink all of this wine by myself."

Carrie laughed. "Then you'll be in bed early again tonight. Seriously, thank you for having me over. I had a great time."

Amy gave her a hug and all three of them drifted toward the door. "Call me and we'll see a movie this weekend."

"Can I come too or is this a girl-only thing?" Tyler asked, tongue in cheek. Surely he had girls lined up for miles waiting to date him?

"Girls only," Carrie replied firmly. "Besides, won't you be in Paris?"

He held up the key. "I will but when I get back let's get the whole group together and go dancing."

Amy's eyes lit up. "Like last time?"

He nodded. "Like last time. Now how about a hug?"

Launching herself into Tyler's arms, Amy giggled as he swung her around in the air before setting her on her feet to open the front door. He stepped back so Carrie could exit first and then followed as they descended the porch steps. He turned back to Amy who was waving goodbye.

"Don't forget we're all going out when I get back. Mark it on your calendar. That first Friday night after."

Amy closed the door behind her leaving Carrie with Tyler.

"I'm afraid to ask about the last time you went dancing. Amy seems pretty excited about it."

Tyler laughed and led the way down the path to the gate. "I rented out a big nightclub so we had the place to ourselves. The stories from that evening will go down in legend. You'll see for yourself this next time."

Carrie's brow shot up. "Now I'm really afraid. Legendary, huh? An epic story for the generations?"

"Ask your boyfriend," Tyler suggested. "He'd remember. You're still with Max, right?"

Suddenly shy, Carrie pulled her phone from her purse and pretended to check her messages. "Still with Max."

"He's a lucky man."

That voice. He might be tired of hearing it but the world wasn't. It made her look up into his intense blue eyes. She could never figure Tyler out. One minute he was casual and friendly and the next flirty and seductive.

Carrie found him attractive but she wasn't attracted *to* him. There was a difference. Now Max...he was another story.

"Thank you. I'll let him know."

Stepping closer, Tyler's head dipped so his lips were close to her ear.

"He knows. See you later, Red."

Carrie would have laughed in Tyler's face but he'd already turned and strode down the street. He had Max and her all wrong. It was all make-believe.

A fact she'd do well not to ever forget. Not for one minute.

# CHAPTER
## *Twenty*

MAX WATCHED as two of his fellow actors worked out a scene on stage while the rest of the cast studied their scripts, caught up with messages, or had a cup of tea. The excitement was beginning to build as they neared opening night but the first real hurdles would be the preliminary performances to shake out any bugs in the production.

"Here's your tea." Gemma was right at his elbow acting like the other night hadn't happened, which was fine with him. The last thing he wanted to do was talk about her feelings. "I also picked up a paper for you."

He accepted the tea but balked at the tabloid she was holding out. Another piece of trash not even good enough to wrap fish in. "I'll pass on the reading material."

She smirked, only pushing it closer to him. "I think you might find it interesting."

Close to losing his patience, his grip tightened on the back of the metal chair. "What could possibly be interesting in that rag?"

Gemma let the folded paper drop onto the chair next to him. "I just thought you'd like see the pictures of Carrie and Tyler Gaylord. Now excuse me. I have to make some calls."

Whirling around, his assistant was gone in a blur of her brightly colored clothing. With a growl he fell back into his chair and reached for the tabloid, hastily paging through it until he found what she'd been referring to.

*Fuck.*

Carrie. Tyler. Standing outside a black wrought iron gate. Tyler was leaning down whispering something intimate in Carrie's ear and she was smiling about it. The headline was as nauseating as the photos.

*Has Max's bird flown the coop?*

Was Carrie spending her days making a fool of him while he worked his ass off on this new play? The photos showed them in a cozy position, that was for damn sure.

The rest of the day passed in a blur. Every break he had in rehearsal, he found himself looking at those photos over and over again as if picking at a scab. Intellectually he was pissed off because she was supposed to be in a showmance with him, letting people know he wasn't heartbroken. But he couldn't deny that his feelings - those pesky things - were involved here. He hated to admit it but it...hurt. Seeing Carrie and Tyler so close to each other wasn't something he enjoyed. They both looked happy, but not in love. Whatever their relationship was it hadn't gone that far. Yet. Max didn't think they'd slept together either but he was no expert.

It was with great trepidation that he stomped up Carrie's front steps that evening and pounded on the door.

Things had been going so well but he was angry and they were sure to argue. They'd had no definite plans to see each other tonight but this couldn't wait. He'd had to call his publicist to try and get the pictures pulled down from several websites that had picked them up, which had only stoked his emotions even higher. She'd better have a damn good explanation for making him look like a fool in front of millions of people. It was her job to keep that from happening.

The door flew open and Carrie stood there in her pajamas, lavender with little puppies scattered all over. Her long hair was pulled up into a messy bun on top of her head and a pair of spectacles were balanced on her pert nose. She looked innocently adorable and some of the anger leaked out of him like the air in a balloon.

"Max, did we have plans?" She tucked a pencil behind her ear. "I don't have anything written down."

He brandished the paper he'd been clutching in his hand in front of her face, frantically trying to get his righteous anger back despite how cute she looked. "We don't but we definitely need to have a discussion about this."

For a moment she didn't move, her eyes narrowed as she studied him. He shifted on his feet under her scrutiny but eventually she stepped back and opened the door wider.

"Then you better come in and tell me all about it. Can I get you a beer?"

He could definitely use a drink. "I'd rather a whiskey if you have it."

"Nate has everything. Just have a seat and I'll get it."

He sat stiffly, feeling out of place when he was so angry

and she was so calm. Like she had nothing to feel guilty about, but she'd caused a mountain of trouble with those pictures.

He accepted the glass and held out the newspaper. "You might find this of interest. I know I did."

Sitting next to him, she gingerly opened the paper as if there might be a nasty spider hidden within its depths. She'd see the photos immediately. He'd made sure that he'd folded it just right so they would be on top.

"I'm not sure I see what's so fascinating in here. Just pictures of me and Tyler from lunch yesterday."

*Aha.* She wasn't bothering to deny it.

"So you admit that you were with Tyler Gaylord?"

She gave him some serious side eye for a guilty woman. "Are you suggesting these were Photoshopped? Of course I admit I was with Tyler. He invited us to a party when he gets back to London, something I forgot to tell you last night."

He took a sip of whiskey and held it on his tongue, enjoying the smooth flavor before letting it slide down his throat. "You two certainly look cozy."

It was a statement meant to get a reaction but she didn't look up from the photos for a long moment. When she finally did, her normally soft brown eyes had turned dark and cold.

"If you have something to say, Hamlet, spit it out. Don't do this passive-aggressive shit with me. Lift up your balls, insert your spine, and tell me what your problem is or get out. Those are your two choices."

He didn't have to put up with that tone. He was the wronged party here.

"I don't appreciate being spoken to that way. As for my problem, right now these pictures are my problem. They're everywhere and my PR people are trying to get them pulled down. You ought to be more discreet when going out to meet your lover."

———

Carrie had to almost wrestle herself to the floor to keep from smacking the ever-loving crap out of Maxwell Hayes, movie asshole extraordinaire. She took several deep breaths before she trusted herself to respond with words only and not a knuckle sandwich.

"Are you insinuating that I am sleeping with Tyler? Because you couldn't be more wrong, Max."

He poked at the photo with his finger. "Photos don't lie, Carrie."

Laughter bubbled up at his pompous, self-righteous statement. "That's bullshit and you of all people know it. Pictures lie all the time. Do you want the truth behind these photos or are you happy that you've caught me doing something bad so you can have the morally superior highroad?"

Max could be a total jerk at times. This was one of them. If he'd come in here and simply asked her what was going on with these photos she would have been happy to tell him. But no. He had to be a douchebag and now they were back to square one.

"The truth," he said, his teeth gritted. "Of course."

She tossed the crumpled paper on the coffee table. "I had lunch with Amy yesterday."

"I know that," he said a trifle impatiently. "What does that have to do with the pictures?"

"That's Amy's house we're standing in front of. Tyler stopped by to get the key to their Paris flat. He and I left at the same time and he walked me to the gate. He went left and I went right. That's it. No big messy affair, I'm afraid. You must be so disappointed not to be the victim in this scenario."

Talk about a drama king. Carrie had thought Nate was bad, but Max had him beat. These actors were a breed unto themselves.

"It looks–"

"Oh, just stop," she broke in, not wanting to hear him justify his actions. "They probably took over a dozen photos and they picked the most damning one. All he's doing is leaning down to talk to me."

Already Max appeared to be shrinking before her eyes. His shoulders were slumped and his gaze was trained on his shoes. "What was he saying?"

She smiled at the memory. "He was saying that you knew how lucky you are to be dating me."

Jerking his head up, Max's face was red. "Was he making a pass at you?"

"He was flirting." Carrie shrugged. "Harmlessly, I might add. I think it's a habit with him. He doesn't know when to stop."

A smile flickered across Max's. "He is an incurable flirt."

"He sure is. Are we done now?"

Scratching his head, Max nodded, his gaze on the floor again. "Yes, I'm sorry I overreacted."

If she'd been a better person she might have just let this go. But she wasn't.

"I'm sorry, I don't think I heard you clearly. Can you say that again a little more loudly?"

This time Max lifted his head and sighed as if greatly put-upon. "I said I'm sorry. I overreacted."

Her evening had certainly turned out much differently than she'd planned. Never a dull moment with Max.

"Tyler flirts and you overreact. Guess which one is more fun?"

He drank down the rest of his whiskey in one gulp, making Carrie wince. That had to burn like a bitch on the way down. "Tyler, I would imagine. Everyone thinks he's more fun."

She picked up the paper again. She'd tortured Max enough. "I'm not sure about that. You can be a great deal of fun when you want to. Now I am sorry these pictures caused a problem though. Is there anything I need to do?"

Shaking his head, Max leaned back against the cushions, letting his eyes close. He looked exhausted. They were working those actors in the play like rented mules. So much for the glamour of show business.

"No, but thank you for offering. I'll make sure the next time we're out that we're a little more affectionate than usual. The rumors will die down."

Considering they barely did anything in public except dance and hold hands that left the possibilities almost endless. "Do you not want to go to Tyler's party? He said something about renting out a nightclub. I guess he'd done this before and the evenings are, and I quote, legendary."

A grin spread over Max's too handsome face. Yep, there

were stories about these parties that she needed to hear. He was thinking of one right at this moment and loving it.

"We will absolutely go. A Tyler Gaylord party is not to be missed. Plus it will give the press a chance to see us when he's around. They'll see that you prefer me."

She poked him in the arm. "Warn me if you plan to get handsy."

"A man simply cannot hear that enough."

She picked up the paper and walked it over to her trash can, stuffing it inside where tabloids belonged. "I haven't eaten yet. Do you want to stay and order a pizza?"

His eyes popped open. She'd said the magic word. Pizza. "You order. I'll buy."

# CHAPTER
## Twenty-One

CARRIE HAD MANAGED three slices of the large pizza with sausage and extra cheese. Max had finished the rest of it while bitching that he was going to have to run twenty extra miles to burn off the carbs.

"You have to be skinny for this part?"

He folded the cardboard pizza box and shoved it down in the trash can with the tabloid.

"Not really. I just have to stay the same size through the entire run of the show so they don't have to make any alterations on the costumes. They can do it but I hate to be an issue for the backstage crew. They work hard enough as it is."

Speaking of working hard...

"I think they're working the actors hard too. You've been doing some inhuman hours the last few weeks."

"We usually get more rehearsal time but one of the cast was working on a movie. It cut our schedule by a week."

"More wine?" She held up the half empty wine bottle.

He shook his head. "Any more alcohol and I won't be able to move from this couch."

He was draped over one end of the sofa, his eyes closed again. He looked so peaceful and young, like a little boy drifting off to sleep. She had to remind herself this was no boy. Max Hayes was all man. A handsome, sexy, talented, annoying as shit man.

"You're welcome to hunker down in the spare room if you like. Nate might even have some pajamas around here that will fit you."

Nate was slightly taller but the friends had the same physique.

"I don't wear pajamas."

"Me neither."

His eyes snapped open and he sat up, his brows pinched together. "You don't?"

"You seem surprised. Don't you remember my list? I don't like wearing anything when I'm trying to sleep. It gets all bunched up and then I can't get comfortable. Besides, I live in Florida where it's warm most of the year."

He stared as if he'd never seen her before. This was fun. She needed to shock him more often. "I guess I just think of you as the buttoned-up type."

That hurt. "You and my ex-fiancé. What is it with you men? Either a female is a precious vessel never to be besmirched or she's a freak in the sheets. There's no in between with you guys."

"And where are you on that spectrum?"

"A hell of a lot closer to freak than vessel."

Those expressive brows that had been pulled together were now raised halfway up his forehead. "Interesting."

"It's freaking fascinating. Now can I ask you a question that will change this frankly bizarre subject?"

"Of course, although I must admit that now you have me intrigued."

She sat down next to him on the couch and snapped her fingers a few times. Men were so single-minded. "Focus, Hamlet."

"I am focused. Ask your question."

"Now that we have seen those photos in the paper do you think paps are following me? Do I need to change up my routine or something?"

Rubbing his bottom lip, Max shook his head. "I don't mean this to be mean but I have to say it's a surprise to me that you were papped at all. Maybe they were following Tyler."

"That makes more sense, and I have to say that I'm relieved."

"They could be following you though."

Contrary British bastard.

"No, they had to be following Tyler. They just got lucky seeing him with me."

"Lucky," Max said softly, his gaze far away and unfocused. "A lot of people around me are getting lucky these days, and not in the Biblical sense."

He was noodling on something, she could practically see the hamster running on the wheel in his head. "What are you thinking or do I dare ask?"

Standing, he towered over her, his arms crossed over his chest. "Alana found me at the hotel that day when no one knew where I was. The paps found you having lunch with Amy. Not to mention the photos of me buying coffee this last week or when you and I were papped going to the movie. I'm rarely even bothered here in London. The photogs know that I lead a fairly boring life."

He did, actually. Max was as much a workaholic as she was and perhaps even more.

"So what are you saying then?"

He shrugged, but she could see the frustration in his features. "I have no idea. I'm tired and all I want is a good night's sleep. Is the offer of the spare room still open?"

Offering him a bed had been an impulse but it had been the right thing to do. He didn't look like he could make it upstairs, let alone to his own house, even if it wasn't far. There was something about him when he was like this that pinged all of her nurturing instincts. Max didn't cut himself much slack when he was working and if he wasn't careful he was going to burn out young.

"Absolutely. The sheets are clean too. I think there's even a spare toothbrush."

She'd try not to think about a naked Max just down the hall. Would he think about her?

————

The smell of freshly brewed coffee lured Max out of bed the next morning. He was feeling refreshed after a good night's sleep and he had Carrie to thank for that. If he had gone home he would have read scripts and answered emails until the wee hours of the morning. Despite fantasizing about Carrie naked just a few doors down he'd managed several hours of quality rest.

Dreaming of Carrie in his bed. Nude and saying his name over and over.

An image he needed to erase from his memory bank immediately. He was never going to see her unclothed and in a state of ecstasy. Never.

Quickly brushing his teeth, he pulled on his clothes from last night and bounded anxiously down the stairs. More delicious aromas had been added to the air and he couldn't wait to see what Carrie was up to in the kitchen. Other than his mum, no one ever made him breakfast unless he was paying them to do it. Alana had never even made him a cup of tea. It had been his job to cater to her.

Standing in front of the stove, Carrie was dressed in faded blue jeans and a teal t-shirt that dipped low on one shoulder exposing creamy flesh that begged to be kissed and caressed. Her hair was in a long ponytail and his fingers itched to reach out and give the band holding it back a tug so the silky curtain of hair would fall loose and wild.

Tortured with visions from last night's dreams, he might have made an audible whimpering sound because she whirled around, revealing a face completely devoid of makeup, just her fresh, glowing skin on display.

She was so amazingly beautiful.

No need for artifice; she was a natural beauty. He was so used to women caked in makeup, designer clothes, and jewels that when he saw Carrie like this it was like a punch to the solar plexus. She took his breath away.

"Good morning." She smiled and waved the spatula in the air in greeting. "There's a pot of coffee so help yourself.

I'm making waffles with Paige's new waffle maker. I think it was a wedding gift. I hope you're hungry."

"I am," he replied, his throat tight. He had to drag his gaze away from her delicious curves. He'd much rather have her for breakfast but she wasn't on the menu.

Business. It was only business. Unfortunately for him, the more time he spent with her the harder it was to remember that fact. Damn if she wasn't flying right under his usually impressive defenses.

He filled a cup and sat down at the table, resisting the urge to stand behind her and slip his arms around her waist while kissing that exposed shoulder. Like they were a real couple having breakfast together and she did girl-friend things like this for him all the time.

His imagination was going to get him in trouble. She wasn't his to fantasize about but when he'd seen those photos of her and Tyler yesterday...something inside of him had shifted.

Which reminded him, he needed to have a chat with his assistant today.

"What do you have planned?" he asked after inhaling the melt-in-his-mouth waffles. "Would you like to meet for lunch?"

"Will the slave drivers give you a break?"

She picked up their plates and placed them in the sink and then refilled their coffee.

He smiled at her characterization of the director who was actually quite relaxed, considering the schedule he'd been given.

"Every day. Come by at noon. There's a little cafe just round the corner."

"Sounds good. I like getting outside at lunchtime. It's breaks up the work day a little bit."

"Then it's a date. I need to get to my place to shower and change clothes."

He was ridiculously excited about seeing her in a few hours. It was pathetic, really. A grown man and he was sweating like a teenager on his first date.

Giggling behind her coffee cup, she had to slap a hand over her mouth.

He was afraid to ask but he had to know what had made her laugh. It was a delightful sound. "What is so funny?"

She was laughing so hard she had to set down her coffee cup. Her cheeks were a lovely shade of pink and her brown eyes sparkled with mischief. What had given the little minx a case of the giggles? Did she know how excited he was and planned to tease him about it?

"Max is doing the walk of shame this morning. Kind of."

If only they had done something to feel guilty for.

"Enjoy your laugh at my expense, wench. Revenge will be mine. I will bring dark days upon your household."

He'd used his Shakespeare voice to deliver that line and it appeared to be a hit. If anything, she was laughing all the harder.

"I like that," she said. "Hamlet and wench. I think that pretty much sums up our relationship."

Slipping his phone into his pocket, he headed toward the front door before he gave in to the urge to kiss her goodbye. That would have been the perfect ending to their domestic morning. A wife sending her beloved husband off to work with a cuddle and a promise of something even better when he came home. Like that imaginary spouse, she followed him to say goodbye. Chastely, of course.

"See you at noon," he said but anything else he'd planned flew right out of his head when he opened the door. A crowd of paparazzi had at some point crowded around the front gate and they'd clearly spotted the happy couple because the flashbulbs went off like a dozen strobe lights. Covering his eyes, Max immediately stepped in front of Carrie to shield her from the cameras. He might think she looked sexy this morning, but being a woman she'd want to be more prepared for a gaggle of photographers that wanted to put her picture in the paper and on the internet.

"What the hell?" she hissed as she ducked down behind him. "How did they even know you were here? I think they are watching me. All I need is some black helicopters and my paranoia is complete."

"I'll handle this. Go on inside and keep the door closed. If they don't disperse after I leave, text me and we can reschedule lunch, but I think they'll go once they get their pictures of me."

The money shot would have been to catch Max kissing Carrie goodbye on her front doorstep but all these vultures were going to get was the walk of shame she'd referred to earlier. Although he hardly considered it big news that a man in his late thirties had spent the night with his extremely attractive girlfriend. It would be news if he hadn't.

The door closed behind him and he put his head down, plowing through the throngs of photographers all shouting questions at him, some of them in rather poor taste. The rabid pack followed him all the way home, snapping picture after picture although Max wouldn't give them the satisfaction of looking up or saying a word. The bloodsuckers had already ruined his morning by upsetting Carrie.

What had they been doing in front of Carrie's house? They hadn't been following him last night. He was sure of that. Had they been tipped off? And by whom?

He had a good idea who it was. But why?

# CHAPTER
## Twenty-Two

AT THE THEATRE, Gemma handed Max his coffee and a lemon poppy-seed muffin before reeling off a few business items he needed to take care of. Call his agent about that new script, remember the interview he was doing tomorrow afternoon, and call his mother.

"I'll give her a call today." Max leaned against a table in the backstage area where they kept the snacks. He was thinking of trading in that muffin for a chocolate chip one. "By the way, Gemma, is there anything you want to tell me?"

With a nonchalant air, his assistant shook her head. She was wearing another of her brightly colored outfits today, the pants yellow and the shirt purple. The color combination made his eyes hurt.

"I don't think so. Will there be anything else?"

He'd given her a chance to come clean. "Actually, yes. Funny thing happened this morning. There was a gaggle of photographers outside Carrie's home. I don't suppose you'd know anything about that?"

The change in her was almost imperceptible but to a stage-trained actor who studied human behavior it was as bright as day. Her shoulders tensed slightly and her hand had fluttered up to cover her throat, the most vulnerable part of the human body. It was a primitive reaction but it never lied.

Unlike Gemma.

"I don't." She shook her head. "I don't."

Ah, she'd repeated her answer twice as if to emphasize her truthfulness. Another tell.

"What is Alana paying you?"

Her eyes widened and she took a step back. "Nothing. She's not paying me anything."

He found that hard to believe. "So you're doing this for free? How foolish of you. She would have paid for the information you've been passing her."

Gemma wasn't the crying type so it wasn't a surprise when she went into offense-mode.

"This is all your fault," she spat, her normally placid expression turned venomous. "You never noticed me but Alana did."

"I told you when I hired you that I do not get romantically involved with my employees."

Rolling her eyes, she gave a snort of disdain. "I don't want you. You're way too old for me. I want to be a star. Why do you think I took this job? Because I love fetching you coffee? Get real."

A star. He should have known. Everybody had their own hidden agenda. But there was literally no path from picking up his dry cleaning to winning an Academy Award. What had Gemma been thinking?

"You want to be an actress? Then be one. You want to be a celebrity assistant? Do that. But the two don't have anything to do with one another."

Gemma tossed her tablet computer on the table hard enough to make him wince. Shit, his entire life was in that thing and if it malfunctioned he had no idea if she kept his schedule and contacts backed up somewhere.

"Alana said that several of your assistants had gone on to get big acting jobs."

Alana? Fuck.

Sighing, he rubbed the back of his neck where a pain was beginning to make itself known. For the millionth time he wondered how he had ended up marrying a woman like Alana.

*Right.* His dick.

"Unfortunately for you, Gemma, that is pure fabrication. None of my assistants prior to you have received any roles of note because of their employment with me."

Gemma shook her head. "No, she said that they're on their way to big things. She said she'd get me an audition with Guillermo Del Toro."

Christ. This was a fucking mess.

"Alana can't even get herself an audition with Del Toro. I'm sorry you believed her."

His non-crying assistant now had fat tears sliding down her face as she took off those oversized glasses to wipe her eyes. "I can't believe this. I did everything she asked me to do."

Scraping a hand down his face, Max gave a half groan

and half sigh. "So you never wanted to be an assistant and see the other side of the business?"

That's what she had told him in the interview. He really needed to pay more attention in those things.

"No," she answered in the most forlorn tone. With black mascara streaks on her cheeks, Gemma looked sad indeed. "I've always wanted to be a star."

She kept saying star. Not actress, which made Max wonder if it was the lights and glamour she was interested in more than the work of deconstructing a character and then bringing them to life for an audience.

"What exactly did Alana ask you to do?"

Max had his suspicions but he wanted to be sure when he threw this all up in Alana's face. Per their prenuptial, a stunt like this was going to cost her.

Sniffling, Gemma wiped her nose on her sleeve. "Keep track of where you were all the time and let her know. Keep her informed of meetings with future directors and producers, plus interviews and public appearances. And Carrie, of course."

What had just seemed like a pain in the ass before was now something far different. Anger built inside of him, making his temples pound painfully.

"Carrie? What about her?"

Gemma had retreated to a metal folding chair and she shifted in it, uncomfortable with the question. "Watch her. What she's doing and where she's going."

That shit stopped today.

"Tyler Gaylord."

He didn't phrase it as a question. He knew for sure.

Tears started all over again. "I'm friends with Gaylord's

stylist and she overheard him making plans to get a key from Amy and Mike. We had a drink and she told me about it. I already knew that Carrie was having lunch with Amy that day."

He gritted his teeth and wondered what Gemma said to other people about him. "And you told Alana?"

She nodded, sobbing pitifully into her shirt. "Are you going to sack me?"

Gemma had to be kidding. What did she want? An Employee of the Month plaque?

"What do you think I should do?"

She looked up, her eyes red-rimmed. "I think you should help me get an acting job. You're a huge star and have a lot of clout."

Max was fucking sick and tired of people - mostly women - wanting something from him, using him. Despite evidence to the contrary, he was a sensitive human being who wanted to be liked for himself. Too many relationships in his life were about what they could get from him.

"If you want to be a star," he began and Gemma's eyes lit up with hope. "Then you need to be ready to work hard and make your own opportunities."

Her smile immediately turned down.

"I started at the bottom and worked my way up," he continued. "I took any job in theatre I could get, often working for free. I studied the craft and sought advice from those more experienced than myself. Even now I don't rest on my laurels. I endeavor to make every performance better than the last. This profession isn't about fame, Gemma, it's about creation."

Standing, she slid the strap of her backpack over her

shoulder. "You're a selfish asshole. Alana was right. You won't help anyone. I guess you're afraid of the competition. Well, fuck you. When I'm a star I'll ruin you, and I won't rest until I do. You'll wish you'd been nicer to me."

The young woman stomped out of the backstage area and hopefully out of the theatre. She had much to learn about the acting profession and if she wasn't careful it was going to chew her up and spit her out. What she didn't realize? He was trying to help her. He was happy to assist those who were putting in the work, busting their asses. But those only interested in Twitter followers and parties? They'd have to get there on their own.

"And a lovely morning to you too," he muttered, picking up the discarded tablet. If it worked it would be a miracle. He was due for one too. He pressed the on button and nothing happened. Zip. Nada. Zilch.

His entire life was stuck in this hunk of plastic. Now what?

———

"Can you fix it?"

Max hovered impatiently over Carrie's shoulder as she tapped away at his laptop computer. Apparently he'd fired Gemma this morning and being unused to terminating employees he hadn't had the foresight to get the tablet from her before he told her the bad news.

"I don't know but please back up. Your hot breath is uncomfortable on my neck."

It wasn't really but his nearness had set off alarm bells that were loud and insistent. As Max had begun to show her his authentic self, her attraction to the movie star had deepened. She'd long passed enjoying his looks superficially and now she was well and truly besotted. The only answer was to keep him somewhat at arms' length.

"Sorry," he apologized instantly but barely budged from his perch right behind her. "Have you found anything yet?"

"I don't know." She clicked around the file folder structure. "You said that Gemma backed up her tablet to your laptop so you would always be in sync with each other, but you didn't change the password after you fired her. It looks like she went in here and tried to delete a bunch of stuff."

A string of expletives fell from his well-shaped lips. "I had my accountant mail her a check for what I owed her but I should have held on to it until she fixed the mess she made."

"I don't think that's legal, Hamlet, although I'm unfamiliar with the laws in this country. But generally you have to pay people what you owe them whether they destroy your life or not."

A smile spread across her face and the heady buzz of triumph had her chuckling evilly. Gemma was a smart young woman. But not smart enough. Carrie had been around this block a time or two.

"I got it," she crowed, throwing a mental fist pump into the air. "This software package automatically backs up a copy every night at midnight. She got rid of the live version but she forgot about the spare. I can restore it but any changes made since then won't be there. Is that okay?"

She was amused to see Max doing a little jig behind

her, his precious dignity be damned. If he'd shown her this side of him from day one... *No, don't think about that*. She'd be his willing slave and that would be bad. Oh so very bad.

"It's bloody fantastic. There shouldn't be any changes since midnight." He was grinning and laughing like a loon. "I can't believe you fixed it. It's all going to be alright."

It took mere seconds to restore everything, then she plugged in the spare tablet computer she was letting him borrow so it could sync with the software. This way he could be mobile.

"Since this is the first sync it's going to take awhile." She stood up with a satisfied smile. "We should probably go ahead and eat dinner. Hopefully it will be finished by then."

"You are amazing," he stated, grabbing her into a big bear hug, his strong arms wrapped snugly around her body. Max's delicious scent hit her right in the olfactory senses and she couldn't stop herself from taking a second whiff. No man should smell this good. It ought to be illegal. It was certainly unfair. "You've saved my life. Seriously. I don't know what I would have done without you."

She opened her mouth to tell him it was no big deal but their gazes locked and the world around her seemed to stand still. Sound disappeared. The room blurred. Every molecule in her body was focused on this one man that was driving her crazy. One second she wanted to throttle him and the next she wanted to kiss him.

Right now it was the latter and she was getting desperate. It appeared she wasn't the only one with lascivious thoughts on their mind when his tongue snaked out and wet his lips. His head dipped down, moving inexorably closer, one millimeter at a time. Their breaths mingled and she could swear she felt the heavy drum of his heartbeat as he pressed her closer to his heated frame.

*This is it. It's finally going to happen for real.*

The chime on his phone jarred them both back to his living room and the present. She thought she heard a low growl from Max's throat but it might have been her imagination. Or it might have been her. She was frustrated and wanted to tell whomever had called him that they had seriously lousy timing.

His gaze still hot, he fumbled with his phone and pressed it to his ear. He didn't seem done with their "moment" quite yet.

"Hello, Mum. It's good to hear from you."

Nothing like a parental intervention to throw cold water on any hanky panky. Chilled as if she'd been doused with icy water, the arousal that had been so acute only moments before dissolved.

She wasn't the type for casual liaisons at this point in her life. She wanted to care about the man in her bed. They had a contract and she would fulfill it. But anything more was simply not in her best interests. This infatuation was just a passing fancy. She'd get over Max. Eventually.

# CHAPTER
## Twenty~Three

**SEXUAL TENSION MADE CARRIE CRANKY.** A fact she was trying hard to hide from Max.

Since firing his assistant, she'd tried to help him out a little which meant they'd spent even more time together than before. Max was hopeless when it came to any sort of organization whatsoever and almost completely dependent on his calendar to get him anywhere on time. Carrie had set him up on new software so that he wouldn't be at the mercy of anyone ever again since she was sure he'd learned absolutely nothing from the situation with Gemma.

The problem was the more time she spent with Max the more attracted to him she was. Paige had been right. He was a nice man, genuinely caring, but reticent to expose his real self to the people around him until they'd earned his trust. Carrie couldn't deny she felt special now that she'd reached that magic circle of friends.

It didn't hurt that he was gorgeous, either.

Max opened the door to the car, giving her a smile that would have made a lesser woman swoon. "You look very nice tonight."

Max's deep baritone sent a shiver up her spine. If he hadn't been completely oblivious to how he affected her, she would have accused him of doing it on purpose. It was that devastating.

"Thank you. So do you."

Her reply came out sounding more prim than she'd intended but Max didn't seem to notice, relaxing back in the soft leather of the limousine next to her. They were heading to Tyler's party at an exclusive nightclub in Chelsea and he'd sent cars for everyone so they could drink as much as they wanted without worrying about getting home.

Max did look handsome in a pair of tailored black trousers, white button-down shirt, and black jacket. No tie, the shirt open at the neck showing off the strong column of his neck and that Adam's apple she was dying to kiss. She'd started fantasizing about it at the most inopportune moments.

Twisting her black velvet purse between her fingers, Carrie tried to make small talk to fill the quiet. Normally she excelled at chatting, even about innocuous topics, but Max didn't always make it easy. He was a man given to bouts of brooding silence.

"It's good that you have tomorrow off. They've been working you hard these last few weeks."

"I'm ready for opening night. It feels like we've been rehearsing forever."

"Not much longer to wait. Next week is the shake out performances, right?"

He looked down at her, his blue eyes intent and serious. "I'd like you there for at least one of them if possible. Can you do that for me?"

He had no idea the things she wanted to do for him. Or to him.

"Of course, whatever you need." She shoved an imaginary knife in her own heart. Just as a reminder of why she was sitting there. "That's what we agreed to."

Something flickered over his features but it settled into a smile. "It is but I can still say thank you. It means a great deal to me to see a friendly face in the audience."

"If Nate and Paige were here, I know they'd be there for you. They're trying to make it for opening night."

"Poor Nate," Max laughed. "He's working overtime to get here. I told him they could come later in the run but he's insisting."

The drive to the venue was short and the limo smoothly pulled up to the curb. Carrie checked her lip gloss in the mirror one last time.

Max reached for her hand and gave it a squeeze. "You're not nervous, are you? You look stunning. Every man in the room will be envious of me."

"And it's all about you," she teased, allowing him to open the door for her. They'd become much more comfortable with each other and he didn't take offense at her words.

"It most certainly is. Are you ready? This is a private party so there's no red carpet or paps. There might be later if they figure out we're here."

It was novel to be this dressed up with no one taking photos but she wouldn't complain. Max led her into the dark nightclub illuminated by flashing lights and strategically placed lamps that looked more like candlelight. The heavy beat of the music could be felt under her feet and the song was one of her favorites.

She tugged at Max's arm. "I love this song. Let's dance."

"You don't want to greet everyone first? Or get a drink?"

He was simply teasing her now. "I don't. Please?"

She stuck out her lower lip in a pout and he threw his head back and laughed. "We can't have you all sad tonight. This is a party. Alright, lead the way, love."

Dragging him out on the dance floor, Carrie found a spot right next to Mike and Amy. The two women quickly embraced before Max twirled Carrie in a circle before pulling her close, his arm wrapped around her waist and her head tucked under his chin.

There she stayed most of the evening, sweaty and happy, as she and Max danced the night away. He was an excellent dancer, comfortable with his body probably because of his profession, and not self-conscious in the least. The perfect partner, he was almost impossible to tire out due to his strict fitness regimen. She, on the other hand, needed a drink and a chair.

"I need a drink," she gasped as the song ended and another fast one came on. "And my feet are killing me."

Max led her to the edge of the dance floor. "Find a place to sit and I'll get us a couple of drinks."

Amy and Mike had already left the dance floor and were sitting off in a quiet corner on a cluster of small couches. Wincing at her sore feet, Carrie joined them, collapsing against the cushions with a sigh of relief.

"Every time I wear heels I ask myself why women got stuck with them and not men."

Mike raised his beer in welcome. "Men wear ties and that's cruel enough. There's no way it's a man's world as long as we wrap nooses around our necks for no good reason."

Amy giggled, her cheeks pink. She was ahead of Carrie on drink count. "What my handsome husband is trying to say is that he looks terrible in pumps. Please ask me how I know that."

Max chuckled in her ear, his breath warm on her cheek as he bent down to hand over her drink. "We said we'd never speak of it again, Amy, now here you are threatening to spill the beans to Carrie."

Amy wriggled her finger at Max. "You just don't want her to know about the time all the boys dressed up in drag. I have pictures, you know."

This Carrie had to see before she left this earth. One more item was just added to her bucket list.

See Maxwell Hayes in a dress.

Max cleared his throat. "It was a bet and we lost. We did not put on dresses because it was the thing missing from our lives. It was a bet."

Carrie took a sip of her cool drink. "Photos or it didn't happen."

Max gave her a smug smile. "Then it didn't happen."

"Yes, it did," Amy declared. "I don't have the pictures with me, but I do have them. I think Nate was the prettiest."

Lifting his nose in the air, Max sniffed with disdain. "Are you saying I was an unattractive female? That's hardly a polite thing to say."

"You had a five o'clock shadow," Mike jeered. "We all looked terrible. My lipstick was smeared. Tyler's chest hair stuck out of his neckline. It was awful."

"I must know about this bet. Who did you lose to?"

Max pointed to Amy who was almost doubled over in laughter. "You boys never learn your lesson. I make a yearly bet with them and they always lose. Every. Single. Time."

"World Cup," Mike said grimly. "My lovely wife is something of a savant when it comes to picking winners. It's one of her more annoying qualities."

"Go Amy," Carrie laughed. "Seriously...there are pictures? I must see these. I bet Paige would want to see them too."

"I'll dig them out." Amy smiled and then stuck out her tongue at her husband. "Maybe I'll even get one framed for the living room."

"I'll see you in divorce court," Mike retorted. "Or better yet, I'll tell my mum. She'll never let you hear the end of it."

Amy's smile only grew wider. "My only love, your mother has already seen them."

Choking on his beer, Mike's face turned beet red. "Woman, you are treading on thin ice."

"Then dance with me," Amy challenged, nudging Mike with her foot. He jumped up from the sofa with a grin and swept her back onto the dance floor leaving Carrie and Max alone.

There was that tension again. It had been simmering below the surface all evening but now it was in full force, practically sucking all the oxygen out of the room.

Max fidgeted on the couch cushion. "Are you having a good time?"

"I am but we haven't talked to too many other people tonight. Everybody is either on the dance floor or..." Her gaze swept the intimate space. "Is there an upstairs or something?"

Max nodded. "There is so there might be some guests up there. Most are dancing and many won't show until after midnight. Tyler has some...interesting friends."

"I've read some of the stories. Is he really that wild?"

She doubted it. One thing she'd learned in the past year was that the press loved hyperbole.

"He can be at times, although when he's working he's quite focused. Extremely serious and dedicated."

"So it's best to keep him busy," Carrie concluded with a giggle. "Idle hands and all that."

Shit. Now she couldn't stop herself from noticing Max's hands. Strong, with long fingers that could reach...

*No. Don't think about all the places he could reach.*

Max leaned forward and she caught a whiff of his cologne. At this rate she was going to lose her mind. "Another drink?"

Alcohol wasn't the answer but she wasn't even sure what the question was, so why not? Maybe it would help relax her. Maybe it would help her forget how attracted she was to Max.

*Because that's what booze does. Makes the opposite sex less desirable.*

She held out her glass. "Absolutely. Then can we dance again?"

# CHAPTER
## Twenty~Four

DRINKS WERE FLOWING, people laughing, and the party was in full swing. The only missing component was Paige and Nate. Tyler had spent some time up in the DJ booth but he was now making his way toward Carrie and Max on the dance floor.

Tyler bowed low, a smirk on his handsome face. "May I dance with this beautiful woman, Max?"

Brow lifted, Max took a step back. "Best ask the lady, mate. I don't want to get my arse kicked tonight for being too possessive."

Carrie tapped her chin as if giving the question a great deal of thought. "I suppose a dance would be okay. I'll even let you lead."

Tyler shooed Max away. "Be gone with you. Go have a drink with Mike. Or better yet, there's a pool tournament going on upstairs. Show them you're more than a pretty face."

Max didn't argue, leaning down to brush her cheek

with his lips before he disappeared into the crowd on the dance floor. Her skin tingled from his touch and her gaze lingered where he'd been even after he was gone.

"You have it bad."

Tyler's words pulled her from her reverie. "I beg your pardon?"

His lips twisted but he pulled her into his arms as the music slowed. "You and Max. It's obvious you really care about him."

Too obvious? That wasn't good.

"He's a good person."

"He cares about you too," Tyler chuckled, twirling her before pulling her close again. "So stop worrying. I've never seen him this smitten before, and I was around when he was dating Alana."

Max's ex-wife. The entire reason he was doing this showmance. Not because he was enthralled by Carrie's beauty and charm but because he was embarrassed and ashamed.

"I'm not worrying."

"Honey, as an actor I study people, and you're worried. Do you honestly believe that Max isn't as crazy about you as you are about him? He's head over heels."

Leaning back, Carrie looked up into Tyler's eyes. He couldn't be serious. "That's how Max Hayes acts when he's head over heels? He might want to hold up a sign or something because it's not obvious to us mere mortals in the world."

Tyler bent his head, his lips close to her ear. "He let you in. That's all you need to know."

It was true that Max wasn't the easiest man to get to know.

Or like.

"He could have anyone–"

She broke off, embarrassed that the words had even been uttered. Baring her soul to Tyler Gaylord wasn't going to happen. He might be a nice man but he didn't deserve her mooning about Max during his party.

"He wants you," Tyler stated firmly. "Besides, you're as gorgeous as any of the women in Hollywood. Better yet, you're real. Although you could be an actress if you wanted to. You have the most amazingly expressive face. You say more with a look than most people do with a hundred words."

Bullshit. She recognized it when she heard it.

"I'm not one of your fangirls, Tyler. You don't have to flatter me."

"It's true," he insisted, his brows pulled close together. "You're gorgeous, smart, funny, and down to earth. I'm surprised Max isn't beating the men off with a bat to keep them away from you. And I do think you'd make a good actress. You have the emotional depth to be able to understand a character. So many people go into this profession for the wrong reasons. It's work and to do it well takes talent."

"Of which I have none. I guess I'll have to stick to boring old business."

*It's not boring to me.*

"I'd give you a part in my new movie in a heartbeat, Red. You just say the word. In fact, I know of one you'd be perfect for. She only has a couple of scenes but they're juicy ones. Lots of anger and strong emotion. What do you say? Should I send the script over so you can take a look?"

He looked serious but he couldn't be. "Are you joking?"

"Not in the least." He stopped in the middle of the dance floor. "I think you could be great."

"No way." She shook her head. "I'm no actress. I'm just a normal, average working woman."

His gaze raked her head to toe. "There is very little average about you. Follow me, Red."

Not giving her a chance to say no, he led her off the dance floor and into a small office in the back that probably belonged to the owner or manager of the club. Closing the door firmly behind him, he positioned her so she was in front of a mirrored wall that made the room look bigger. Or was supposed to. Mostly it made the room decor look cheesy, like a bad disco.

Standing behind her with his hands on her shoulders, he didn't let her turn away, keeping her facing forward so she was looking directly at her reflection.

"So?" she challenged, keeping her gaze directed somewhere in the vicinity of her knees. "I look at myself every day in the mirror. This is nothing new."

"Have you? Look at yourself, Carrie. See what I see."

Giving herself a cursory inspection, she shrugged. "I look fine. Listen, Tyler, I'm okay with myself. I'm not one of those insecure women begging for compliments. I'm attractive and smart. Successful, too. I agree that I'm a catch. But Hollywood has standards few women can live up to and that's something I've never aspired to be."

Chuckling, he didn't let go of her, his expression determined. "Being a great actress has little to do with being genetically perfect. There is more beauty in imperfection. It draws the eye and adds interest. It's more approachable. Look at yourself through that lens and tell me what you see."

"Well, I'm certainly imperfect," Carrie laughed, trying to get in the spirit of his game. "But I'm not sure what you're expecting me to do here."

"I'll help you." He stepped back and dropped his hands. "Close your eyes and think about a time you were angry and how that felt. The hurt and betrayal. The utter devastation. Remember how you felt and really relive it."

This was some touchy-feely stuff but she'd comply. Obediently she shut her eyes and thought about how Mark had left her in the lurch. She wasn't so much hurt anymore as disgusted with his chicken shit behavior. He should have come clean long before he actually did. The anger she felt was mostly directed at herself. She should have seen through him a long time ago.

"Okay, I've got one."

"Really think about it. Play it over and over in your head. When you're ready, open your eyes and look at yourself in the mirror."

Slowly she opened her eyes and gazed at her reflection. A conflicted woman with red cheeks and dark eyes stared back. She'd done it. Brought anger to life.

Tyler leaned over her shoulder. "Passion. Character. It isn't enough to look good. An actress or actor has to be able to bring emotions to life. You have no idea just how expressive you are even at this moment. You're looking at me like I've lost my mind. I can assure you I haven't."

There was a part of her that felt like it had to protest. "It can't be that easy. I'm not an actress–"

"You could be, if you wanted to. I'm just giving you options. There are people that would kill for the opportunity. Do you want to do another emotion? Close your eyes again."

Did she? Digging into an emotion was kind of fun and challenging. Is that what Max did to bring a character to life? No wonder he earned the big bucks. He made it look easy and it wasn't at all. Even if she didn't want to act, understanding what Max did for a living seemed like a good idea so she let her eyes drift shut.

"Close your eyes and think about being passionately in love. The candlelight. The warmth. The sex. The way he feels and speaks. Even the way love smells."

No. Hell no.

Her heavy lids snapped up. "Max is probably wondering where we are."

Their gazes met in the mirror, his seeing way too much. She wasn't fooling him or anyone and for a long moment she thought he was going to call her on it. Point out her cowardice but that wasn't Tyler's way. Instead he nodded and gave her shoulders a reassuring squeeze as if to say *Don't worry...I won't give away your secret.*

"We should head back to the party. We don't want Max to get jealous."

Fat chance of that happening.

She gave herself one more look at her reflection. More kindly and less critical. She didn't want to be the kind of person who tore themselves down and only saw the nega-tive. There was so much good in her life. She was an attractive woman who was way too hard on herself at the best of times. "Thank you, Tyler."

"You're welcome. Did you see anything you liked?"

Smiling, she nodded, thinking there were several kinds of beauty. Tyler was right. Physical perfection was boring. "I did and that's why I'm thanking you."

"You're a beautiful woman, Red, but more importantly, you're fascinating. That wins hands down over looks every time. I'd still like you to look at that script."

"I don't think so but thank you for the offer. I needed it today."

He smirked and reached for the door handle. "Anytime you want me to tell you the truth about how amazing you are just let me know. I'm at your service. In fact, any time you want to dump Max and let me take you out give me a call."

"Some friend you are, hitting on me like this." She shook her finger at him. "You should be ashamed."

It was good-hearted joking but Tyler's expression had turned sober. "If I thought he was treating you right I wouldn't say a word. But I kind of get the feeling he hasn't said these things to you and that's a serious omission."

"Maybe he doesn't agree with you," she said lightly as they headed back to the main nightclub area.

"Then he doesn't deserve you," Tyler shot back. "Don't let Max treat you less than you deserve, Red."

Good advice and she immediately took it to heart. Max might not want her the way she wanted him but it wouldn't be because she wasn't enough. She was plenty all by herself and if he couldn't see that then it was his loss.

He would be lucky to have her, especially after his night-mare ex-wife.

"Damn right. I'm a catch. Now are you going to dance with me again?"

Carrie was going to have fun tonight. She was going to laugh, dance, and drink with her friends. Life was too short to moon over Maxwell Hayes. He either wanted her or he didn't. It was really that simple.

Frankly, she'd survive either way.

———

Max was leaning against the bar when a heavy hand clapped him on the shoulder. Tyler, of course.

"When was the last time you told Carrie how beautiful she is?" the other actor queried, his eyes narrowed. Tyler Gaylord was pissed off. "You should be down on your knees thanking whatever god you pray to that she gives you the time of day. You don't deserve her, mate, and if you don't straighten up I'll steal her from you and not feel a bit sorry about it."

"I have no idea where this is coming from," Max replied slowly, watching Tyler closely. He was known to take a swing out of nowhere upon occasion and Max didn't want to be a recipient. "Did she say something to you?"

The idea that Carrie might be angry or disgusted with him didn't sit well with Max. Of all the people in his life, he wanted her approval. He wasn't sure when that happened exactly but he couldn't deny it. She was special and he wanted to be the same to her in return.

"She would never tell me anything so personal," Tyler

said, dismissing the idea entirely. "But that's a woman that needs attention, Max. She needs to be told she's pretty every now and then. Jesus, have you ever bought her flowers or a gift?"

Max hadn't and clearly that was a mistake. He'd wanted to send her flowers but Alana had always complained about the smell which made her sneeze. He'd also thought about cooking Carrie dinner but Alana had said his culinary skills were mediocre at best.

Alana. There was the problem. Carrie wasn't Alana. Where his ex-wife wanted her space, Carrie clearly liked to spend time together, whether talking or just hanging out. He had to stop living his life as if he was still married to that witch.

Max looked over the crowd but Carrie was nowhere to be found. "You've made a very good point. Have you seen her recently?"

"She was heading into the ladies' room when I left her just a few minutes ago." He leaned close to Max, eye to eye. "I meant what I said. I'll romance the hell out of her and steal her away."

Max had known Tyler Gaylord for about six years and he knew good and well the man would never do that. These were idle threats.

*Probably.*

Either way he wasn't going to let Tyler anywhere near Carrie.

"You won't be able to."

Tyler gave him a cocky grin. "Do you want to take that chance? I don't know what's going on with you two but you better get your shit together. I'll enjoy every minute of convincing your woman that you're the biggest loser on the planet. In fact, I better make sure I give my agent her home phone number so he knows where to contact me...tomorrow morning."

*Over my dead cold body.*

"Stay away from her," Max growled, no longer amused by his friend's antics. "Carrie doesn't want your playboy games. She's looking for something real."

Tyler turned to walk away. "Then give it to her."

That was the one thing Max couldn't do.

# CHAPTER
## Twenty~Five

IN THE THIRTY minutes Carrie had been apart from Max at the party something had changed. He'd left her on the dance floor with Tyler acting completely normal, but who was the man that had returned?

She wanted to keep him.

Pulling her closer to the heat of his body, they moved in rhythm to the slow, romantic ballad. His thighs brushed against her with every step, and there was no mistaking his arousal pressed against her belly. He slid his hands down her spine until they rested at the small of her back while her hands looped around his neck, her fingers playing with the silky hair at his nape. Nuzzling her temple, his lips grazed her skin and she had to stifle the moan that tried to escape from her throat.

At this moment he filled her senses, completely blocking out the rest of the world. She could feel his warm flesh, smell his heady male aroma. The muscles of his shoulders bunched under her palms as he breathed softly in her ear, crooning words she'd longed for.

How beautiful she looked tonight.

How good she felt against him.

How amazing she was.

Like a thirsty man in the desert, she drank up his compliments as if her very life depended on it. She didn't even care if he meant them. It simply felt wonderful to finally be in his embrace. She'd craved this since she'd come to London.

It wouldn't be the same with another man. No one else would do but Max.

Pressing a kiss next to her ear, she heard him whisper softly, "Do you want to go home where we can be alone?"

*Yes. With all my heart.*

That was her heart speaking. Whatever her brain might have had to say about this moment she'd never know because every single cell in her body was screaming at the top of its lungs to say yes, drowning out any rational thought. Yes. Go home with Max. Make love. Get sweaty in the sheets and do debauched things to one another until dawn. She was already more aroused just by dancing with him than she'd been with her ex the entire last year they were together.

Carrie might have regrets later but right now she longed to live in the moment. Grab the brass ring and hold on tight for all she was worth. Maxwell Hayes was the ride of a lifetime and she wasn't going to miss out. He wanted her and she wanted him. It might not be true love but he was a good man and he wasn't making her any promises he couldn't keep. This was about this one night and that was fine with her.

Reaching up, she traced his lips with a fingertip, feeling him shudder under her touch. It made her feel even more powerful knowing she affected this man so much.

"Take me home, Max."

———

Carrie barely registered the limousine driver who opened the car door for her. Her focus was on the man at her side. Max too seemed preoccupied but managed to nod and thank the driver before pressing the button that slid the privacy shield between the front and the back of the vehicle.

They were finally alone.

The good girl Carrie would have waited patiently until they arrived home and then allowed Max to lead her to bed where they would have polite sex in the missionary position. She might even have an orgasm. But she didn't want to be good and patient and all that other crap.

She wanted to be bad.

She wanted to be wild.

Specifically, she wanted to be naughty with Maxwell Hayes. Being sweet and nice was fucking overrated. If she was going to regret this later then by God she was going to make it worthwhile. Tyler might throw legendary parties but Carrie was about to throw one unforgettable after-party. Only two guests required.

Checking that the dark screen was indeed in place, she swung her leg over Max's thighs so she was straddling him as she ran her hands up his muscular chest, looping them around his neck. His smile grew as he realized her intentions were decidedly debauched.

Carrie's fingers tangled in his thick dark hair and she immediately felt him hard and ready. Rubbing against him, she heard his tortured exhale as his hands slid up her legs and under her skirt. His touch sent swirls of pleasure through her abdomen and she leaned forward to capture his lips with her own. He tasted of fine whiskey and sin, a deadly combination.

But Max wasn't the type to sit passively as her greedy fingers explored his torso. With a muttered oath, his mouth covered hers and his tongue demanded entry, easily taking control of the kiss and ultimately their encounter. This was the dominant man she'd come to know in the last weeks. Max plundered her mouth as if he was a pirate and she was his treasure to find and win.

His surprisingly gentle fingers traced patterns on the sensitive flesh of her inner thighs and his thumb probed the elastic of her panties, making her shake with arousal. He would find her wet, swollen, and wanting, desperate for more of him. *This.* It had been so long and she couldn't get enough. She needed his kisses, his fingers, his tongue, and ultimately his cock.

She ground against him and his fingers tightened on her hip as he growled her name against her skin, sending vibrations straight to her clit. His teeth nipped at the pulse point of her throat and then his tongue swept out to soothe the tiny hurt. Her world tilted and spun and her head fell back, her lids drifting closed as she trembled with the force of her need. She'd never craved a man the way she did

Max. He was a fever in her blood, a dream that wouldn't let her sleep, a nagging ache in her heart that wouldn't give her peace.

Right now, he was her entire world.

"Max," she breathed, sucking in a lungful of his addictive scent along with the aroma of expensive leather. "Yes."

His devilishly talented fingers found her hot center, slick and ready. Two fingers easily glided in as his thumb played with her clit, almost sending her over with that simple touch. Instead of teasing her, he seemed to recognize her desperate need, or perhaps he had his own barely controlled desires. His fingers moved in and out, slowly, maddeningly, giving her just the rhythm she needed to go over.

"That's my girl," he urged, his lips next to her ear and that deep baritone doing evil things inside of her. "Come on my fingers. You can do it, darling. Come hard for me and then I'll let you ride my cock. That's what you want, isn't it? For me to be deep inside of you? But first you have to give me your first orgasm of the night. The first of many."

*Fuck yes, that's what I want. Give it to me.*

His dirty talk was exactly what she needed. Carrie's entire body tightened, her channel clamping down on him as she fell over the cliff. If she hadn't been sitting she would have collapsed and in a way she did, falling forward against his chest as his fingers wrung out orgasm after orgasm before giving her a moment's respite.

"Little one," he whispered, his chest rising and falling rapidly and his voice strained. "Are you on birth control? Are you clean?"

She'd had herself tested after Mark's betrayal and she knew from talking to Paige that the actors had complete physicals and bloodwork for every film. No studio would hire an actor that couldn't be insured.

"I'm healthy and I get the shot."

The metallic sound of Max's zipper was loud in the silence. "I'm clean too, sweetheart. Do you want this? Do you want me? You can still say no."

There was literally no chance of that happening.

She had to take a breath to be able to answer. "I'm saying yes."

His hands went to her hips and he gently lifted her up onto her knees. "Ride me."

Lowering herself down onto him, she panted as he entered her inch by glorious inch. He was big and thick and it had been a long time.

*So good.*

Panting, she groaned as her walls stretched to accommodate his size. When she was fully seated, she paused for a moment to revel in the feeling of being so amazingly and wonderfully full. She leaned forward and pressed her lips to his cheek, his chin, his jaw, and then finally his mouth.

As they began to move together the musk of arousal and sex hung in the air. Gasps and moans broke through the quiet along with the slap of skin against skin. Underneath her Carrie could feel the smooth roll of the vehicle as it sailed down the road, occasionally veering to the left or right.

"So tight, so hot," Max ground out, his teeth gritted together and his jaw snapped tightly shut. "That's it, baby.

Fuck yourself on me. Use me and make yourself come. I want you to scream my name when you do."

The pleasure continued to build as she slammed down on him over and over, more urgently than before. His fingers had found the tips of her breasts, hard and needy through the fabric of her dress, and he pinched them into tighter points as his cock rubbed all the spots deep inside of her that no man had ever seemed to find before.

It was as if her body didn't belong to herself. It took commands from Max and she was his willing supplicant. She cried out his name when he reached between them to rub her swollen clit, sending her straight into the stars, vaguely aware that he reached his pinnacle right after.

Shattered and exhausted, she fell against his chest, the fabric of his suit coat rubbing against her cheek. Both of them sweaty and satiated, they didn't say anything the rest of the ride, content to simply be close. As the limo pulled up in front of Max's house, he tilted up her chin so she was looking into those crystalline blue eyes.

"I don't want this to be over. Come inside with me, Carrie. Be with me tonight."

There was only one possible answer. It had been that way since the moment she'd stepped foot in London. Maybe it was something in the water or the rain. Whatever it was she was hopelessly hooked on this man.

"Yes."

Even if it was only for one night.

# CHAPTER
## Twenty-Six

MAX WOKE SLOWLY the next morning, the bright sun streaming in the windows letting him know in no uncertain terms that the night was over. A new day was upon them. A fresh start.

But what a night it had been.

Carrie had been delightfully wanton, unashamed of her sexuality and her clear enjoyment of Max's lovemaking. Vocal in her applause, she'd exhorted him to a performance even he hadn't believed possible. His appetite for her was insatiable and he couldn't get enough of her hoarsely calling his name when she found her release.

Ah yes, the orgasms. He'd lost count of how many times she'd climaxed last night. It had been twice in the limousine. Once on the stairs when he'd pressed his face between her creamy thighs and used his tongue to elicit the second screaming of his name that evening. Then several more as they'd rolled around his king-sized bed for the better part of the night.

He'd never known a female as responsive or as giving. Her generosity as a lover went far beyond what he'd experienced in the past. As hungry as he was to explore every square centimeter of her body she seemed just as eager, pushing him back on the mattress and kissing and caressing him from head to toe until he was ready to explode.

Clearly his body as well as his brain remembered their activities because his cock was at full attention. Pressing against her pert little bottom, he wrapped his arms around her, allowing his fingers to trail up her ribcage and then cup her full, round breasts. Her flesh was warm to the touch and as smooth as satin against his much rougher skin. He couldn't help but be fascinated with their differences. Carrie was so much smaller than he was, more delicate, and she brought forth all of his protective instincts.

Chuckling at his flight of fancy, he traced her belly-button with the tips of his fingers and her hips jerked in response. Carrie would laugh at the direction his thoughts had traveled. She considered herself to be a strong, independent woman.

And she was...

But she also needed to be cosseted and spoiled a little bit too, not that she'd ever allow him to do that.

"Max," she sighed, stirring slightly, her plump lips falling open and her eyelids fluttering as she awoke. Her long, fiery red hair was like a silk curtain on the pillow and it was all he could do not to bury his face in it. Tyler was right. Carrie had no idea how beautiful she was nor how she affected him and every other red-blooded male in her orbit. Her fiancé had been a bloody idiot.

*His loss. My gain.*

"What do you think you're doing, young man?"

Chuckling, Max bit down gently on her earlobe and then traced a wet path down her neck with his tongue. "Good morning, love."

Carrie stretched and pressed her cute little derriere more firmly against his cock. "Good morning, although I should be mad at you. You kept me up half the night and then woke me early as well. Cruel, Max, very cruel."

Burying his face in her luxuriant hair, his fingers wandered down to the cleft between her thighs. He groaned when her found her already wet and ready.

"Funny, I thought it was you who kept me...up...all night."

Lifting her leg up and back over his own, he pushed into her slowly, savoring every moment of her tight walls pulling him in. Her soft sigh was his reward when he was in to the hilt and set a leisurely pace, content to take it easy in the bright light of day.

"You're a bad boy, Maxwell Hayes."

"The worst," he agreed, his voice still morning-rough to his own ears. "The devil incarnate. Want me to stop?"

Carrie moaned as he hit an especially sensitive spot. "Don't you dare."

He hadn't honestly been planning to.

Their lovemaking was tender and gentle, almost lazy in its complete unhurried pace. Max was cognizant of how they'd ravaged each other during the nighttime hours and she might be sore. He wanted to make Carrie feel amazing, not hurt her.

His fingers traced circles around her swollen and sensitive clit, hopefully pushing her closer to the edge. His own arousal had built, the pressure in his lower back becoming almost unbearable in its intensity.

"It's time, my pretty one. Will you come with me?"

Gasping, she nodded as her head fell back on his shoulder. "Yes, faster. I need more."

Max sped his fingers up and thrust in once...twice...three times. That was all it took. Carrie's tiny frame stiffened as her orgasm hit, her fingernails digging into his scalp where she'd burrowed her hand into his hair. His own climax came quickly after, a torrent of exquisite pleasure so strong it was almost pain.

It was only later when their breathing and heart rate had gone back to normal that he was able to speak. No one was more aware than he that they'd crossed a line last night but he didn't want her to be unsure or nervous. They were both joyful participants in this and he hoped she wouldn't feel any sort of misgivings this morning. He didn't regret a thing.

"That was amazing," he finally said, dropping a kiss on the tempting curve of her shoulder. He could spend all day finding things about her that he adored. "How about we go out for breakfast?"

If Carrie was having second thoughts he wanted to know sooner rather than later. Because if she didn't regret last night...

He was going to want to make love to her again as soon as possible.

————

Her stomach growling, Carrie quickly slid her feet into her high heels and smoothed down her rumpled dress. To anyone with half a brain cell it was going to be obvious that she was doing the walk of shame this morning after spending the night with a man. The outfit that had looked so glamorous and sexy last night now looked trampy and garish. Her smeared makeup and rat's nest hair didn't help. She wouldn't be surprised if mothers moved their children to opposite side of the street when they saw her. She might as well have a flashing neon sign on her forehead.

*I had sex last night and it was awesome.*

Frankly it was the best she'd ever had so the walk home in her eveningwear was the price of pleasure, she supposed. Funny how things turn out. She wasn't frigid, defective, or too good of a girl to have great sex. She'd simply needed a man who knew what he was doing. Max certainly could navigate his way around the female anatomy. He knew what to do and wasn't afraid to do it. He'd encouraged her inner vixen to make an appearance and then spent the evening making her glad she'd...come.

Several freakin' times. Last night was going to be hard to top.

She tromped down the stairs where Max was waiting, if a bit impatiently. He stood next to the door, his foot tapping while he checked his watch. To her shock it hadn't been incredibly awkward this morning. He hadn't tried to make too much eye contact and he'd kept the conversation incredibly impersonal. He was so good at not making her uncomfortable it made her wonder how often he woke up with a woman in his bed.

"How is it possible that I took a shower and changed into fresh clothes and I'm still ready before you?"

He wasn't mad or even frustrated. There was a teasing smile on his face that she returned. He did have a point.

"I'm a girl."

That smile become more evil and wolfish. Now this was interesting. The impersonal Max was gone and his evil twin had appeared. "You certainly are."

"Seriously, I tried to fix my destroyed hair and makeup but eventually gave up. I think this is the best I can do for the walk home."

Frowning, his gaze swept her up and down. "I think I can help with that."

Striding to the foyer closet, he pulled out a trench coat and held it up.

"This should cover everything but your shoes," he said with a smile. "I don't want you to feel uncomfortable walking back to your place."

Thoughtful was the first word that sprung to her mind. Gentleman was the second. She let him hold it up for her while she slid her arms into the sleeves.

"Thank you. I promise when we get to my place I'll be quick."

"Take your time."

Snorting, she retrieved her purse from the table by the front door. "I'm not hurrying for you, Hamlet. I'm starving here. Wasting away to nothing."

He bowed low, his lips twitching with a grin. "How tragic. We'd best get a move on then. After you, my dear."

The weather was mild but the gray clouds had begun to gather so she didn't look too out of place in Max's raincoat. They didn't get halfway down the walk when a man showed up at the wrought iron gate brandishing a large envelope. For a split second Carrie froze, thinking it was a paparazzi capturing their morning after but the man didn't appear to have a camera. He waited patiently until Max opened the gate and then thrust the envelope into his hands.

"Package from Arthur Blaisdell. Sign here."

Max scribbled his signature on a small receipt and the messenger hurried away without another word, clearly not interested in the movie star he'd come into contact with.

Turning the legal-sized envelope over in his hands, Max gazed at it as if he was afraid to open it. His ebullient mood had fizzled away, leaving the frowning man she'd become accustomed to since they'd met.

"Arthur is my solicitor," he finally said, his voice low. "These must be the final divorce papers."

His words struck a blow straight to her chest, sucking the oxygen from her lungs. Was Max regretting the split from Alana? Carrie wasn't sure how she was supposed to respond, especially considering she'd just spent last night naked in Max's bed.

"That's good. Right?"

He looked up, a strained smile on his face. "It's very good. It's just that it's a reminder that I'm a failure at marriage, love, and relationships."

Alana sure hadn't made it easy.

"It takes two to fail at matrimony."

"Perhaps," he conceded. "Either way, it's done and over with. I can move on now."

Was he not moving on before? What had last night

been? Carrie had hoped something had shifted in their relationship. The way he'd held her this morning with such tenderness didn't speak of a man getting his rocks off with a one night stand. But what did she know about movie stars and their sexual habits? He was an actor and that made his actions and words automatically suspect. She genuinely liked Max and she had harbored a hope - a tiny one - that he might feel the same. That maybe he wanted to...date her.

He held up the folder. "Let me put this inside and then we'll walk to your place. Just give me a minute."

Carrie could use a moment or two alone as well. She'd known going into last night that she would probably regret making love with Max. Even if she was his type - which she clearly wasn't based on his ex-girlfriends and wife - he was fresh off of a marital breakup and she didn't want to be his rebound girl.

There might not be a great love and passion between them but they did have great sex. Was it enough for her? With every single relationship in her past, she'd had an eye on "forever" and damned if they hadn't all crashed and burned eventually. It might be time to simply have some fun. Enjoy Max and her time in London while she could. It would be something she'd remember for the rest of her life. She could look back fondly in her old age. Tell her lady friends at the nursing home about the movie star she'd shagged that one summer.

Because she had to face facts. Walking away from Maxwell Hayes wasn't something she was prepared to do. Not yet. She wasn't in love with him but he'd definitely wormed his way into her affections despite all her defenses. If a fling was what he offered her, then that is what she'd take. She was tired of being the organized, efficient, *predictable* Carrie Johnson. It was time to shake up her life and this was the first step to a new her.

Scratch that. Second step.

The first step had been the wild sex they'd had last night.

That had worked out pretty well after all.

*I can have casual sex. I'm just fine with it.*

That only left one question and it was surely going to be discussed at breakfast.

Just what did Max want?

# CHAPTER
## Twenty-Seven

BY THE TIME Carrie and Max made it to breakfast it was actually midday. They ate, made small talk, and compared notes about the party the night before.

They didn't talk about the sex and the tension between was beginning to build to an uncomfortable level. He'd tried to keep it low key and casual this morning but the moment to talk about what had happened had arrived. They couldn't avoid it any longer.

The hard part of this entire situation was that Max wasn't sure what he wanted out of all of this. He definitely wanted to make love to Carrie again. He'd never had such a physical connection to a woman before and it would be a shame to waste it.

But he cared about Carrie too. It wasn't just her body he wanted; he liked spending time with her, even when they weren't doing anything special. Hanging out with her was more fun than a Hollywood party with anyone else.

There was the question... Just how did he feel about

her? Was he falling in love? He hoped not as he wasn't sure he was ready for something that serious. Fuck, he'd just received his divorce papers this morning and here he was contemplating entering into another relationship with hardly a breath in between.

Max simply couldn't let her walk out of his life or have things go back to the way they were between them. They'd crossed a line and things were different now. They'd been intimate. What was the saying? A person cannot unring a bell. It had happened and they needed to deal with the reality of their situation. They were more than friends but less than...lovers? No, they were certainly lovers. They weren't *in love*. They weren't looking to move in together, get married, and have several children all named after dead relatives.

They were definitely *in like*. Like-like. The variety of like that might become something. Someday. If they could survive the beginning part of a relationship which always seemed to be the part that tripped him up.

"So..." he said, needing to cut through the thick wall of tension between them. Could he convince her to take a chance on a casual dating "thing" that might be something at a future date? Maybe.

Take a chance on him. It was like betting on horse who had lost every race. One might think the animal would win one, if only by accident, but the odds weren't in their favor.

"So..." she replied, her brows raised. Waiting for him to say something.

"I suppose we should talk about last night," he said in a rush. Now that he was speaking the words seemed to want to run out of his mouth faster than his brain could process them. "We're both adults here and neither of us was a virgin last night. I think we should simply speak honestly about what we want to happen from here. I hope you know that you can be open with me about any of your concerns regarding our future."

Placing her fork on the corner of her empty plate, Carrie picked up her napkin and wiped off her hands, slowly and deliberately. She was stalling and that made Max's nerves twice as bad. Sweat began to pool at the back of his neck and on his palms as he waited for her to respond.

"Well...I can say...openly and honestly...that for me last night was quite...pleasurable. I hope it was for you as well."

"It was," he assured her, nodding in encouragement for her to continue. "Fantastic. Brilliant. I don't have the words to describe how good it was between us."

The diarrhea of the mouth - caused by the strange expression on her face - continued and now he was on a roll and couldn't stop.

"That's why I think that we should give this a chance between us," he explained, leaning forward as far as the table between them would allow. "Last night was too bloody good to turn our backs on it. Add in the fact that we get along well and we could have something quite enjoyable."

Shoving a piece of toast in his mouth, he finally - mercifully - shut the hell up. Appearing too eager was going to turn her off completely. No woman wanted a desperate man in her bed.

*I'm not desperate. There are plenty of women that want me.*

Folding her hands on top of the table, she looked him straight in the eye. "So what exactly are you proposing here? Fuck buddies? Friends with benefits? Some sort of dating? A full-fledged relationship? Where is your mind at on this? And please be straight with me."

Damn, this woman had a spine of solid steel and she didn't take any crap. No wonder he liked and admired her. She was tough and strong and formidable.

Max cleared his throat and straightened in his chair. "Nothing so crass as fuck buddies. I care about you as a person, Carrie. I have a great deal of respect for you. But I'm also not in the place in my life where I'm ready for a serious relationship. I'm thinking that there must be something in between those two extremes that we can agree on."

The corner of her mouth quirked up. "Is this a negotiation? Am I going to need my lawyer?"

Snickering, he shook his head. "Nothing so extreme. I think we can work this out ourselves, don't you? What did you have in mind? If anything at all, of course. Perhaps last night was enough for you?"

That thought was too awful to contemplate and for a moment he panicked until she spoke again.

"As I said before, last night was incredible and I do want it to happen again."

Whew. Okay, they'd decided they wanted to shag again. That was something, at least.

Her gaze skittered away and her cheeks turned pink. He felt some relief in that she seemed as embarrassed as he was by the whole subject. "I'll be honest with you, Max. It is not my habit to have sex without some sort of commitment. Before you get all nervous, I'm not talking marriage or an engagement. I am talking physical fidelity. If we decide to continue sleeping together, I would ask that you not sleep with anyone else. I, of course, would do the same. We're contracted to spend the next few months together in a dating situation and people who date often have sex, right? How about we just...date? Exclusively."

Slowly exhaling, he felt his heart galloping against his ribs. Date. Exclusive. It was really what they already had, although they'd be doing it in private too, not just for the cameras. As for not sleeping with anyone else, she'd muddled his brain so thoroughly he couldn't bring one woman to mind that he wanted to have sex with other than her.

Carrie wasn't asking much of him and that kind of hurt. More than he'd expected. If she'd demanded a relationship, he didn't know what he would have done though. Did he want her more than he was afraid? He wasn't sure and she hadn't pushed him for the answer.

"I can do that," he answered quickly, not wanting her to think that her request was more than he could handle. "Date exclusively."

She fiddled with the paper napkin. "So we sort of just go on as we are, but with the added element of dating for real. I mean, it's not like we live together or anything. You have your place and I have mine. We won't spend every moment in each other's pocket."

This conversation had turned out better than he'd ever dreamed it would. He got to have Carrie and some much needed space to breathe. It was the perfect solution.

He signaled the waitress for the bill. "We can reevaluate

when the contract is over. See what we want to do then. You might be sick and tired of me after a few months."

Although he couldn't imagine ever being tired of Carrie. She fascinated him on so many levels, more than any woman before her.

Carrie stood, so it appeared that their discussion was over. "Who knows what the future will bring? Now if you'll excuse me, I need to visit the ladies' room. I'll be right back."

Max watched her as she walked away, his thoughts firmly on the woman who had shown so much patience and generosity. His future was up in the air but Carrie just might make him want to take a chance and share it with her.

If he didn't fuck it all up first and drive her away.

# CHAPTER
## Twenty~Eight

CARRIE STARED into the bathroom mirror and took several deep breaths, her face paler than usual. She'd known going into this discussion that it wasn't going to end the way she wanted it to. She'd been hoping for more emotion from Max but while that might have been a possibility before he received those divorce papers...afterwards? No way was that going to happen. After the tenderness he'd shown her this morning in bed, he'd literally closed in on himself right before her eyes. That armor he'd first worn wasn't back completely but he was frantically trying to build his shields back up, terrified of being used again.

*Reevaluate when the contract was up.*

Max had actually said that. The words had come out of his mouth and she'd heard them with her own ears. He wanted to reevaluate in a few months.

Like this was a trial period.

Or in actor terms...an audition.

She might get cast in the part of the woman in his life

but she might not. There were, without a doubt, many other women who wouldn't mind auditioning, some that might even be better for the part of his girlfriend than she was.

At least he'd agreed to be monogamous while they were together. That was a victory of sorts. If she couldn't find the strength to walk away from him at least he wasn't juggling her and a few other women. Carrie would be the only female in his life. For awhile, anyway.

After freshening her lip gloss, she straightened her shoulders and exited the bathroom. She wasn't a shrinking violet who could blame this situation on someone else.

This was all her doing. She'd gone into last night with her eyes open, knowing that it had disaster written all over it. But here she was running at the brick wall full speed like a blooming idiot. Now that she was sleeping with Max the chances were high that she was going to fall in love with him, especially as their chemistry was beyond hot. She'd known this going in, had assumed she'd be hurt at the end of this...whatever it was. Bizarre, strange, weird relationship? Yep, that about covered it.

Was he worth it? Last night she'd certainly thought so but then she'd been so consumed by lust she would have rationalized sleeping with him in any way she could. That light at the end of a tunnel was a runaway train and she was going to become roadkill. But damn, she was going to have a good time first. Step out of her boring everyday life - her practical, mundane, organized little life. There was nothing wrong with wanting a little excitement, was there? After all, broken hearts happened every day and people survived. She had in the past.

This was pathetic, really. She'd played it safe for so long that she had to give herself a pep talk to date a guy when she knew the relationship wasn't going anywhere. *Most* relationships didn't go anywhere but if people just stayed home and watched Netflix the human race would die out.

*Get out there, girl. Have some fun. Do something unexpected.*

When she returned to the table, Max was paying the check and he looked up and smiled, the corners of his blue eyes crinkling. Why did that look so good on a man?

"Are you ready to go, love?" He glanced out the front window of the restaurant. "Looks like it's starting to rain. Should we brave the elements or try to get a taxi?"

Carrie had quickly learned that finding a cab in London when it was raining was like finding the Holy Grail.

"I'm okay with getting rained on if you are."

And she would have been too if the heavens hadn't opened up a little less than a mile from Max's place. The deluge pelted her skin and made it almost impossible to see in front of her face as everyone else on the sidewalk scurried about to get out of the rain. Max's long legs were eating up the distance and she had to jog to be able to keep up with him. But the faster she went the more he sped up too, so it wasn't long before she was flat out sprinting to stay next to him.

It was on the corner as they raced down the street that she went down like a ten-pound sack of potatoes. They'd crossed to the other side of the intersection and she'd raised her leg to step up on the curb but the sole of her drenched Chuck Taylors hit wrong somehow and her foot slid out from under her. She landed in an undignified

sprawl, her legs thrown in different directions in a modi-
fied version of the splits. Her jeans were ripped at the knee
on her sore left leg but it was her right that was going to be
a bitch of a problem. Dagger-like pains shot up her calf
from her ankle and Carrie felt the first prick of tears behind
her eyes as she struggled to breathe and control the agony
her jaunt in the rain had caused.

Max was at her side on his knees in an instant. "Are
you hurt? Jesus, of course you are, I can see you're in pain
by the look on your face. Can you move?"

Taking a slow deep breath and not bothering to answer,
Carrie grabbed onto Max's hand as she gingerly slid her
left leg from its awkward angle and out straight. With a
huff of relief, she now had two legs both pointing in the
same direction. It was progress.

As long as she didn't move her right leg she was okay.
She could bear the white hot pain radiating out from her
ankle, down her foot and up her calf.

*As long as I don't move.*

Of course that meant she had to just sit on her ass in the
rain, soaked to the skin while she recovered. Then she'd
die from pneumonia. It would probably take a few days to
expire and a crowd might gather to wonder what in the
hell she was doing. She could hear them talking now.

*What's that Yank doing sitting on her arse on the pavement?
Crazy American.*

The rain was still coming down in buckets so now they
were both sopping wet, Max's dark hair plastered to his
skull.

"Carrie, love, can you stand up?"

His tone was anguished and clearly he was worried

and upset. His skin was pasty - although probably not as pale as she was - and his lips were pressed together so tightly they'd disappeared into his face. The only color he had was his blue eyes that were dark with emotion.

She shook her head and pointed to her right ankle. "I don't think that's a good idea. I've sprained my ankle and I don't think I can put any weight on it. I'm going to have to sit here until I die."

A smile flickered and he squeezed her hand reassuringly. "You are not going to sit here until you die. I'm going to take you to the A and E to get that looked at. You may have broken something."

Her dignity wasn't looking too healthy right now either but that was something she'd lament later. Her biggest concern was how in the hell she was going to stand up.

Putting his hand on her shoulder, he used the other to push her sodden hair out of her eyes.

"Just stay here while I get us a taxi."

What did he think she was going to do? Hop up and start breakdancing? Her gaze flickered to her ankle and then back at him. "That is the one thing I can actually do. Sit and don't move."

Carrie had no idea how he did it but within a few minutes, he'd procured a cab despite the odds against him. The rain had petered out to a drizzle but they were both completely waterlogged. She hoped the cabbie wasn't fussy about his upholstery.

He knelt down again and gave her a reassuring smile that she knew was total bullshit because her ankle still felt like some asshole was stabbing it with knives and beating on it with a hammer.

"Okay, I'm going to lift you up and put you into the cab. I'll be very careful but I apologize now if I jostle your foot. Put your arms around my neck, love."

Apparently he'd lost the use of his common sense in the rainstorm. "You can't lift me up and carry me. You'll end up in traction and you won't be able to take some award-winning role and it will be all my fault. Then when people talk about you they'll say 'He could have won an Oscar but he tried to carry that not so skinny American woman and injured himself. He's never been the same'."

Rivulets of water ran down his too handsome face as he threw back his head and laughed, his shoulders shaking with mirth. Dammit, this shit wasn't funny.

"My sweet, nothing bad is going to happen to me and you are not too heavy. Now I'm going to lift you up and you are going to let me. The only way you'll hurt me is if you fight me. Are you ready?"

Carrie had no other options other than sit there until she became a part of the pavement. Nodding, she wrapped her arms around his neck and tried to stay as still as possible. Without even a grunt of effort he easily lifted her from the sidewalk and strode over to the cab idling at the curb. All that physical training for the *Thunder* movies obviously paid off. Those muscles weren't just for show.

Carefully he set her on the backseat and she inched her way toward the opposite door, keeping her right leg elevated. At one point it touched the edge of the seat and she sucked in a breath and whimpered as fresh pain stabbed at her limb.

"Fuckity fuck," she muttered as softly as possible but Max heard her, stripping off his raincoat, wadding it into a ball, and making a nest - albeit a sodden one - under her leg to keep it elevated. Damn these British gentleman. They knew how to get a girl right in the feels.

"Now sit tight while we get to the A and E. Don't you worry about a thing, love. I've got you."

Boy, did he ever. Did Max have any idea how much?

# CHAPTER
## Twenty~Nine

LUCKILY THE DOCTORS had given Carrie something for the pain, and whatever it was, it was strong as hell because she was smiling and chatting as if she hadn't a stage two sprain of her ankle. It was immobilized in a boot with Velcro straps and she wasn't supposed to put any weight on it for a few days. That particular fact didn't appear to bother her at the moment but when the drugs wore off she was going to be upset about it. There was no way she could care for herself alone at Paige and Nate's house.

Which is why he'd brought her to his house.

She'd giggled when he'd carried her from the taxi into the living room, setting her on the sofa and elevating her leg with a pillow. Apparently in her current state, being ferried around like a fainting heroine in a historical novel was amusing. She'd been given a set of crutches but frankly she scared Max to death with them. At best Carrie could only be described as awkward when she'd tried them out at the hospital but then she was under the influence of some powerful painkillers. It was much easier and simpler, not to mention safer, to simply carry her where he needed her to be.

He put a few pillows behind her back and handed her the remote for the television. "Now why don't I get you a nice cup of tea? Are you hungry? I can fix something."

Carrie shook her head, placing the remote on the end table. "Still full from lunch but thank you. No tea, but maybe a nice glass of water? The pain medication is making me thirsty." She blinked a few times and yawned. "And a little sleepy too."

Hurrying into the kitchen, he quickly fixed a glass of ice water and brought it out to her only to find her fast asleep, her head lolling against the cushions. With a chuckle, he retrieved a wool throw from the closet and covered her up, careful to tuck the blanket around her feet and shoulders. They'd both been chilled to the bone after getting caught in that rainstorm.

After running upstairs to change clothes and into an old pair of sweats and a t-shirt, he checked on Carrie again still peacefully sleeping although the blanket had slid off and onto the floor. He tucked it around her again and settled into a chair opposite the couch to check his emails on his laptop. His attention, however, kept straying back to his houseguest as she slept, her expression in sweet repose.

In deep contrast to pretty much all of her waking moments.

He winced as he remembered her whimpers of pain when they'd manipulated her ankle in the hospital to see how badly it was damaged. Her full lower lip had trembled but fighter that she was, she'd held back the tears that had surely wanted to fall. A few expletives had escaped from her potty mouth but all in all Carrie had been quite brave. He'd expected a few of those curse words to fall on his head but so far, nary a one.

After all, this was Max's fault.

Like the stupid idiot that he was, he'd been running too fast on the wet pavement. His legs were twice as long as Carrie's, so of course she'd been struggling to keep up. He'd wanted out of the rain and because of his thoughtlessness she'd been hurt. He was supposed to be taking care of her and now she'd been injured. Paige and Nate were going to throw a fit when they found out. Max had some groveling due for Carrie and he would gladly do it. Hopefully when the pain medication wore off and she started to think more clearly, she wouldn't hate him.

His gaze traveled back to the couch where she lay sleeping, her long, dusky lashes fanned out on her cheeks and a dainty hand tightly clutching the blanket to her chest as if it were her favorite stuffie. When awake, Carrie was a formidable and strong woman but right now she looked almost like an angelic child. His protective instincts had already kicked in but now they seemed to take up every part of him until his chest was painfully tight at the mere thought of anything bad happening to her. He'd keep her safe and happy no matter what.

Time ceased to be meaningful as he studied her head to toe. The long fiery red hair, her stubborn chin and graceful neck, her perfectly polished toes peeking out of the boot. Every time he saw her again he was struck by how much more beautiful she was than the time before. Was she growing more lovely or was something changing inside of him?

Going back and forth between watching her sleep and checking his email, he didn't know how much time had passed when her lids fluttered open and a smile curved her lips for a split second before a grimace took its place. The medication must be wearing off.

"Shit, I hurt."

Quickly tossing his laptop aside, he was up and out of the chair. "I'll get you the pain pills the doctor prescribed."

"Wait," she called, struggling to sit up, her forehead furrowed with the effort. "I don't want to take those unless I have to. Maybe just at night. I have some ibuprofen in my purse. Fuck, where is my purse? We didn't leave it in the street, did we?"

There was panic in her voice and Max hurried to her side and knelt down, taking her hands in his. "I told you I have this handled, didn't I? Your purse is on the foyer table. Do you want me to get it for you?"

Not waiting to hear her answer, he snagged the over-sized handbag from the table and placed it down next to her. Knowing Carrie, she wouldn't have rested until she saw the damn thing with her own two eyes.

She pawed through it, placing odds and ends on the coffee table before tossing back two pills and chasing them with the now tepid glass of water. Her gaze followed his to the items she'd unloaded from her purse.

"What?"

Picking up the small bottle, he flipped the lid and sniffed. Alcohol.

"Hand sanitizer," she offered, her brows raised.

He held up a second item.

"Hair tie. You never know when you're going to need to pull your hair back."

"Obviously." He held up a third. "And this?"

"Band-aids or as you call them, plasters. I get a lot of paper cuts."

There was a tin of mints, a brush, a comb, a tiny notebook with a pen, a head band, an e-reader, an Oyster card for the Tube, chocolate, dental floss, tissues, safety pins, a mobile charger, a bottle of nail polish, and several tubes of lipstick.

And the purse wasn't yet empty. It had been heavier to carry than she was.

"Well, my sweet, should there be a zombie apocalypse you are all set."

Carrie stuffed everything into her bag. "I think you're making fun of me."

"I'm just surprised. You're usually one of the most organized women I've ever seen but in this one area you have a giant bag of odds and ends."

Pulling open the top of the purse, she held it up so he could see inside. "It is organized. I have a place for everything and I know where it all is. It only looks muddled to the untrained eye."

It was his turn for his brows to shoot up. "Am I the untrained eye in this scenario?"

"Are you an expert on women's handbags?"

Max had to admit that he was not.

"No, but I'm trainable."

"My point exactly. Now do you think I could trouble you for some ice for my ankle? It hurts like someone took a sledgehammer to it."

Shit, he needed to get on the ball if he was going to take care of her. "Of course. One ice pack coming up."

He refreshed her water while he was at it and then handed her a stack of menus. "Choose whatever you want."

Gingerly she accepted them but didn't open any. "You don't need to go to any trouble. I can just order something when I get home."

Home? Carrie had no clue. He'd expected an argument when she figured out she was just about helpless but it appeared...she hadn't figured it out yet.

"Sweet," he said gently, lowering himself into the chair next to the couch. "You aren't going home tonight. Or probably tomorrow night either. Or the next. Don't you remember that the doctor said no weight on that ankle for at least a few days? That means you can't be on your own."

It took her a long moment before she seemed to understand, panic crossing her features.

"I can't stay here."

Why not? She hadn't minded last night.

He kept his voice even and calm, not wanting to get pulled into an argument about this. She wasn't leaving and that was final. "You need someone to take care of you. I'm sure Paige would want to do it herself if she was here but she's in LA. It's not a problem because I'm glad to do it. This is all my fault anyway."

Carrie shifted position, wincing as she moved her tender ankle. "How is this your fault? I was clumsy and I fell."

"Chasing after me," he shot back. "My legs are twice as

long as yours are. I was thoughtless and you paid for my inattentiveness. I truly am very sorry, Carrie. I never meant for you to be hurt."

"My shoe slipped," she said, shaking her head. "That's not your fault."

"Because we were running. If we had been going at a more reasonable clip it might not have happened."

"Or I might have been flattened by a London taxi. Seriously, you don't have to feel guilty. I'm sad to say this isn't the first time I've fallen ass over teakettle and it won't be the last."

He clapped his hands on his knees. "Be that as it may, I do feel responsible. Now what would you like for dinner?"

Her expression turned mutinous. He had a fight on his hands.

"I cannot stay here, Max."

"Why not? You clearly cannot stay by yourself. How will you get around?"

She pointed to the crutches he'd leaned against the doorway. Far away from where she was lying so she wouldn't be tempted. "With those."

"Oh? How will you carry food or drink back and forth? Or get in and out of the shower? Or climb the stairs? You haven't thought all of this through, love. The hospital was very clear in their instructions. You're to have someone to look after you for a few days until you're getting around better. They wouldn't have released you if they thought you were going to be on your own."

Her mouth was hanging open and he had to stifle a laugh. She appeared positively scandalized. "The shower? You're planning to help me bathe?"

In every way possible if she'd let him.

He gave her an evil grin. "It will be my pleasure."

Her mouth opened and closed a few times as her gaze darted to the crutches then back at him. Every alternate scenario she could think of was whirling through that brilliant mind of hers but she was going to come back to the same solution he'd come to hours ago. Falling back against the cushions, she gave a sigh of defeat.

"Fine, but we'll...*reevaluate*...in the morning. I might be a lot better."

"We'll see," he replied, picking up the menus again and handing them to her. "Now choose some dinner and then a movie perhaps? Whatever you want to do tonight."

Max was simply grateful she'd given in and stayed. But he had a feeling that this might just be the battle and not the war. Victory was far from a sure thing when it came to Carrie.

# CHAPTER
## *Thirty*

MAX HAD MISSED HIS CALLING. He should have been a nurse, not a movie star. He'd fetched and carried for her all evening, doing everything but cutting her meat. With the gigantic boot on her leg she was terribly awkward, making it difficult to do even the simplest of tasks. There was one thing it didn't impede and that was eating. She'd scarfed down the pizza they'd ordered in no time.

There was a movie playing on the huge television on the wall but Carrie wasn't all that interested. She couldn't seem to get into a comfortable position on the couch and going to bed with a good book sounded like an excellent option. But one question had hung in the air all night like a neon sign in her favorite watering hole back in Florida.

Would she be in that bed alone?

More than likely, no. He'd said he intended to help her bathe although he might have been pulling her leg, which would be cruel considering she had an injured one. She wanted a shower or bath desperately, having been baptized with buckets of rain water earlier in the day plus the grime she'd picked up on the city pavement. There was something about being freshly clean when she slid between the sheets. It was a primal feeling that she never got tired of. It required, however, Max's cooperation.

The man that was currently dominating her thoughts reached for the empty ice cream bowl sitting in her lap. "More? I think I have biscuits—I mean, cookies—as well."

Patting her stomach, she handed him her dishes. Turns out he was domestic too, cleaning up the kitchen and dirty dishes while she relaxed.

"I'm stuffed, thank you. But..."

Pausing on the way to the kitchen, Max waited for her to continue.

*Crap. I could just go to bed dirty. But...ewww.*

"I was wondering...if maybe...you could help me take a bath? I feel filthy after rolling around on your London sidewalks."

To his credit, he didn't give her the wolfish smile she'd seen in the past. Simply nodding his head in assent, his expression solemn. "Whatever you need. Just let me tidy up the kitchen."

The image of Max elbows deep in suds was doing strange things to Carrie's libido. A man was never more attractive than when he was cleaning or cooking. Unless it was holding a baby. That blew everything else out of the water. Maxwell Hayes with a child in his arms would simply not be fair to womankind.

It didn't take him long to finish whatever he was doing in the kitchen. "Are you ready?"

"More than ready. I just want to curl up in bed with a good book."

She wasn't in any condition to curl up with Max. Was she?

Throwing off the blanket, she sat up but before she could swing her legs down to the floor, Max had bent over and scooped her into his arms bridal style.

"Hold on, love. We're going upstairs."

He didn't have to tell her twice. He'd carried her to the taxi from the hospital and then into the house but it hadn't involved dizzying heights. Burying her face in his neck so she couldn't look down, she tried to pretend she was lighter than she actually was, although he didn't appear winded at all.

He settled her onto the long bathroom vanity. "I know you said you wanted a bath but getting in and out of the tub might be problematic and slippery even with me lifting you. I'd suggest a shower. You can sit on the seat and be comfortable."

Carrie had pictured herself sitting in bubbles but he had a point. Getting in and out of that tub was going to be a bitch and a half even with him lending the muscle. She didn't want to put the poor man into traction.

"That's a good idea. I'll do that."

Max stripped his t-shirt off and tossed it aside. "Excellent."

Eyes wide, Carrie held up her hand. "Whoa there, Hamlet. What are you doing?"

He didn't answer, instead shooting a question back at her. "How are you planning to get in the shower?"

Studying the path from here to there, she considered her options. "I'll take off the boot and hop over there."

He crossed his arms over his extremely attractive chest. "On a floor that might be wet? That doesn't sound all that safe, does it?"

No, it didn't but for some reason she was feeling self-conscious, which was incredibly stupid. He'd seen - and touched - every part of her last night and this morning. But while it was one thing to get an eyeful during sex it was something else entirely during the clinical process of being hygienic.

Dropping her gaze to her toes, she swung her good leg back and forth nervously. "I'm a little shy."

His sock-clad feet appeared in her view and his fingers lifted her chin so she was looking up into those crystal clear blue eyes. "Shy? Whatever for? I've seen what you have as you've seen me too."

And it had been glorious.

She shrugged, heart suffusing her cheeks. "I know it's silly but this... It's different."

Leaning down, he brushed his lips against hers, light as a feather. "Please let me help you, Carrie. I know I'm difficult and grouchy but I swear that I can take good care of you if you'll let me."

The lump in her throat wouldn't let her speak so she simply nodded. He gave her a triumphant smile before stepping back and stripping off the rest of his clothes, which ended up in a heap on the tile floor. Completely unconcerned about his nudity, he twisted the water on in the huge shower stall.

*Damn, he looks good.*

"Now let's get you undressed." He knelt down, his fingers going to the Velcro ties on the boot. "Should we start here?"

"It's as good a place as any," she said, plucking the buttons on her blouse until it fell open. Taking off the boot wasn't as uneventful as she'd expected, however. Pain shot up to her knee as he set it aside but then it subsided. It was just like earlier on the sidewalk. Don't move and it won't hurt.

"I saw you wince. Are you okay? Should I get your pain medication?"

Shaking her head, she shrugged off her blouse. "I'll take some when I get in bed. It just hurt for a moment when you took the pressure off the ankle."

Max took the blouse from her hands and carefully folded it and placed it on the hamper lid. Next came her jeans which was a bigger deal but with his help easily dealt with. The lone sock on her left foot followed. Now she was only clad in her bra and panties, a fact that Max seemed to appreciate. His warm gaze roved all over her body and her skin tingled in response.

He hadn't even touched her. Yet.

Reaching for the butterfly clasp between her breasts, Carrie unclipped it and pulled it away, her nipples puckering in the cool air. She set it on top of the neatly stacked pile of clothes before reaching down for her panties but his hands had made it there first. He hooked his thumbs into the elastic waistband and tugged them down as his other arm lifted her bottom off of the vanity, his rough skin skimming her sensitive flesh all the way to her toes. The scrap of red satin joined the rest of her clothes, almost like the cherry on top of a silk and lace hot fudge sundae.

"Thank you," she whispered, her eyes locked with his.

"You're welcome."

His voice was husky with a desire that his naked body couldn't hide. His cock was at full attention and she had to drag her fascinated gaze away from it. Staring wasn't polite.

She tried not to squirm too much when he lifted her into his arms and placed her in the shower, setting her down on the tiled seat. The steam and hot water felt heavenly and she immediately felt her muscles loosen and the tension she'd been carrying in her neck and shoulders dissolve.

"This is one fancy shower, Hamlet." Her gaze took in the multiple showerheads at different heights. There was even a handheld near where she was sitting. "And big too. We could fit three or four more people in here."

Sticking his head under one of the sprays from the ceiling, his throaty laugh echoed in the space. "Who would we invite? I think this is a party just for two. Now let's get you all scrubbed up."

"I don't need any he–"

"Nonsense." He waved away her objections and knelt down, squeezing a bit of body wash into his palm. "Correct me if I'm wrong, but the more you move the more it hurts, yes?"

Shit, she couldn't argue with her own logic.

"Yes, but I can still bathe myself."

Picking up her uninjured left foot, he braced it against

his chest. "I'm sure you can but I'm here to help you. Now stay still like a good girl."

Easier said than done. His large hands were sliding up and down her leg, each stroke coming closer and closer to her core. His fingers brushed the sensitive flesh of her mound before gliding back down to her toes, scrupulously washing between each one. By the time he finished with her left leg, she was almost a puddle on the tiled shower flower, ready to slide down the drain and into the mysterious London pipe system. Would she end up in the Thames?

Max picked up the handheld showerhead and rinsed her limb, giving his wrist a twist when he arrived at the top of her thighs so the spray ran over her already swollen clit. Carrie gasped at the sensation and would have jerked sideways but he was thinking far ahead of her befuddled mind. His hand had wrapped around her knee, bracing it against his hips so she couldn't jar it or herself.

"Jumpy, aren't you?" he said with an evil grin. "One might think you're...aroused."

"Asshole," she said just loud enough for him to hear. "You might want to look in a mirror."

Glancing down, he seemed unperturbed by the turgid state of his impressive manhood.

"And?"

"Well, you're..." Her toes grazed the base of his cock. "Aroused too. Doesn't it...hurt?"

"I'm getting used to being hard around you all the time. I've pretty much had a hard-on since the day I met you."

She remembered Thanksgiving all too well.

"Bullshit. You were drunk as a skunk when you came to

Paige's house for Thanksgiving and you certainly didn't notice me in that way."

His smile widened, showing off even white teeth. "That's where you were wrong. I was contemplating a shag when I saw your engagement ring. It put a real damper on my plans."

Funny how the mention of her ill-fated engagement didn't bother her in the least anymore. In fact, with each passing day she was more grateful that Mark had cheated on her and they'd ended their relationship. It would have been a disaster.

"Male whore movie star. You'd just met me and you were thinking about having sex with me. Disgusting."

Tut-tutting, Max shook his head sorrowfully but the grin stayed in place. "Yes, I was contemplating some rather naughty positions while getting quietly drunk. Believe me, if you'd given me even a smidgen of encouragement I would have had you on your boss's desk."

That declaration had Carrie laughing. "Paige would have killed you. She loves that desk." She arched a brow at the man kneeling before her, her earlier shyness forgotten. "What kind of naughty positions?"

He lifted her left leg and pressed a tender kiss to the instep of her foot. Carrie sucked in a breath as heat flowed through her veins at his touch. Max could make her crazy so effortlessly.

"How about this one?" he asked, running his tongue up her calf and sending sparks straight to her clit.

Beautiful but almost feral. That's how Carrie would have described Max if someone had asked her. Rivulets of water ran down his face and torso as he kissed a path up her leg, stopping to nip at the skin every now and then. His dark hair was plastered to his head and his pupils were blown wide. Each time she gasped or moaned, he'd chuckle darkly and she had to quell the urge to reach out and make horns on top of his head with his hair as if he was Lucifer himself.

"Easy, love." He picked up her left leg and placed it over his right shoulder. "We're going to do this slowly and carefully. If at any time you feel pain you're going to tell me and I will stop immediately. Do you understand?"

Barely. She was floating out in the ether and he'd sent her there with his too-talented mouth.

Slowly so she could object if she needed to, he lifted her injured leg and placed it on his left shoulder, anchoring it in place with his hand on her thigh. His warm breath caressed her slit and somehow her fingers ended up tangled in his hair.

"Relax, my sweet. This will be easier on you if you just let me do all the work."

She should have thrown herself down on the pavement days ago.

# CHAPTER
## *Thirty-One*

MAX TRAPPED Carrie's leg against his body so she couldn't hurt herself when she climaxed. And she was definitely going to do the latter if he had anything to say about it. His tongue traced her folds before running in circles around her clit. He'd planned to tease her a little bit but her nails were already digging into his scalp while his name fell from her pretty pink lips. He was becoming addicted to her voice calling out to him when she was on the edge.

She'd been through so much today and all he wanted to do was make her feel incredible.

"That's it, baby," he urged hoarsely. " Come for me. Let yourself go. I've got you."

His mouth closed over the sensitive button and he sucked lightly, sending her over in a rush. Her head was thrown back and her eyes closed as she shook with the power of her orgasm until eventually she sagged against the tile wall, a satisfied smile on her beautiful face.

Ever so carefully, he placed her foot on the floor before reaching for the body wash again. As gently as he could he soaped up her right leg, using as light a touch as possible on her ankle and foot. He thought she might flinch or protest but she sat still and quiet, her trust in him absolute as he soaped her from top to bottom.

After rinsing her off, he poured a dollop of shampoo in his hands and lathered up her long hair, reveling in the feeling of the silky damp strands between his fingers. He did a quick rinse and then reached for his rarely used conditioner bottle.

"This hotel has great service."

Max liked her when she was playful like this, her guard down completely. Like earlier when she'd been sleeping, she looked innocent and guileless. So opposite of the women he was used to in his life.

"Be sure to leave your review on Yelp," he said, trying to keep a straight face. "A small business like this lives and dies on word of mouth."

Clearing her throat, she was laughing at him. "*Mouth* being the operative word here. Seriously, I'd like to return the favor."

Her deft fingers had slid down his abdomen and were reaching for his overeager cock but he managed to capture them while he still had the willpower. He kissed her knuckles and then set her hands at her side.

"Not tonight, love. You're injured and tired. You need your rest."

Her brows pinched together. "But you–"

"That was for you and I loved doing it. In fact, I may

want to do that every day while you're here. Maybe twice a day."

"If you think I'm going to stop you or pretend to protest you're mistaken, Hamlet. I'm not that kind of girl."

He also liked this brazen female that he'd only gotten a glimpse of last night. He needed to coax her out to play more often. Just not tonight.

"Let's finish your shower and then we'll get you into bed. I think you said you wanted a good book and your pain medication?"

When she yawned widely, Max knew he'd made the right call. She acquiesced and he finished up her hair and then lifted her out of the shower, setting her back on the vanity while he dried her off.

Leg first and then right back into the boot. He didn't want her to jostle it by mistake. Within a few minutes he had her tucked up in his bed, wearing one of his t-shirts with a book in hand, the television on a low volume in the background.

It looked...right, having her here. Too right, perhaps? Already he was thinking of reasons for her not to go back to her place.

That was amazingly scary.

———

Max couldn't leave Carrie at home by herself the next day so he loaded her into the car and took her along with him to the theatre.

Carrie. A giant flavored coffee. Her laptop. Crutches.

Pain pills. A pillow for her leg. Her humungous handbag with half the house stuffed in it.

That was just what he knew about. She wasn't much for traveling light, even if it was only to the West End.

"That's more sugar than coffee," he said, gently placing her on a chair with a good vantage point to where he'd be working. "It will make you hyper."

She took a sip and sighed, smiling and closing her eyes as if in bliss. "Yes, it is and no, it won't. I'm not a toddler, Max. You should try it. It's heavenly."

He pulled a face, not as fond of sweet things as she was. "I'll take a pass on that. I prefer my coffee to taste like coffee. It has a job to do and that's why I drink it."

"I'm not sure how to respond to that."

"Then don't respond at all." Chuckling, he lifted her right leg and placed it on another chair, propped up with the small pillow he'd brought along. "Now, did you take your pain pills or some ibuprofen?"

"Ibuprofen," she answered, opening her laptop and setting it on her thighs. "Honestly, I'm good here. Go work and have fun. If I need anything I'll let you know."

That was the issue. He couldn't have her interrupting a scene when they were rehearsing.

"I'll come back and check on you periodically. Do you need anything before I go? A water? A trip to the bathroom?"

She reached into that nightmare of a bag and pulled out a water bottle. "I've got water and took care of nature's calls before we left home. I do have my crutches, you know. If I can't wait I can get there by myself."

They'd argued for ten minutes about those damn crutches. He hadn't wanted to bring them, didn't want her on them, but like most discussions with Carrie he came out on the losing end. It was easier to agree.

"Hopefully you won't need to use them. I'll only be a few feet away."

Her fingers were poised over the keys of the laptop. "You're working. I don't want to be a bother when you're busy."

"You're not a bother," he said automatically but he meant it sincerely. He'd loved spoiling her yesterday and he planned to do it again this evening no matter how much she fought him about it.

She tapped his chin playfully. "Max, go to work. I can't admire your talent if you're not onstage."

*True.*

"If you need any–"

"Max." Carrie's tone was firm and she gave his shoulder a light push. "Please go and pretend to be someone else. Why are you delaying? Did you forget to study your lines or something? Do you have a pop quiz today? Do actors even have pop quizzes?"

"You're pushy."

"You're stubborn."

If he was he'd learned it from her.

———

Max must have called out the cavalry. About every five minutes someone stopped by where Carrie was sitting inquiring whether she needed anything. It was sweet and polite and it was driving her insane. She couldn't get anything done so eventually she gave up and watched Max rehearse instead.

He was magnificent. It wasn't enough that he was incredibly talented, an actor among actors. No, he also oozed charisma on stage. Her gaze was riveted to his every word and action. His face was expressive but in this arena so was his voice. Effortlessly, it carried all the way to the cheap seats, mesmerizing her with its tone and resonance. He was able to convey so much emotion with a flicker of an eyebrow and a single syllable. What must it be like to have a gift like that? No wonder he was often arrogant and full of himself. He had reason to be. She'd seen him onscreen and it didn't do him justice. Only in person did she feel the fullness of his performance.

"He's good, isn't he?"

The soft voice behind her made Carrie jump but she easily recognized it. "Amy, I didn't expect to see you today. Don't tell me...Hamlet up there was worried and asked you to check on me?"

"Good guess." Amy settled into the chair next to Carrie and leaned down to get a good look at the offending ankle. "How does it feel?"

"When I'm in this boot and I can't move it's all fine. Honestly it's more awkward than anything. I'm not exactly graceful at the best of times and then add in an injury and I'm screwed."

"Oops, I almost forgot. I brought you this." Amy dug into her purse and pulled out a small bag of chocolates.

"Thought you might need it. Is there anything I can do for you? Help you to the bathroom? Get you another coffee? Call Tyler and have him sweep you off your feet?"

Carrie accepted the chocolates with a grateful hug. "You are a mind reader. This is just what an injured girl needs. As for needing anything, I'm good. Max has people stopping by every few minutes, but I'm still glad you popped in."

Amy cleared her throat. "No comment on Tyler?"

"None. He and I are just friends and you know it. There will be no sweeping."

"I have to say I'm glad about that. You and Max make such a cute couple."

Carrie sometimes had to remind herself that Amy - and others - didn't know about the contract.

"Thank you but I think as good-looking as Max is he'd make any couple cute."

Amy's gaze followed Max, who was rehearsing a sword fight onstage with another actor.

"I've never seen Max look this happy though. You bring out the joyful side of him that's been missing for a long time, especially after that bitch Alana. I hope he doesn't screw it up and do something stupid."

*I hope so too.*

"Is that likely?"

Shrugging, Amy shifted in her seat. "He hasn't always made the best decisions when it comes to relationships. It's made him terribly gun-shy, if you know what I mean. He can be a cynical bastard too."

Carrie had seen all of that up close and personal. "We're not rushing into things. We're just...enjoying the here and now."

Amy frowned. "He needs to find a good woman and settle down, have six kids and a dog. I'll be honest, Carrie, all of his friends are hoping you're the one."

The one. That wasn't frightening at all.

"You don't even know if I want children, and I could be allergic to dogs."

"Do you?"

Carrie's attention was pulled back to the stage where Max ripped off his sweaty t-shirt and used it to dry his damp chest after the sword fight. *Damn.*

"Do I what?" Carrie had forgotten the question.

"Do you want children?" Amy pressed, her gaze following Carrie's. "I bet making a few babies with Max wouldn't be much of a chore."

Remembering the last twenty-four hours, Carrie had to admit he'd make a wonderful father. His nurturing was second to none.

"He'd be a good dad," Carrie said since Amy was still waiting for a reply. "And yes, I want children. I always have. In my family there was only me and my brother. I'd like to have four or five kids."

Amy's smile grew wider. "That's exactly what Max says. Four or five. But he's frustrated because he can't find a woman that wants more than two."

Carrie needed to slow this conversation down. It was getting out of hand.

"We haven't talked about kids," she stated firmly. "Or commitment or anything like that. We're taking it slow."

"Slow," Amy echoed, her expression smug. "You do that, but I have a feeling I should start crocheting a baby blanket. I think yellow since we don't know whether it will be a boy or girl."

Way out of hand.

Carrie shook her head, her own stomach doing somer-saults in her abdomen at the images her friend had wrought. "No crocheting. No baby blankets. Please, I am begging you, do not go overboard here. I like Max. I really do. But there isn't going to be any happily ever after here. There will be no fairy tale wedding. It's just a casual rela-tionship. Max isn't in love with me. Heck, I piss him off pretty much on a daily basis and that's the reality. This won't last forever."

Her speech had been more for herself than Amy. It was a good reminder when she sometimes had fantasies of more. He'd made "more" easy by taking care of her so thoroughly.

Amy's features softened and she grabbed Carrie's hand and squeezed. "You're in love with him."

Carrie's denial came swiftly.

"No."

"Yes."

"No."

"Okay, then you could easily be in love with him."

One push and all of Carrie's defenses would go tumbling to the ground. That's what kept her up at night.

"I don't want to talk about this anymore."

Sighing, Amy took the bag of chocolates and ripped it open, handing two to Carrie. "Pretending it's not happening isn't going to make it go away."

"But it makes today so much easier."

Popping the chocolate into her mouth, Carrie didn't say

another word. There was nothing left to be said really. She knew the reality of the situation. Carrie was going to have a broken heart when all was said and done but she'd known that for awhile now. She simply couldn't play it safe for the rest of her life. She didn't want to either.

She had Max, for now, and that was enough.

# CHAPTER
## Thirty-Two

CARRIE DID MANAGE to get a little work done in between ogling Max and his minions checking on her constantly. She didn't mind her non-productivity as it gave her a chance to watch him work and that had been a true pleasure. If rehearsals were any indication, the play was going to be fantastic.

He'd disappeared back into the dressing room area about fifteen minutes ago but now he had reappeared looking freshly showered and wearing a cocky grin. He knew how good he was in the role and he was feeling the well-earned confidence.

"So what do you think?"

"Be gone with your false modesty." Carrie playfully shook her finger at him. "You're amazing and the play is wonderful. But you very well knew that, didn't you?"

"I'd hoped," he confessed, beginning to pack up their things. "I have a good feeling about this production but there are still many things to iron out. The sword fighting scene we were rehearsing today, for example. It's still quite rough."

Carefully, she lowered her foot to the floor so he could pack up the pillow. "Do they give you a real sword for the actual play?"

He'd used a wooden one today and it reminded her of a cute little boy pretending to be a pirate.

Chuckling, he slid her laptop into her handbag. He wouldn't let her carry it, saying it weighed a stone. Whatever that was.

"We get fake swords but they look more real than what we had today. Now, are you hungry? I hope so because my parents called while I was cleaning up. They're in London and they want to have dinner."

"Dinner? Your parents?"

It had been the last thing Carrie was expecting to hear. She'd known he had parents and he mentioned them quite often but somehow she hadn't thought that they might meet.

"Don't worry," he assured her with a smile. "We have time to go home and change."

Carrie glanced down at the boot on her leg. It wasn't exactly what was on every fashion catwalk this year but she had a dress that might cover it up a little. At least make it less noticeable.

"You don't have to be nervous."

"I'm not nervous. Moms and dads love me because I have a good career, no discernible drug habit, and I'm not on the run from the law. It doesn't hurt that I'm a ray of fucking sunshine. I'm like the girl next door."

In truth, she'd never had an issue with the parents of

any guy she'd dated. That didn't mean she wasn't concerned about putting her best foot forward, however. How was mummy and daddy going to like it when Max insisted on carrying her into the restaurant and out? Even to the bathroom?

"That's the spirit. I like your confidence. Now I'll take all of this to the car and come back for you."

"I don't suppose you'll let me use my crutches?"

"Perish the thought. Just give me a minute."

Max was loaded down like a pack mule. She needed to learn to pack lighter.

"On the way home I want you to tell me all about your parents so I can dazzle them with my knowledge."

If she was lucky they had a few items in common and it would help fill any breaks in the conversation. Books, movies, and music were fertile ground for dinner topics. If Carrie was honest, she was curious as to what Max's parents were like. It was always a clue as to how Max would look and act later in life. An older, silver-haired, distinguished Maxwell Hayes was something to look forward to.

---

Max's parents were actors themselves, although never as successful as their son even at the peak of their careers. In their early sixties, they easily looked a decade younger and not *regular-person* younger. They looked *actor-younger* which meant that not only was their skin remarkably unlined but their teeth were white, their hair perfectly coiffed, and their clothes fashionable. Smiling and vibrant, they looked like they'd just stepped out of an ad for a luxury automobile or a fine liquor.

They also hated Carrie's guts.

Not that they were overt about it. They weren't. Karen and Tim Hayes were too wily to simply throw their rancor out there for all the world to see. They were actors, so they were going to *act* as if they liked her. So far Carrie wasn't buying it but Max seemed to be. Frankly, Karen and Tim weren't the thespians they thought they were. Even the waiter was getting the vibe that they wished Carrie was anywhere but with their precious baby boy.

So far they'd barely acknowledged Carrie's presence at the table, instead peppering Max with questions about award shows and parties. It appeared to her that Karen and Tim were infatuated with their son's fame and fortune. They wanted to hear the latest juicy gossip, talk about the glamour and glitz, hear about the famous directors he was working with. Perhaps they were living vicariously through Max?

Sadly they decided to bring Carrie into the conversation when Max wouldn't be more forthcoming about his possible award nominations nor would he divulge any details about his contract negotiations.

Karen sipped at her red wine. "What is it that you do, Carly?"

*Virtual slap.*

"Her name is Carrie, Mum. Carrie Johnson."

*I don't think your mother gives a shit, Max.*

"I'm Chief Operating Officer of a publishing company but we dabble in other things as well, such as merchandising and now moviemaking."

Max nodded in agreement. "Carrie is basically in charge of Paige Mitchell's entire business, top to bottom."

"That must be...challenging," Tim said. "But so mundane. I'd sooner jump from the top of Everest than be in an office all day long. Lucky you have the temperament for it."

*Another virtual slap.*

Carrie didn't work in some sterile office and her job wasn't mundane in the least. Tim must have strained a muscle jumping to all those conclusions.

Max was doing his best but he was clearly uncomfortable getting in between her and his parents. Not that she was asking him to. If she was his real girlfriend she'd expect it but not in this situation. Frankly she felt sorry for him being put in this position.

But he'd been smiling and complimentary all evening, raving about the maxi dress she'd chosen. The length covered the boot and the color highlighted her tan which was holding on by its fingernails in this gray weather.

Karen pressed her palms together and smiled. "That reminds me. We're going to spend the weekend in London for your opening night. Gavin and Emily would like so much to come too. You can get two more tickets can't you?"

Shaking his head, Max fussed with the napkin. Maybe he was more perturbed than he was letting on. "Mum, you know I can't. I can get them tickets for a performance on a different date but not opening night."

Pouting, Karen appeared quite put out. "But Gavin and Emily are some of your best friends."

"No, they're your best friends and I'm sure they'll understand."

Tim cleared his throat. "We already asked them to go with us so you'll need to find two more tickets, son."

An edict. Just like that.

Then again, the way they were treating Carrie was head and shoulders above how they were treating Max. Did they really expect him to drop everything and find two more tickets to the absolute hottest show in London?

Better question...would Max do it? Carrie waited, holding her breath for his response.

"I'm afraid it's just not possible." Max shook his head and she thought she saw a muscle tick in his jaw. "I've used my entire allotment for opening night and then some."

Not happy. Karen and Tim were visibly upset.

"Can't you just move a few of your opening night guests to later?" Karen gave Carrie a pointed stare. "I'm sure they wouldn't mind. Gavin and Emily are practically family."

Max's teeth clicked as he snapped them together. "Mother–"

"Never mind," Karen interrupted, waving a hand in the air. "We'll just go whatever date you can get Gavin and Emily tickets. We'll miss your opening night but if that's the way it needs to be then we'll have to understand."

Now the guilt trip. It was fascinating to watch and no way was Carrie going to open her mouth at this juncture and say a word. Nope, this was Max's show.

His knuckles had turned white as he held onto his wine glass but his expression was supremely calm. Damn, he was a good actor.

"If you don't want to attend the opening night I can

assure you there will be no shortage of takers for your tickets. Just say the word."

He'd said it politely but there was an undercurrent to his tone, an edge, warning mummy and daddy to back the hell off.

Tim signaled the waiter. "Of course we want to be there..."

Max smiled. "Then it's all settled then. You'll attend opening night and your friends will attend another date. So what else is new these days? Any upcoming roles?"

*You smooth motherfucker. I saw what you did.*

"I have a small role in an indie film being shot in the Cotswolds," Karen said, her facing lighting up. "And do you know who is also in the movie? Susannah Dougherty. How long did you and she date? A year? Or was it two? I never understood what broke you two up. You were such a handsome couple and you seemed so happy. She's single again. You should give her a ring."

*Hello? Am I invisible? Did I fade into the upholstery of the chair? I hate it when that happens.*

Max's gaze flickered to Carrie, his cheeks slightly pink. At least he had the decency to be embarrassed.

"I don't think I'll be giving her a call, Mum." He reached out and placed his hand on Carrie's, squeezing her fingers reassuringly. "Perhaps I wasn't clear earlier. I'm dating Carrie and we're very happy."

Karen's smile faltered. "I guess I didn't realize it was exclusive. You haven't known one another long."

"Since last Thanksgiving," Carrie heard herself pipe up, but wincing inwardly. She should have stayed silent.

Stupid, stupid, stupid. All she'd done was remind Max's parents that she was American. As in not British.

"Do you ride?" Tim asked Carrie, his faced scrunched up as if something smelled bad. Like her. "We like to go riding as a family when Max comes out to visit."

This was the exam part of the evening. When faced with Carrie as a potential future partner to their son, it was now time to make sure said son knew how inadequate she was as a significant other.

*Well played, parental units. Well played.*

"I've never ridden," Carrie confessed. She had a feeling this was a grave sin in the Hayes family.

Karen looked shocked. "Ever? Why not?"

Max was rubbing his temple as if a vein was about to pop out of his skull. "For heaven's sake, Mum, she doesn't ride. Leave her in peace about it."

What the hell. She wasn't going to win over these people no matter what she did or said. Time to throw caution to the wind.

"Actually, horses kind of scare me. They're so much bigger than I am."

Apparently Tim and Karen had nothing to reply because they turned back to their son just as the entrees arrived. Carrie happily ate her chicken and let the trio carry the conversation as they discussed acting roles, directors, producers, and poorly written scripts. It was too good to be true though as Karen's attention swung back to Carrie.

"We must be boring you terribly with all of this shop talk. I'm sure you don't understand a word of it. Creative people are so different than everyday worker bees."

*Virtual slap number three.*

Max threw down his napkin. "Mum, you are being very rude. If you can't at least be polite to Carrie then she and I will have to leave."

Brows up, Karen smiled sweetly. "I meant no offense. It's just that you and Carrie are so very different. You're a famous actor and she's more a behind the scenes person. An administrator who handles the paperwork. Of course after dating you that could all change. Being Max Hayes's girlfriend could open up several doors for her."

*And...virtual slap number four. This one I cannot ignore.*

"I can assure you, Mrs. Hayes, that my career is fine and on solid footing. I have no need to date anyone to bolster it. I'm with Max because I like him."

"Everyone likes Max," Karen said, a gleam in her eye. "He's smart, funny, and talented. He could have any woman he wanted."

*Virtual slap number five.*

At this rate, Carrie was going to be dizzy from getting knocked around by Max's parents.

"Mother," Max's tone was decidedly frosty. "If you cannot say anything nice, than please keep quiet. Carrie is a lovely woman and she has no interest in show business. We are together because we like each other. As for getting any woman I want, I can assure you that is patently false, not that it matters. We're extremely happy and if you don't like it I can pay the check and we'll go. Carrie has tolerated a great deal of abuse from you tonight and I'm determined she won't have to deal with any more. Either be polite or you won't be seeing me for quite awhile."

This forceful Max was quite attractive.

"I meant no harm," Karen murmured. "I was just trying to get to know her."

Scowling, Tim set down his fork. "Apologize to your mother, Maxwell. You've hurt her feelings."

Christ on a crutch, this family put the *fun* in dysfunctional. Christmas had to be a hoot.

Max set down his own fork. "I'll happily apologize to Mum if she apologizes to Carrie."

The evening had just gone from bad to fucking worse. Karen looked livid at her baby boy's declaration.

Wanting peace more than she wanted a fake apology, Carrie raised her hands in the universal sign for "stop." "Okay, how about we just start over here tonight? Pretend the first part of the evening never happened. Let's pick a topic that isn't controversial. Do you think it will rain tomorrow?"

"It rains every day," Tim said gruffly, his lips in a thin line. "It's London."

"Carrie's from Florida," Max offered with a smile. "She says they call it the Sunshine State."

Karen looked horrified as if Max had confided that Carrie liked to wrestle alligators in the mud for tip money.

"You mean...like Disney and Mickey Mouse?"

Carrie didn't have a chance to respond. Tim replied to his wife instead. "Now, darling, Disney is a very influential movie studio. They do much more than just cartoons. Max, is your agent still talking with them about that big budget film that starts shooting next year? Didn't your character have parents in that script? Your mother and I would be available and honestly, wouldn't our casting make the most sense?"

Just like that they were talking about movies and acting again. Karen and Tim certainly had a one track mind when it came to their son.

Dinners like these were always educational and tonight was no exception. Carrie might have found herself slapped around a little bit but it had been worth it. She'd learned how Max had ended up with Alana. Now that Carrie had met his parents, she could see how he would think it was perfectly normal for someone to want something from him.

Even mummy and daddy.

# CHAPTER
## Thirty-Three

MAX KNELT on the floor in front of Carrie, gently pulling off her boot so she could get out of her dress.

"I'm just so fucking sorry," he said for the tenth time, his expression contrite. "I had no idea they'd act that way. We shouldn't have stayed. I should have picked you up and marched out of the restaurant the first time she forgot your name."

"She didn't forget my name," Carrie said wryly. "That was a little passive-aggressive game to see if I'd react. Although maybe they would have liked me better if my name really was Carly and I rode horses."

*And disappeared, never to be heard from again.*

He tugged her dress over her head. "I'm just mortified about the way they acted. I don't know what got into them. They're usually quite polite and outgoing. They love meeting new people."

Should she just lay it on the line? Be brutally honest? It

wasn't like she was going to be their daughter-in-law, after all.

"I kind of got the feeling they like meeting new people in the movie business."

*People that can help them get roles. Not nobodies like me.*

Max held up two pairs of pajama - one pink and the other purple. She pointed to the purple pair. "They do tend to be very focused on the industry. I think it comes from being jobbing actors all these years. They weren't famous enough to be sought after for projects so they had to scrap and claw for each one. Yet somehow they managed to make a good living and put me through the best schools."

That was something his parents should be commended for. It was clear that he was the apple of their eye, their pride and joy. Karen and Tim simply wanted the best for him.

And themselves. They didn't seem to realize they were using their son as a business contact. For all Carrie knew, Max encouraged them to do so. It would be just like him to want to help his mom and dad now that he was rich and famous.

"Still, I'm very sorry," he said again, helping her into the soft cotton pants, his hands brushing her bare skin and giving her naughty ideas. The best ending for this crappy evening would be to shag Tim and Karen's son all night long. "I thought tonight was going to be a pleasant dinner and it was anything but."

"It is not your fault so please stop apologizing." She slipped on the t-shirt as he knelt down to replace the boot. "Who is this Susannah, by the way? It sounded like you dated her for a long time."

Carrie didn't want to know because she was jealous. She was simply curious.

Now that she'd been taken care of, Max began to strip his own clothes off. "I have no idea why they thought she and I were together that long. We dated for about three or four months and she was very focused on her acting career so needless to say the relationship fell apart rather quickly. We were on opposite sides of the world filming different projects. It wasn't conducive to commitment. I daresay we never got past what you would call the casual stage."

Lounging back on the bed, Carrie had been enjoying the strip show Max performed for her. It was giving her even more ideas. Even injured, she could get him out of those boxer shorts and t-shirt in record time. "Still...your parents have a point."

"I'm not following you, love."

That was because he was scrolling through his phone, barely paying any attention. It was a bad habit that drove her crazy.

"You and that damn mobile. Would you two like to be alone?"

Cheeks flushed, he set in on the bedside table next to hers. "Sorry. I was hoping Mum or Dad had sent an apology. Now what were you saying about a point?"

"Just that they kind of had a point. We do live very different lives."

Max pointed the remote at the television. "It wouldn't be near as much fun if we were just the same. I might as well date myself."

What was it with men and gadgets? Now he was clicking through the channels.

"I simply meant that you're world famous and I'm not. Although I can see how it affects your life, Hamlet, I truly cannot understand what it's like to be you. The sacrifices you've had to make for your career. The loss of privacy, for example."

Max shut off the television and turned to Carrie. "Have you ever sacrificed anything, love?"

"Well, of course I have."

"Then you understand."

Carrie pointed to the window. "Max, will you go stand by the window and look outside for me?"

Frowning, he did as she asked, peeking out the curtains. "It's raining again. Is that what you wanted to know?"

"Nope. Please count the number of photographers camped out across the street with their lenses focused on your home."

"Carrie–"

"Humor me."

He sighed and let the curtain drop back into place. "Four. What is your point?"

She couldn't help but laugh. Didn't he *know* the point?

"Hamlet, there are four photographers across the street and their entire focus is to get pictures of you and your life. There were six earlier when we came home to change but two of them must have had to go home to their families or maybe get a bite to eat. The point is that there are a bunch of people on this planet that are extremely interested in where you dine, what kind of coffee you drink, and what you wear. So interested that they buy tabloids with photos of you with bedhead getting a pastry and a newspaper. That...right there...is the difference in you and me."

His expression was somewhere between annoyed and defeated. "I never asked for this. They normally leave me alone but dating you has captured their interest."

"I never said you did, but it's a reality whether you wanted it or not. You wanted to act and you wanted to be successful at it. This is what happens when you are. I am also successful in my chosen profession." Giggling, she reached for his hand to tug him back into bed. "Thankfully though, no one cares to know my personal details. No one gives a shit if I like vanilla lattes. That's my point. I can see it happen to you but I can't truly understand it because I don't live it every day."

"You've had cameras pointed at you on more than one occasion."

She poked him in the ribs. "Because of you, not for anything I've done. If we weren't a couple the only way I could get those paps' attention was if I stripped off my clothes and ran screaming down the street, bare-ass naked and boobs flying everywhere."

His smile grew and he leaned over to steal a kiss, his fingers insinuating themselves under her shirt. "Now that's an image that warms a man's heart."

Blowing a raspberry, she wriggled in delight as his hand cupped her breast. "And somewhere in a more southerly direction too, I'll bet. Are you going to just lie there or make me scream?"

"Scream."

The chirping of one of their phones broke apart a kiss so hot it had singed her toes.

"Yours or mine?" Max asked as he lifted his head, a scowl on his handsome face.

She reached for both of them and wrinkled her nose. "Mine and it's my sister-in-law."

"You should take it then." He growled and rolled off of her. "How about I go get us some wine?"

"Damn, you're brilliant. That fancy boarding school education is paying off."

Another growl and she was on the receiving end of an extremely nice view of his backside as he headed downstairs.

"Hi, Jeannie. What's up? Is everything okay?"

"Everything is fine. Just fine. In fact, things couldn't be better. We've had some exciting news."

"Are you having another baby? That's awesome."

Jeannie's laughter was the only answer Carrie needed. "Heavens no. We're done having kids. Two is plenty for me. No, this call is about Greg. He was made a full partner today at the firm. It's so exciting and it's what he's worked and slaved for."

Fingers tightening on the phone, Carrie stammered with shock. "Full partner? Wow, that's amazing. Fantastic. Greg must be over the moon. You're right, this is everything he's ever wanted. Tell him congratulations, okay?"

"I will, definitely. The reason I'm calling is that we're going to throw him a party on the twenty-third to celebrate. I know you're over in London working and this is short notice and everything but I thought - what the heck - the worst thing you can say is no. We'd love it if you could come. We'd make it a surprise for Greg."

A party. In Florida.

Apparently, Carrie had been so stunned by the invitation she hadn't replied. Jeannie rushed in to fill the silence.

"Listen it's okay if you have to say no. Like I said, this is really short notice and kind of unreasonable to ask you to fly twelve hours to spend an evening at a party and then fly another twelve hours back. I just had to call and ask you because, well, Greg is just so excited and happy. I know he'd want you to share this moment with him if it was possible."

Time to get her mouth in working order.

"I'll be there," Carrie said, her throat tight with emotion. Suddenly she was swamped with homesickness. Everything was so much simpler outside of London. "Nothing could keep me away."

"Oh, thank you so much, Carrie. Now remember, not a word to Greg. The party isn't a surprise but you being there is."

"I'll remember. I'll call you when I have the travel arrangement made. Thanks for calling me and give that brother of mine a hug."

"Will do," Jeannie laughed happily. It truly was fantastic news. "Thanks so much, Carrie. I can't wait to see Greg's face when he sees you."

Carrie ended the call and placed the phone back on the table. Greg was a full partner now in the law firm. His entire career had been focused on this day. Mom and Dad would have been so proud of him. There was no way Carrie was missing that party. Her ankle would be much better by then and Max would be busy with the play. He'd be fine for a few days while she was home.

Home. It might be a good place to find some of the answers she'd been seeking.

———

From where Max was lying on the bed, he could see a sliver of the moon through the gap in the drapes. It was late, well past midnight, and he couldn't sleep. His mind was too active to let his body rest.

Sliding his arm out from under Carrie, he levered up from the bed and reached for the boxers and t-shirt that had been discarded earlier during a bout of passion. After a glass of wine, they had both been pleasantly relaxed which had led to more pleasurable pursuits that didn't require clothes. They'd carefully - mindful of her ankle - made love and fallen asleep in each other's arms, Max as the big spoon and Carrie as the little one.

The sex between them only seemed to get better and even the cuddling afterward was better than he'd ever experienced. Everything was better with this woman, even a simple coffee and toast in the morning.

Padding downstairs on bare feet, he grabbed a juice from the refrigerator and sat down in the big leather chair near the front window. A peek out told him that the photographers had finally given up and gone home, but he knew from experience they'd be back. Now that he and Carrie had gone public they were following him around endlessly.

They always came back no matter how hard Max tried to be boring and normal. Alana had loved the attention and had cultivated it by making sure her life was as exciting as possible. Or at least controversial. One was just as good as the other to her.

Carrie, on the other hand, didn't care or need the paps following her around. Already she'd shown a poise and calmness regarding the attention that some people with years in the business didn't have. If it all went away tomorrow it wouldn't bother her a bit.

He'd watched her tonight at dinner with his parents as the wheels turned in her head. As smart as she was it wouldn't be difficult to figure out the dynamic between Max and his parents. He loved his mother and father and was grateful to them for all the sacrifices they'd made on his behalf but he wasn't an idiot. They loved his fame. Not as much as they loved him. No, not at all. But they were quite...enthusiastic about what was going on his life.

He was living their dream and he was able to in part because of all the things they'd done for him. They'd been his first role models and his biggest cheerleaders. Still it was a little embarrassing when they wouldn't leave him alone about a party or a director. He was well aware that his success gave them more opportunities and they liked that a whole hell of a lot. If his career disappeared tomorrow they'd be sad and a little let down but they'd support him in any way that he needed.

After tonight though he could only imagine what Carrie was thinking. His parents had treated her terribly when in fact they were usually quite normal. Normal *involved* parents. Karen and Tim had an opinion about every subject under the sun. Why had he thought this would be any different?

It could cause a problem if the relationship with Carrie

lasted past the end of the contract. Already he couldn't imagine not having her in his life and in his bed. The barriers he'd erected to keep his emotions safe had been useless when she was around. If they became serious there would have to be apologies made by his mum and dad at the very least. She wasn't like Alana who could be bought off with a few diamonds.

The contract. That was another issue.

A good thing because it gave Max time to ponder what he really wanted from Carrie. Friendship? A roll in the hay? A relationship? Forever? That last one struck fear into his heart. He'd tried that once and look how it had turned out. The divorce was just as much his fault as Alana's. She'd cheated on him but he'd married her in the first place. He had lousy judgment when it came to women. He'd thought she'd loved him. She'd only loved what he could give her.

But the contract had its dark side as well. Because they were bound for a certain period of time, Max wasn't concerned about Carrie bolting if he didn't tell her she was pretty. He didn't have to be on his best behavior, courting and wooing. There was no pretense, no putting his best foot forward. He was out there, warts and all. If he went too far or showed who he was a little too much...would she run when their time was up?

There was a chance he'd be ready for her to leave. Tired of having a woman around all the time and having to think about her needs and wants. He'd been selfish for many years now and in his profession it was not only allowed but encouraged.

Where it left them, Max had no idea. A big part of him wanted this to work. Carrie was a wonderful woman and he doubted he could do any better.

After years of playing make-believe, he mostly just wanted to believe that it could be real.

# CHAPTER
## Thirty~Four

MAX'S OPENING night was a triumph. He was amazing as Carrie had known he would be but more than that, the entire cast pulled together and made her believe that this world existed right in the here and now. Like everyone else, she stood and applauded, blinking back tears of happiness as the crowd went wild. It wasn't even her accomplishment but the pride she felt for Max overwhelmed her, clogging her throat and making her chest hurt.

*Damn, he's utterly fantastic.*

As he took another bow he caught her eye, giving her a smile that promised so much. Later. When the audience went home, the partying was done, and the champagne all gone, Carrie would be there for him. She wanted to be the one constant in his life, by his side whether it was a happy occasion or a sad one. Her loyalty didn't hinge on his success or failure.

Nate and Paige had made it back from Los Angeles for

the event and Carrie couldn't help but notice how happy her friend looked. Radiant but tired, perhaps Paige was slightly jetlagged. Carrie couldn't wait to spend some quality time with her friend even if it was only a few days. Nate had to get back on set by the end of the week.

The afterparty was a rowdy one. Lots of booze, lots of dancing, and lots of loud and boisterous people celebrating what was a triumphant opening night. Thankfully Max's parents didn't stay but she'd felt their gazes on her during the performance. Once again they weren't openly nasty but they did look slightly annoyed as if they'd expected her to be dumped and gone by now.

The group found a corner that while not all that much quieter, at least was out of the main center of frivolity. At one point, the partiers were pouring beer on each other's heads and that was something that Carrie didn't want to happen to her.

Instead she sat next to Paige while on the opposite side of the table the actors – Amy, Mike, Max, Nate, and Tyler dissected the play scene by scene and line by line.

Paige's gaze flickered over to Max who was huddled with the other men. "He looks happy."

"He ought to," Carrie laughed. "He's the toast of London tonight."

"I think it's because of you. I saw the way he looked at you from the stage. He's smitten and so are you. Admit it."

Paige knew Carrie better than anyone on the planet so there was no reason to deny it.

"I...like him. A lot. I see now what you were saying about his kind heart."

"He keeps it hidden."

"Massive understatement," Carrie giggled, reaching for one of the appetizers in the middle of the table. "But we've made real progress. I think he might even trust me."

Paige gave her a smug smile. "The real question is do you trust him? Is he someone you could have a future with?"

The short answer was yes, but the long answer was much more complicated and involved.

"I'm taking things one day at a time. He wants to reevaluate at the end of the contract."

It still stung a little.

Wrinkling her nose, Paige shook her head. "He's not the type to throw caution to the wind and do something spontaneous."

Carrie nodded to where Nate was sitting. "You cornered the market on spontaneity. Your handsome husband could be the poster child."

"I love it," Paige confessed, her gaze loving as she caught Nate's eye. "But it can be exhausting never knowing what he's going to do next. He's full of surprises."

"You love it."

"I love *him*."

Paige and Nate were made for each other. If anyone had a chance at happily ever after it was those two.

"When do you come back to London?" Carrie asked. "I miss you."

"I miss you too and it should be soon. I think. I'll have to check the schedule. After shooting's finished Nate has some voiceover work that has to be done in LA but it should only last a week or so. Personally I'm ready to get back home."

"Did I mention that I'm headed back to Florida later this month? Greg made partner and they're throwing him a party. I'm the surprise."

Paige lifted her drink so they could toast. "That's awesome. Tell him congratulations from me. He must be thrilled."

"I'm sure he is although I didn't talk to him, just Jeannie. I can tell she's proud of him."

Nudging Carrie with her elbow, Paige glanced at Max. "You should always be proud of your man."

"I am proud but I'm not sure I can classify Max as *mine.*"

"There are worse things he could be."

Tyler signaled the waitress for another round and then turned to Paige and Carrie. "Our manners are terrible. We've been ignoring you beautiful ladies all evening."

Max's cheeks were red. "I apologize also. I think we got a little carried away with the play."

Carrie waved it off. "It's all good. You deserve to bask in the glory."

Paige nodded in agreement. "Bask away. Just don't forget to eat something to go with that alcohol. Trust me on this. Nate has a lovely story of me falling on my ass when I had too many hard ciders. It was humiliating."

Nate gave his wife a look of pure worship. "You were adorable."

Paige blew a small raspberry. "I was drunk but since you're married to me I guess you have to say things like that. I'm being restrained tonight. No getting drunk, but I make no promises for the movie wrap party. I'm going to

be so happy when you're done making this film I'm definitely celebrating."

Laughing, Nate brushed Paige's temple with his lips.
"I'll be right there with you, love. I'm ready to be back in
London." He turned to Tyler. "When does shooting begin
for your new movie? That has to be coming up soon."

"We start filming in New York City right after Labor
Day. I'm looking forward to this one. It's a great script and
the director is top notch." Tyler grinned and waggled his
brows at Carrie. "And if this one would just say the word I
could get her a small part in the movie. I know the director
hasn't cast it yet and I've already told him about her."

Heat rose in Carrie's face and she inwardly groaned.
Tyler wasn't going to let this go and the last thing she
needed was more people piling on and putting her under
pressure. She knew what she wanted out of life and being
an actress wasn't it. It was a perfectly good profession and
she had a great deal of respect for them as a whole - Alana
not withstanding - but it wasn't the career for her. Still
Tyler thought he was helping so she couldn't be mad.

"You can just un-tell him," Carrie playfully shook her
finger at him. "I am not doing the movie."

"Really?" Max wore the strangest expression, those blue
eyes almost silver. "A part, you say? I'm sure you'd be
wonderful, love. Tyler has an eye for talent."

What the fuck was Max up to? He didn't want her to
take the damn role any more than she wanted it. It only
took a moment for her to realize what he was upset about.

He thought she'd used him to get a part in a big budget
movie.

So much for trust. That wall she'd torn down was not

only rebuilt magically but he was in the process of forti-
fying it. She had to cut him off at the pass. Quickly.

"I am not under any circumstances doing the film,"
Carrie said as firmly as possible. "I am not an actress nor
do I have any interest in becoming one. I am having far too
much fun with my own career to think about getting a new
one so banish it from your thoughts, Tyler. It ain't gonna
happen, my friend. However, it is sweet that you thought
of me. Terribly misguided, but sweet."

Shrugging, Tyler accepted a fresh beer from the waitress. "I think you'd be great, Red, but I understand. If you
ever change your mind..."

"You'll know that I've had a severe blow to the head,"
she finished for him, noticing that Max looked much more
relaxed than he had just minutes ago. "Really and truly. I'm
happy with my career. In fact, I'm thrilled. I'm having a
ball."

Paige had been nursing her hard cider all night but she
finished it off with a flourish. "That's right. Keep your
hands off Carrie. I need her."

Aww, that was sweet. Carrie was looking forward to
being a producer on Nate and Paige's film. She wanted
nothing to do with being in front of the camera but behind
it? It was an exciting new challenge. One she was looking
forward to. All they needed was for the studio to sign off
on the final deal. Until then the plan for her to be part of
the production team was hush-hush. She didn't want to
jinx it by announcing it before it was official.

Max's warm gaze landed on Carrie and she squirmed
in her seat, the blood singing through her veins. He was
looking at her with a combination of lust and admiration.

*I can't wait until I get him home.*

"She is special, isn't she?" Max said, his deep voice sending tingles straight to the most intimate parts of her. If they had been alone, she would have reached out and let her fingertips trace his lips. But with all of these people around them she had to be content with smiling back, hoping he got the message.

*You are getting so lucky tonight, Hamlet.*

# CHAPTER
## Thirty-Five

MAX WAS in an excellent mood as they climbed the front steps to his home, Carrie in front of him. His hands were on her hips and his lips were exploring the side of her neck and making it more difficult than it should have been to fit the key into the lock. She slapped playfully at his hands that had roamed to her front.

"Can you just hold on one cotton pickin' minute? I can't get the door unlocked."

Instead of pausing, Max nipped at her shoulder with his teeth sending a shiver up her spine. "You wouldn't let me kiss you in the limo. You said to wait until we got home. Well, we're home."

Technically, he had a point.

"That's true, Hamlet, but you might want to watch those hands because there is about a dozen cameras trained on the front door of this house tonight. We could end up on the cover of a tabloid with our knickers down."

"Only girls wear knickers."

Success. She got the darn key in the lock. Twisting it, the door fell open and they stumbled inside.

"Funny about that. I forgot to wear my knickers tonight."

The door immediately and loudly slammed shut and she found herself pressed up against it by one male, six feet tall and all muscle. His warm breath feathered over her shoulder as he ran his tongue from her earlobe down to where her pulse beat madly at the base of her throat.

"You naughty girl," he chuckled, pressing damp kisses to her flesh and making the room spin. "You've been walking around all night without your panties? Are you trying to kill me?"

His questing fingers slid up her thigh and she relaxed, surrendering to his carnal explorations. Her lips captured his, their tongues playing together as his hand slipped between her legs. Breaking the kiss, she moaned as his touch found her wet, swollen, and needy. She'd been fantasizing about this all night.

"I wasn't trying to kill you. I was trying to please you."

His laugh was pure male pleasure and dominance. "My darling girl, you always do that. Now I'm going to please you."

Max slid down her body and to his knees, hooking one of her thighs over his shoulder. Gasping at the first stroke of his tongue, she was grateful for his strong arms as he braced her firmly against the smooth oak of the door, allowing her to abandon herself to the maelstrom of pleasure his expert mouth evoked. Wave after wave of heat swept through her veins and her eyelids fluttered shut, closing out the world beyond the two of them.

"Max," she whispered as her fingers dug into his soft, springy hair. A coil of arousal was tightening in her belly, inexorably pushing her closer to release as his tongue flicked over her sensitive clit. "More."

Usually he liked to tease her but tonight he didn't make her wait. His mouth closed over the sensitive bud, the tip of his tongue drawing circles around it until she thought she might lose her mind. Her body exploded into a million tiny pieces like confetti showering down from the sky.

His name was on her lips when he lifted her and wrapped her legs around his waist. At some point he'd unzipped his pants and now he was pushing against her core, hot, hard and ready. She groaned as he bottomed out, every steely inch of him buried to the hilt.

Every time he sank into her, stretching her walls, Carrie clenched around him. Her nails dug into his shoulders as his strokes picked up speed, rubbing that spot inside of her that drove her mad with want. This would be no gentle, romantic coupling. They were frantic and needy, their hands pawing at the barrier of their clothes so they could touch the bare flesh underneath.

The sounds they made were obscene. Damp flesh. Grunts. Wild, breathless panting. The door he'd braced her against shook on its hinges with the power of his thrusts. She'd have bruises on her hips tomorrow where his hands gripped her bottom, holding her still for their mating. He was in his all-male domination mode and although she wouldn't want a steady diet of this cock of the walk attitude, tonight she relished his passion and ardor. Never in her life had a man wanted her this badly. It was as if he couldn't get enough.

Or maybe it was she that couldn't get enough of him.

It didn't matter which because they were both getting what they wanted. He'd driven them both to the pinnacle and now she was climaxing around him, screaming his name so loudly the paps across the street probably heard her. His own orgasm was no less spectacular. He threw his head back, his eyes closed as if in prayer. The veins on his neck stood out in stark relief, his jaw tight. His skin was covered in a fine sheen of sweat and she leaned forward to run her tongue along his Adam's apple, tasting the salty tang.

As quickly as the storm had come upon them it was over. As gentle as ever, Max pressed baby soft kisses onto her face as he stepped away from the door and headed up the stairs, carrying her the whole way. Once in his bedroom, he laid her on the bed and began to undress her, slowly this time, savoring every moment of it. His own clothes melted away and he cuddled against her, his front to her back. His fingers methodically stroked her skin as their heartbeats slowed and their breathing evened out.

Max made Carrie feel infinitely precious and protected. Snuggled and safe in his arms, nothing could touch her. No doubts. No fears. This was a man worth believing in.

———

Max shifted on the mattress slightly, trying not to wake the woman peacefully slumbering at his side. The clock on the bedside table read three-thirty but he was wide awake. Despite their passionate lovemaking that should have burned whatever energy he'd had left after tonight's performance, he couldn't seem to settle down and sleep. His mind was buzzing as he replayed Tyler's words over and over in his head.

*I think you'd be great. Just say the word.*

Carrie had quickly put the actor in his place, turning him down in her no-nonsense tone. Max believed her. He believed that she wasn't interested in being an actress. A star. Mostly. He couldn't deny, however, that little voice in the back of his head that was whispering again and again.

*She wants something. She's using you. You can't trust her.*

After all, who didn't want to become a star? They thought it was all riding around in limos, drinking champagne, and shagging fans. Carrie, of course, knew full well that it was a hell of a lot more work but was the glamour any draw for her at all? She certainly enjoyed wearing designer dresses and attending parties.

Shaking his head, he gazed down at her innocently curled against him and silently berated himself. This was no barracuda looking for a big payday. Carrie was ambitious and hardworking but there was no way she was planning to become the next Meryl Streep. She loved her work and her life and it showed. There was no way in hell that Carrie was using Max unless it was for hot sex.

Snickering at his own joke, he leaned down to drop a kiss on her shoulder, the skin like satin under his lips. Her warm scent surrounded him, swamping his senses and his chest tightened in response. The emotions this woman created inside of him were so incredibly strong, almost bringing him to his knees with their awesome power. In one breath he wondered how he could ever survive feeling like this and in the next he wondered how he could live without it.

Carrie confused and bewildered him, keeping him off balance and reveling in it. Max was a man that was unused to not knowing what he wanted and how he felt. He needed to figure it out quickly though, as the clock on their relationship was ticking away and the last few granules of sand would soon be at the bottom of the hourglass. She wouldn't be obligated to be with him and he had doubts as to whether he'd given her enough reasons to stay without the ties that bound them together. He'd spent so many years putting distance between himself and others that when it came time to pull someone closer he had no idea how to accomplish the task.

For Carrie...he'd better figure it out and fast.

# CHAPTER
## Thirty-Six

CARRIE COULD BARELY KEEP her eyes open after a twelve hour flight to Tampa from London. Thank goodness she'd gained five hours with the time difference. She'd napped in the air but sleeping on a plane when she was alone always made her uneasy. If Paige or Max had been there she would have been able to drop off without any problems, but by herself she simply felt too vulnerable.

While waiting for her luggage, she dug her phone out of her purse and sent a quick text to Max letting him know she's arrived safely. He'd been adamant that he would worry so she'd promised to let him know as soon as she landed. Her ankle was almost back to one hundred percent but he'd fussed about her luggage and walking through the airport.

She'd had the distinct feeling he hadn't wanted her to go on this trip but that was probably all her imagination. He hadn't said anything outright about not going so she was sure it was just her that didn't want to be away from him. Max might even be celebrating having the bed and remote control to himself. She'd spent every night at his place since her sprained ankle.

Technology was an amazing thing. Soon after she shot off the text, her phone rang. Max.

"Shouldn't you be sleeping in after last night's performance?"

His gravelly chuckle told her that he was still in bed and had just woken. That was her favorite time. Warm and sleepy, he curled himself around her, whispering filthy suggestions in her ear that were definitely going to make him late for any morning appointment. Now with the play underway, he worked late and - usually - slept late.

"Hell of a way to greet a man who just wants to hear your voice. How was your flight, love?"

"Long," she sighed, making herself comfortable on a bench by the elevators while she waited for her bag. "The food was decent though and I got a bunch of paperwork done, so that was good. How was the play last night?"

Her flight had taken off at eight in the evening so she'd had to say goodbye before he left for the theatre. He'd given her the puppy dog eyes that made her feel like she was abandoning him at the pound.

"It was good, although someone's bloody cell phone went off during. Can't people turn those things off? It's hellishly rude."

It was but he might not be the best spokesman for that particular cause.

"Uh...Hamlet? Your phone is never more than a few inches from your fingertips. You get twitchy if you haven't touched it for awhile. It's the first thing you reach for in the morning."

"That's not the case at all." His tone was indignant and it sounded like he was waking up fast. "*You* are the first thing I reach for in the morning. But your point is well taken. Which reminds me...you were not here this morning when I woke. Tell me again as to how long that will be the sad and lonely situation?"

"Geez, you are so formal. Just ask me how long I'm going to gone for."

He gave her a long-suffering sigh. Such a drama king.

"How long are you going to be gone?"

Too long. Carrie already missed him.

"Four days. It didn't make much sense to fly twelve hours to attend a party and then turn around and fly out hours later so I'm going to visit with my family and a few friends before I return. Think you can hold out?"

*I'm not sure I can. Max-withdrawal.*

"If I must, I suppose I can."

"Concentrate on the play and I'll be home before you know it."

Oops. What the hell did she just say? Home? Was London home? Was *Max's house* home? Was he over-thinking this like she was? Damn, she needed a dose of caffeine and a slap to the face.

"I know I'm complaining but I do want you to enjoy yourself, love."

A man with a huge suitcase smacked the side of his bag into her knee as he walked by, luckily the left this time and not the right. Stifling a groan, she rubbed at the spot that would surely turn into a bruise as she saw her flight number flash on the overhead screen.

*Luggage on conveyer belt B.*

"You're such the gentleman. Don't worry, I will. It will be good to see everyone but I have to admit I'm getting used to London. It's going to be so bright here with all the sunshine." The conveyor belt began to move, spitting out suitcase after suitcase. "I think my bag is here so I better let you go. Go back to sleep."

Standing, she hurried over to wait with everyone else on her flight. Tiny as she was, she was able to slip through the crowd and make her way to the front.

"Call me later."

No way was she calling him at the theatre. "No, you call me when you have a minute. I don't want to interrupt rehearsals and everything so I won't be reaching out to you. Now...seriously...go back to sleep. You need the rest."

"I'll call you then. What time would be good?"

Now he was simply stalling.

"Just call me. I'll talk to you later."

"Bye, love."

If he said any more she didn't hear it, ending the call with a press of a button. She could have chatted with him all damn day but he needed to get some rest or he'd be out of sorts for the performance tonight.

Grabbing her luggage from the belt, she was aware she had a goofy smile on her face. Her heart was beating fast, and just like in the movies, she wanted to break into song, singing at the top of her lungs. Maybe even do a dance step or two. She just couldn't help it.

Max missed her.

———

Greg's party was a huge success and he was shocked but pleased to see her standing in his living room. Carrie didn't know about half of the people there but they were all friendly. Her picture had been plastered on a bunch of tabloids with images from Max's opening night and a few of the guests recognized her. Cornered by the buffet, she patiently answered their questions until a few of them became way more personal than she was comfortable with.

She was happy to tell people that Max was smart and sweet. That he liked chocolate ice cream more than vanilla or that he listened to Vivaldi when he was trying to concentrate. But the more personal questions such as did they live together or was he a good lover or were they getting married? Nope.

And yes, someone at the party had the gall to ask her those questions. One woman in particular looked like she wanted to smack Carrie across the face, her lips twisted with dislike. Carrie could have told the female that the chances of ever meeting Maxwell Hayes, getting asked on a date, falling in love, and getting married were fairly remote but she didn't bother. If the woman was delusional enough to think that all that stood between her and Max was Carrie, then there wasn't much to be done about her grip on reality.

"I still can't believe you're here, Sis, and that you flew all this way just for me."

Greg was pouring her another glass of wine which she desperately needed after her interaction with that woman and her nosy questions.

"It's your big night so of course I'm here." She placed her hand on his arm and gave it a squeeze as her throat clogged with emotion. "Mom and Dad would have been so proud of you."

"And you. You're all over the papers. I wish Jeannie and I could come to London and see your man's play. The reviews are amazing."

*My man. I hope so.*

Shrugging, Carrie sipped her wine. "I'm not sure dating a movie star and getting my picture in a supermarket rag is something to strive for but I think I see your point. I hope they'd be proud of all that I've achieved."

Greg nodded. "They would be. You've worked hard to get where you are, and might I say that I'm glad you broke up with that waste of skin Mark. He was never good enough for you. Not even close. Now this Maxwell Hayes guy, he's more your type. The kind that has goals and works toward them. Makes something of themselves."

"He did do me a favor by cheating on me. I'd been dating him so long that I forgot how relationships were supposed to be."

Greg rubbed the back of his neck, looking uncomfortable. "So...this Max Hayes? He's good to you? I don't need to catch the next flight and beat his ass or anything?"

Every time someone mentioned his name she smiled.

"He's a good man."

Greg gazed at her for a long moment. "I can tell he is just by your expression when you talk about him. You're in love."

There was no denying it. She had all the symptoms and frankly she was happy about it. She'd fallen in love with a

wonderful marvelous man who might even love her back.
He had all the signs too. Or at least some of them. Enough
to give her real hope.

"I am in love but it's early days yet. Let's not book a
church or anything."

"Fair enough," Greg laughed. "But when the day comes
don't run off to Vegas or anything. I want to be there,
okay?"

"I promise." The buzzing of her phone had her digging
in the pocket of her dress and checking the screen. "Crap,
this is Paige. I need to take this. She wouldn't call unless it
was important."

Paige would normally text if it was a routine message.
A call was something much bigger.

"Hey, what's going on?"

Carrie could hear Paige groaning through the phone.
Her boss was frustrated and not a happy camper.

"The studio wants a meeting in the morning regarding
the budget numbers. That's your territory."

Since being made part of the production team on the
Flynn movie, Carrie had taken over most of the number
and schedule crunching. "Can I dial in for it?"

"Normally I would say yes but this is Hollywood. They
like to schmooze and do the face to face thing. Nate thinks
you should be here in person. I don't suppose..."

The reason for Carrie's visit was the party and it was
almost over. These were adults with children and they
weren't going to dance and drink until the sun came up.
"Let me see if I can get a flight out of here. What time do
they want to meet?"

"Ten in the morning so with the time difference it gives

you some cushion. Can I tell you how grateful I am and how much I love you? I know this is a gigantic pain in the ass. As for a flight, Nate is holding up a sign that says we'll set up a charter for you. I can call you with details as soon as it's set up."

Already making a mental to-do list, Carrie put talking to her brother at the top of it. She wouldn't be staying a few days to visit with everyone after all.

"Don't worry about it," she assured a worried-sounding Paige. "The party was the most important thing and it's already winding down for the evening. This place will be cleared out by eleven, I'm betting. I was going to visit with a few friends but I can do that another time. This meeting is important and I'll be there."

"I'm still grateful as hell. I just want to thank you about a million times. How about I book us some spa treatments for after the meeting? My treat."

"Now that's the right way to thank me," Carrie giggled. "Call me when you have flight details. I'm going to tell my brother that I need to leave in a few hours."

Carrie ended the call and headed straight for Greg who was deep in conversation at the other side of the room. Plans were changed and she better get used to it. She was making a movie with Paige and Nate, becoming a *producer* of all things. She'd never even dreamed of a job like this but now that she had it, she wanted to be the best damn producer Hollywood had ever seen.

She'd make Greg...and Max...proud.

# CHAPTER
## Thirty-Seven

MAX WOULD HAVE BEEN happy to never see Alana again for the rest of his life but it was not to be. After the play, he and some of his castmates went for a pint down at the local pub and Alana strolled in with his ex-assistant Gemma. At first he'd tried to hide behind his friends, keeping his head down as much as possible. The two women sat down at a table on the opposite side of the room but apparently someone outed him because Alana was now crossing the pub with a very determined expression on her face.

That was never a good thing.

She sidled right up to the table and leaned over to speak to him, her breasts almost spilling out of the ridiculously low-cut blouse she was wearing. It was loud in the large room but she was close enough that she didn't have to yell to be heard. His friends had tactfully turned away and were speaking quietly amongst each other. No one liked Alana. She had a terrible reputation in the theatre community.

"Max, I didn't expect to see you here."

Bullshit. Alana wasn't the pub type but she liked to be where theatre people hung out. This was all about making a connection with Max's director and producer, probably hoping for a part in an upcoming production.

"I didn't expect to see you either," he said wearily, his gaze pointing at Gemma who still sat at the table. "Nor did I expect to see my former employee."

Alana smiled and laughed but it sounded too sharp to be from happiness, in contrast to Carrie's laugh which always seemed to come from her heart. "She's my assistant now. Does a good job too. You shouldn't have fired her."

Max was tired and didn't have the patience for this. Time to cut to the chase.

"What do you want, Alana?"

Running a finger over her collarbone, she gave him a look that once would have set his blood on fire. Now it simply left him cold. He felt nothing for this woman and he could only wonder how he ever had. It didn't say much for the man he was...or at least had been.

"Aren't you going to introduce me to your friends?"

*Fuck no.*

"No, you're done using me to get acting jobs. Now what else do you want?"

She ran her fingers up Max's arm but he wasn't having any of it, shaking her off.

"Don't be so mean. You didn't care that your little redhead used you to get a part in a movie. Why would it matter if you introduced me to a few of your theatre friends?"

Frozen in place, Max silently tried to count to ten but only made it to five.

"What are you talking about? Carrie didn't use me to get a part in a movie. She doesn't want to be an actress."

Carrie had said so and he believed her.

Tapping her chin, Alana shrugged carelessly. "Are you sure? Because Gemma was talking to Tyler Gaylord's stylist a few hours ago and she said that Carrie was in Los Angeles today at the same movie studio where Tyler Gaylord is making his next picture. There's a rumor that he's offered her a part in it, which isn't all that surprising. They were photographed together, weren't they?"

"Thanks to you," Max growled, his mind desperately trying to come up with a million reasons for Carrie to be in Los Angeles when she'd told him she was in Florida. "It probably wasn't even her."

Alana's smirked. "It was her and she was with Tyler, walking around and laughing like they were old friends. Why don't you ask her about it? I'm sure she'll tell you the truth."

Anger burned in Max's gut and bringing an end to this little conversation was imperative.

"Get out of here, Alana," he said through gritted teeth. His jaw ached from the tension but the pain gave him something to focus on instead of the bombshell she'd dropped. "You're on thin ice here. I don't think you want these people to know what I truly think of you."

She should have been afraid but Alana had absolutely no sense of self-preservation. Instead of leaving she learned down farther and bit his earlobe, giggling the entire time.

"Take care, lover. I'll be around."

With that she turned on her heel and sauntered away, her hips swaying back and forth, capturing the interest of more than a few males in the room.

They were welcome to her. God help them.

Max just sat there, his thoughts in turmoil as he contemplated what Alana had said. It couldn't be true. Not his Carrie. She was different, he was sure of that. She cared about him.

Him.

Not his career or what she could get from it.

Him.

She was not in Hollywood. She was in Florida visiting her family and friends. She'd attended her brother's party and he'd talked to her right before that but not since. He'd been busy with the play and the promotional interviews with the press. She'd sent him a vague text about her plans changing a bit but he hadn't thought much about it.

It was certainly possible that she was in Los Angeles. Airplanes and all. But not probable. Not bothering to say anything to his colleagues, he stomped outside where it was quieter and pulled out his phone, dialing Carrie.

Max could clear this all up with one phone call and then go back to his evening.

She was in Florida with her family. Not at the movie studio with Tyler.

Carrie picked up on the third ring.

"Hamlet, how was the play tonight?"

Just hearing her voice had his heart beating faster. He

missed her more than he'd ever thought possible. The house was an empty shell when she was gone.

"It was good. Very good. Just out for a pint with some of the boys."

"And you thought of me. How sweet."

Her giggle was like music to his ears. He wanted to make her laugh every day for the rest of their lives.

"I am sweet, aren't I? Love, I know this is going to sound like a strange question but just humor me. You're in Florida, right? You aren't in Los Angeles."

A small silence that had Max holding his breath before she rushed in to answer.

"How did you know? Did Tyler or Nate tell you?"

Max's heart fell straight down to his feet as acid rose in his throat.

No. No, not his Carrie.

"Where are you exactly?"

There was a heavy sigh on the other end of the phone. "I'm in Los Angeles on business. I had a meeting with the movie studio. Listen, I have some fantastic news–"

Her admission took his breath away. He'd never believed it could be true but she'd said it. He was well aware of what her news was and he was disgusted.

"Was Tyler there?" he asked, not letting her finish.

"Yes, he was here. Why?"

He didn't answer. There wasn't much left to say. "Listen, I need to get back to my friends. I'll see you when you get back."

Max pressed the end button, not waiting to hear her reply. He couldn't stand to even hear her voice. Not anymore.

Stumbling and falling back against the stone wall, he sucked air into his lungs, concentrating as he inhaled and exhaled. It was the only thing he knew to do when everything inside of him wanted to scream and rage, pound his fists against the building until they were battered and bloody. He wanted to crawl away whimpering like a puppy as he licked his wounds. He wanted to hide from the cruel world that had led him to this moment.

So this was what a broken heart felt like.

It was funny what happened to a human being when all hope was gone. At first all he'd felt was pain and then he went numb. Completely dead inside.

# CHAPTER
## Thirty-Eight

TIRED BUT HAPPY TO be back in London after the whirlwind that was Los Angeles, Carrie dumped her luggage at Paige and Nate's home and headed straight for Max's place. It was only midday and he should be up but not yet at the theatre. She couldn't wait to share with him all the exciting news about the Flynn movie. Contracts had been signed, I's dotted and T's crossed. The budget and schedule she'd put together had been approved and it was official now. She was one of the producers on the film along with Paige and Nate. Now she could shout it from the rooftops.

Or at least call her family in Florida and tell them the good news. This was a challenge she was going to relish.

First she wanted to tell Max. He of all people knew what a big deal this was, expanding her resume and becoming a continuing part of the business that she and Paige had built over the years.

She knocked on the door and heard some shuffling

behind it before it swung open. Max stood in the doorway wearing jeans and a white button down shirt. He hadn't shaved yet this morning and his chin was covered in stubble that her fingers itched to caress. He looked better than any man had a right to and her heart lurched in her chest. She was in love with this man. So much.

His blue eyes were watching her intently, his focus laser-like. She'd texted him right before she'd boarded the plane but he was acting as if he hadn't quite believed she was coming back. On the long flight back to London she'd given herself quite the pep talk about showing Max her feelings. She couldn't expect him to show his love for her if she wasn't willing to walk out onto a limb and show him the depth of her regard.

Jumping into his arms, she looped her hands around his neck and pressed her lips to his, putting as much adoration into it as she possible could. She pulled back and cupped his cheeks, grinning like an idiot. She was simply so happy to see him.

"I missed you," she said huskily. "Are you going to let me inside or do you want to make love right here where the paps can see us?"

He stood there, his body stiff and unyielding. He hadn't kissed her back and his expression had barely changed. He was like a robot, no emotions or tenderness whatsoever. Stepping back, he moved out of her embrace, his own arms still at his side.

"Yes, of course, come in."

Cold. His house was chilly and not just because of the temperature. Goosebumps rose on her arms and she rubbed at them to ward away the shivers that threatened to derail any sensible thought. He was totally different than when she'd left. It was as if he'd flipped a switch and the pompous, stiff prick she'd first met had taken over and the loving, gentle man she'd known had disappeared.

"Is everything okay?" she asked in a shaky voice. This simply couldn't be happening. Not after all they'd shared together. "Has something happened?"

Max had circled around the couch and was standing by the credenza in the corner.

"Not that I know of. Is there anything I should be concerned about?"

"Not that I know of..." Maybe she could loosen him up with her news. "Listen, I have kind of a big announcement and I want you to be the first to know. I'm so excited I can barely stand it."

His smile was ice cold, not reaching his eyes that were currently grayish-silver. "Actually I know your news. I suppose congratulations are in order."

He supposed? Was there some question there?

Had he talked to Nate and Paige already? She hadn't asked them to let her tell him but they were so busy in LA she thought they wouldn't bother and let her.

"You've already heard? Wow, news travels fast in Hollywood. So...what do you think, Hamlet? Do you think I can do it?"

It was silly to want his approval this badly. She was a professional woman who had taken on big challenges but this one was something very different.

He seemed to consider her question. "Well...I don't actually know."

She recoiled from his terse, bald answer. Where was the

show of support when she needed it? He was back to that rude asshole and had deliberately said that to hurt her.

"I know you can't be sure," Carrie said, wanting to give him a second chance. "But you know my skill set. I have to admit I'm so damn nervous I'm almost shaking. If I fail this will be so incredibly public."

His expression appeared to like that idea. "I suppose it would be quite humiliating."

Her eyes went wide at his callous statement. The bastard could be so nasty when he wanted to be.

So they were back to this. She hadn't even been gone a full week.

He held a stack of papers in his hand as he sat down on the sofa. "I've given this a great deal of thought since I heard about your...new career opportunity...and I've decided that I'm going to hold you to the contract. Every day of it. I'm sure you'd like to be free to begin your adventures early but I'm afraid that won't suit my plans at all. In case you've lost your copy, I've taken the liberty of printing you a new one along with a list of social engagements that I expect you to attend at my side." He looked up from the contracts and straight into her eyes. At one time they'd looked at her with such tenderness but now he had almost...loathing? "This is business, after all, and I expect people to live up to their commitments."

Business. Yes, it was business. Carrie never should have forgotten that fact.

His hateful demeanor almost took her breath away as her guts churned in her abdomen. She had to swallow down the bile that had risen in her throat, not wanting him to see the wounds he had inflicted on her person. They might not have been real and physical but it didn't make them any less painful. Even now she could feel the tears burn in the back of her eyes and she had to steel herself against letting them slide down her cheeks.

She wouldn't give the asshole the satisfaction. He was enjoying this.

"Just business," she murmured, carefully not saying much. If she did she might later regret it. Anger and fury weren't going to change anything. Not with Max. He was impervious to her emotions.

He'd proved it time and again.

"I guess you aren't a big fan of my new job," she finally said, meeting his gaze with her own. She wouldn't be cowed by him. Not now and not ever. "I suppose you think this is a mistake and that I'm out of my league."

There was a part of her that certainly thought that way. She was no Hollywood heavyweight who knew how the games were played. She was a rookie and as such had been hoping for his support and perhaps some advice.

She would get neither.

Max held out the stack of papers. "The biggest mistake I've ever made."

He wasn't talking about her new job. He was talking about her.

Accepting the contracts, she perused the schedule on top. There was nothing there that she didn't already know about. There was nothing left to say.

Lifting her chin, she pretended that he hadn't just shattered her heart into a million little pieces. That she didn't want to crawl away in agony, screaming his name at the top of her lungs. She was no actress but she didn't think she was doing too badly.

"Do you mind if I go upstairs and get the few things that I have? Some toiletries and a few clothing items?"

Max stepped back out of her path to the stairs but didn't say yes or no. Fine. The asshole was done talking and frankly she was finished listening. He wasn't going to say anything she wanted to hear.

With as much dignity as she could muster under the circumstances she marched upstairs and gathered her things into a plastic bag and returned to the living room, her items in hand. Shoving them into her oversized purse, she glanced at the crutches leaning on the wall by the door. The tender caring man that had carried her around rather than let her use them was nowhere in sight. Long gone and never to be seen again.

"I guess I'll see you on the..." She checked the paper again. "The twenty-fifth. Text me if you need anything before that."

She turned but not fast enough because his answer smacked her right on the ass he wanted out of his house.

"I won't need anything from you."

As she walked out of the house and down the walk, the tears she'd been trying to quell wouldn't be denied any longer. They ran down her cheeks and blurred her vision.

He never had needed anything from her. She'd only fooled herself into thinking he did.

# CHAPTER
## Thirty~Nine

IT WAS BUSINESS. That was the mantra that Max repeated to himself over and over for the next three weeks. Because he was in the middle of a play, he wasn't expected to make many social appearances but there had been a few.

As expected and required by contract, Carrie had appeared at his side looking absolutely stunning. What she did with the rest of her time, he had no idea. He didn't speak to her in between and didn't see her either. For her part, she made no effort to contact him.

He missed her. The way she could make him smile and laugh when he wasn't in a good mood. The funny way she worked at her laptop, making faces at the screen and completely unaware she was doing it. He particularly missed her at night. Yes, he missed the sex but it was more than that. The cuddling and tenderness she's brought into his life was something he'd found he wanted. Now that he'd lost it that is.

He had seen her one day coming out of their favorite coffee shop with a paper cup in one hand and a pastry in the other. He'd watched her walk down the street, not sure where she was going because it was the wrong way for Nate and Paige's place. Guiltily, he'd turned and gone in the opposite direction, not wanting to feel like a creepy stalker getting a glimpse of the object of his affections.

Here he was a few days later seeing her again. Tonight was a charity function and Max couldn't even remember what the party was trying to raise funds for. Not that it mattered much. He'd figure it out when they arrived. He was decked out in his usual tuxedo, his hair freshly trimmed and his shoes shined. Carrie was dressed in a strapless gold gown that showed off her incredible curves. The hairdresser had coiled Carrie's long red hair on top of her head, leaving her neck and shoulders bare. And absolutely kissable.

They'd barely touched since she'd come back from Los Angeles.

He'd taken her hand as they'd walk down the red carpet but as soon as they were away from the cameras she'd moved away, putting as much distance as possible between the two of them. She'd clearly received his message that day she'd come back. He should be happy that she wasn't hanging on, trying for more. She'd done as he asked, and perhaps for the first time in their short acquaintance she hadn't questioned him to death.

Then why was he so deeply and unutterably miserable?

The only thing that kept from drinking his days away was work. When he wasn't at the theatre he spent his time lying in bed staring at the ceiling - wishing she were with him - or sitting on the couch staring at the paps across the street and remembering what she'd said about the difference between them. In fact, every single word she'd ever spoken to him had come rushing back, making it harder and harder to sleep. She wouldn't give him a moment's peace. He constantly felt as if he could jump out of his own skin. He was restless, moody, and unpredictable. No one wanted to be in his vicinity.

The limo pulled up to the curb and he could already hear the crowd of fans and see the flashing bulbs through the tinted windows. He was an actor, goddammit, and he could bloody well act happy when the situation called for it. This wasn't the first time he'd had his heart stomped on but for some reason he wasn't bouncing back as he had from Alana.

It was almost as if Carrie was in a league of her own. That she was...*different* than all the others. The one thing he'd wanted to believe was that she was exactly the same as Alana but hid it better. Then she'd be a great actress, though, and he wasn't ready for that either.

"Are you ready?"

It was the first words he'd spoken to her the entire journey there. She barely turned her head but nodded slightly, her gaze averted away. Her tiny frame was stiff, her back ramrod straight as she sat on the sumptuous leather seats waiting for their turn in the car line. In a moment the door was going to fly open and they'd be on display for only the second time since she'd come back to London. Since he'd learned the truth.

"Just follow my lead."

It was the same thing he'd said every time they'd done

this and she'd never failed to do just that, content to sit in the background while he chatted with interviewers and fans. Would this time be different? She had her own career to think about now. There was nothing in their contract that said she couldn't promote herself.

The car door opened and the cool damp air immediately chilled his overly warm skin and dried the sweat that had pooled on the back of his neck. The usual surge of adrenaline that hyped him up when he heard the roar of the crowd was suspiciously absent tonight and he keenly missed it. He hadn't realized how much he'd needed it until he was standing outside the limo holding his hand out to Carrie and wondering just how his life had come to this. As she demurely climbed out, careful not to flash too much leg or cleavage for the paps, she turned up her face and looked at him for the first time that evening.

He could see it in her eyes.

Whatever tender emotion that had dwelled there previously was long gone and in its place was pure disdain. He wasn't even worth her hatred.

Carrie, like every appearance previously, had drifted back away from the crowds and the cameras, letting him soak up the attention alone. Working the red carpet by rote, he barely listened to the questions from reporters, simply repeating the answers he always gave.

*It's a terrific cause and I'm happy to support it.*

*The play is going great and I'm gratified by the reviews and the public's response.*

*I really don't know if or when another Thunder movie will be made.*

*I'm always looking for new and different roles.*

*I'm thrilled to be working in London where I get to sleep in my own bed every night.*

He was almost done and inside the venue when he was tripped up. A pretty reporter from a national entertainment network had finished quizzing him about a new *Thunder* movie and instead of asking another inane question he'd been asked a million times before she went off script. She'd forced him to think about his answer and then scramble to make something up.

The young reporter held the microphone in his face and there was no escape. "You and your girlfriend Carrie Johnson look absolutely adorable together. And I think I speak for the world when I say that we all want to know how you balance having two busy careers and still manage to make time for romance. How do you both make a decision about what projects you'll take? Does your acting and traveling make it difficult for her to make commitments to her own career?"

*What the fuck kind of question was that? This woman spoke for the entire fucking world?*

"You'll need to ask Carrie that question."

Then Max turned his back and strode away, fuming at the reporter. It was a stupid question and he had no idea how to answer it. What did it even mean? They balanced their relationship and careers by...

Fuck it, he didn't have an answer. It had never come up. She'd never put him in the position of having to make those kinds of decisions. His publicist was going to have his head on a platter for the reply that he'd given. What had he been thinking? *Ask Carrie?* She'd say that Max was a complete bastard, although that was tame compared to what Alana had told reporters.

Speaking of Carrie? Where the hell was she?

Realizing he must have walked right past her and into the building, he backtracked slightly only to see her entering with his publicist Garrett at her side, laughing at something she'd said. Jealousy speared Max right in the gut and he didn't stop to think about the consequences of his actions. He marched right over there and insinuated himself between Carrie and Garrett, giving his publicist a glare for good measure.

"I was looking for you."

The smile she'd given Garrett had disappeared, replaced by a sedate expression that kept all of her emotions behind a wall. "And here I am. You walked right by us."

Smoothing his lapels, he heard the orchestra playing a familiar song. If they danced they didn't have to speak to one another. "We need to be seen together. We'll dance."

He didn't make it a request because it wasn't one. Garrett's brows raised but he didn't intervene, which was good as Max was in the mood to fire someone. It was too bad he hadn't rehired Gemma.

Her arm in his, he led her to the middle of the crowded dance floor. He'd meant to keep her at a decent distance but the crush of couples kept pushing their bodies closer together. His thighs brushed her hips every time they moved and he was beginning to think this had been an extremely bad idea. His palms began to sweat and his heart raced at a much faster rate than the song. Concentrating so he didn't stumble, he kept his head down, not daring to look her in the eye and see the scorn she held there.

And who the fuck did she think she was, being disdainful of him? She was the one that had used him. She was the one that had snagged a part because she'd met Tyler Gaylord. Max hadn't done anything wrong. He had the moral high ground here so her little snit was completely uncalled for. She should be thanking him. He could have thrown her to the wolves and ruined her reputation.

Nate would murder Max though. For some reason, his friend was rather protective of Carrie. It turned out she could take care of herself quite well.

For the dozenth time, another couple bumped into Max causing him to press against Carrie's lush body. Her breasts strained against the material of her dress, the creamy skin calling to him. It might have been his imagination but he would have sworn that he saw a small glimpse of a pink nipple as well. Perhaps.

*Kiss. Worship. Devour. Claim.*

If he stayed here on the dance floor with her his baser instincts were going to take complete control of his body. His brain scrambled to speak logically and coolly but his libido didn't give a fuck about rationality. It had been weeks since he'd had Carrie under him, over him, beside him. Like a fever in his blood, he couldn't forget the way she'd felt and tasted. Her scent wrapped around him, driving him slowly out of his mind and directly to one inevitable conclusion.

Thinking was overrated. He was running on pure male

instinct now, letting the more primitive voice inside of him make all the decisions.

"We need to find someplace quiet to talk."

Wrapping his hand around her arm, he tugged Carrie off of the dance floor toward...what? He'd know it when he saw it. He finally found what he sought...a doorway that led to an empty broom closet.

The room was lit by moonlight through a window, casting a shadow over Carrie's face so he couldn't make out her expression. If she was angry, she hadn't acted like it.

"What do you want, Max? What do you hope to solve with this farce? We should go back to the party. I have nothing left to say."

His chest rose and fell with his tortured breathing. There was a part of him that wanted to forgive her and simply sweep her into his arms, but that other part of him was still smarting from her betrayal.

"I..."

Max didn't know what to say or do. Bringing her in here hadn't been the brightest move but then he'd been doing boneheaded shit since the day he'd found out about her role in Tyler's movie.

"You what?" she asked him, shoving against his chest when he would have moved closer. To explain only but she was in no mood to hear his excuses. "I asked you a goddamn question, Max. What are you doing? Why did we leave the party?"

Had there ever been such excruciating pain as the one in his heart at this moment? Carrie stood before him, beautiful, smart, funny, and talented. She was everything he'd wanted and more. He'd loved her, for Christ's sake.

No, he still loved her. He wasn't over her yet. Physically and emotionally he was a wreck and it had begun to affect his entire life. Even his coworkers on the play had begun to notice his distraction.

But it was the constant physical pain that he couldn't take much more of. How much could a human withstand? If he couldn't stop it, he needed something to distract him from it. A different pain. That's what he needed. A small hurt to take away from the massive jagged gash in his heart. Max knew just how to get it too. He knew how to make her react. If he pushed her hard enough she just might strike out at him and he *needed* to feel her wrath.

"Did you fuck him? Did you fuck Tyler?"

A strangled gasp escaped from her lips and then her arm swung in the air. He watched it, fascinated as it came nearer, almost in slow motion, but he welcomed its destination. When her hand connected with his cheek, his head snapped back and his flesh burned. Harder than he'd thought her capable of but that was good. The more his face hurt the less he thought about his other wound. The mortal one.

Without another word or look, Carrie whirled around and strode out of the closet, leaving him behind without a backward glance.

Alone. Again.

# CHAPTER
## *Forty*

HUNKERING DOWN INTO HER SEAT, Carrie silently looked out the airplane window as the lights of London faded into the distance. She'd ran out of the charity event and straight home, throwing some clothes into a suitcase so she could catch the next flight out of London. She didn't much care where it went. As much as she'd learned to love this city, she couldn't be in it right now. Every place she went, every corner she turned would remind her of Max.

How he'd ripped out her heart and then stomped on it.

However, his behavior tonight had been bizarre even for him. Max was a pompous asshole. That was a given. A judgmental bastard? Yep, that too. Spoiled and arrogant? He had his moments. But this evening at the party he'd shown a side of himself that she'd never seen before. Cruel. Callous. Insensitive. Primitive, even. His slick veneer of civilization had been stripped away and all that had been left was fury. The hopelessly polite Brit who drank tea had been taken over by an alter ego who didn't care about the social niceties.

It was almost as if he'd *wanted* her to slap the shit out of him. Something, by the way, she'd been more than happy to do. Carrie could only hope it knocked some sense into that hard head of his. After a little more than three months in his company she could understand why he was single.

"Can I get you anything to drink?" the smiling flight attendant asked. "Pretzels?"

"Soda. Anything with caffeine. And make that a yes on the pretzels."

She was going to need it to stay awake. The first plane she could get out of Heathrow had been to Rome. From there Carrie had a connecting flight to New York and then a final leg to Los Angeles. She'd be traveling the better part of the next twenty-four hours but it was worth it. She was out of London.

She'd sent a text to Paige from Heathrow that she was on her way and would explain when she got there, not mentioning any reasons. She didn't want to get into it on the phone. This was a face to face conversation that required tequila. Lots of it. Paige sent one text in reply.

*Max is going to wish he was never born.*

Ah, friendship. It was kind of funny that Paige simply assumed it was Max that had driven Carrie out of England.

She had learned something tonight, though. The reason Max had turned angry and cold was that he thought she'd slept with Tyler. Why he thought that was a mystery. Carrie knew Tyler would never tell him a tall tale like that. He had enough women begging for his attention that he didn't need to brag about females that weren't.

Max should have just talked to her about it. Like adults do. But then she remembered Max's parents and realized he didn't have much of an example there. They weren't acting much like mature human beings so it wasn't a shock that he had no idea what to do. They'd raised him to be a famous actor. Teaching him to be a good relationship partner? They'd dropped the ball on that one.

He might love her. But he didn't trust her. Without that, the love didn't matter much.

Carrie couldn't try and make a relationship with a man work if he constantly thought she was out messing around. Alana had hurt him deeply but she was not Alana. Carrie wasn't willing to take her predecessor's punishments when she'd done nothing to deserve them. If Max didn't get his head out of his ass he was going to die alone.

She'd be hard pressed to feel sorry for him.

———

The pounding on the front door woke Max out of a dead sleep. After Carrie had left the party last night he had gone on a drinking binge that would have made a college student wince. He was paying for that act of stupidity now. His skull felt like there was an ax splitting it in two, his mouth was as dry as cottonwool, and his stomach was tumbling and twisting. One look in the mirror as he stumbled to the door told the whole story.

What wasn't pasty gray on Max was puke green.

"Just a fucking minute," he mumbled as his hand

wrapped around the doorknob. "Stop the bloody hammering."

His publicist Garrett stood in the doorway holding a giant coffee and a stack of newspapers. Max only had interest in one of those items so he grabbed the coffee and turned around, assuming Garrett would follow him into the house.

"You needn't look so chipper this morning, mate," Max said as he collapsed into a chair wearing nothing but his tuxedo pants from last night. Apparently he hadn't had the manual dexterity to unbutton his trousers.

Garrett dropped the stack of papers next to Max on the couch and then took a seat opposite. He had that look on his face...the one Max hated. Like a disappointed father. Garrett needed to remember who worked for whom. Max was the client, not the employee.

"Are you still drunk or have you finally sobered up?" Garrett's voice seemed overly loud in the quiet room. "I waited until later in the day before I came over hoping you might have slept it off."

The coffee was rich, dark, and scaldingly hot. Just the way Max liked it.

"If I were still drunk I wouldn't feel this awful, so I think it's safe to say I'm sober. Now what do you want on this fine Sunday morning?"

"It's afternoon."

"Fine. Afternoon. What do you want?"

Garrett stood and walked over to the front window, peering out. Were the paps still there? Those vultures were waiting for him to do something newsworthy. From Garrett's presence here, Max had a bad feeling that he had finally done just that. Fleet Street must be cele-brating.

"I'm not even going to yell at you about the way you bungled that question from the reporter about your careers. That's the least of your damn worries." Garrett's lips flattened into a straight line. "You and Carrie had a fight."

Hungover, Max didn't have the mental wherewithal to lie.

"We did. So?"

Max tried to push away the image of Carrie's tearstained face as she'd left him at the party.

"The contract wasn't supposed to end for another two weeks but it looks like things are over. Was it supposed to be so public? Is that what you and Carrie intended? Because if so, you really need to run this stuff by me first. The press is all over this and you are not coming out well, Max."

Gingerly, as if it might bite, Max lifted the top news-paper from the stack. Photos and lurid headlines dripped from the pages. He hadn't meant for this to happen but it looked like he'd dragged them both through the mud. Pawing through the papers, every picture was more damning than the last. Only an idiot wouldn't be able to see the tension and hostility between the two of them from the time they'd exited the limo all the way down the red carpet. One lucky pap had captured Carrie's face as she was leaving the venue, looking heartbroken and miserable, tears streaming down her face.

Max should have felt proud of himself but he didn't

have the energy. The photo caption called him a bastard, a title he couldn't argue.

"It wasn't planned."

Garrett's eyes widened. "Not planned? So you're telling me that you and Carrie had a real breakup last night? As in...the romance was real and now it's over? When did that happen?"

"Does it matter? It's over." He couldn't stop himself from asking, his mind already thinking about the next time he'd see her. If ever. "Have you talked to her about the tabloids?"

"She's not answering her phone. I left her a couple of voicemails but I didn't hear anything back so I stopped by Nate and Paige's place but there's no one there either. Do you know where she is?"

His sluggish brain was beginning to work. "No one there? That's strange."

"My next step is to call Paige and Nate and see if they know where she is. I can't let her walk into this paparazzi mess without preparing her. The papers smell blood, my friend, and they aren't going to give up easily. After the way Carrie looked when she left the party last night, you're being cast as the villain in this one."

Remembering last night, Max took another gulp of hot coffee. "I am the villain."

Garrett shook his head, his gaze taking in Max's disheveled appearance. "I'm not sure which of the two of you is more stupid. You or Nate? Both of you don't have any common sense when it comes to women which is ironic considering the way they chase you. Carrie is an amazing person and I doubt you could do better."

"Thank you for those kind and supportive words." Max put as much sarcasm into his tone as possible. "Now what do we do? Lie low? Call a press conference? Pretend last night never happened?"

Snorting, Garrett settled back into a chair. "Make believe isn't an option after last night. These photos tell a bleak story, one that we need to spin. I'll put out a press release that the two of you are reluctantly and regretfully parting ways. The usual stuff. It's a painful and emotional time but you hope the press can give you the privacy you both need to heal and move on. You'll always respect and care for one another and you're sad that it didn't work out. Then you do need to lie low. Don't date anyone else for awhile. Be boring."

Sad was a weak word for what Max was feeling. As for dating another woman?

There were no other women in the world.

"I cannot believe that I pay you for this."

"And quite well too," Garrett grinned, slapping his knee in what appeared to be glee. "A huge part of public relations is common sense. You know...the stuff you didn't use any of last night. Now I come in and clean up after you. It's that simple."

Everything was complicated.

"I do have to ask you one question before I run off and start giving statements to the press. Is there any chance of a reconciliation? Because if there is, that changes everything."

Max had literally no idea what he wanted or hoped for. He missed her dreadfully, thought about her all the time, but he couldn't be with her if she wasn't going to be honest. He had to be able to trust her. He understood her ambition. If only she'd just told him what she wanted when they'd signed the contract.

An image of her furious expression, stubborn chin, and stormy eyes flashed in front of him and his fingers automatically brushed against his cheek where she'd slapped him.

And rightly so.

"There's no chance of a reconciliation. I'd wager, in fact, that Carrie might never speak to me again. At least not of her own free will."

Whistling and rolling his eyes, Garrett tapped a note into his phone. "You must have had one hell of a blowout last night. I know it's none of my business but what did you argue about?"

Max liked Garrett. The man was a PR genius and he'd helped get Max out of some sticky situations since marrying and divorcing Alana. He'd also helped Nate as well when the shit had really hit the fan. But there was a difference between a professional relationship and a private one. They had the former, not the latter.

"The usual," Max replied, the lie bitter on his tongue. "You know how it is in this business, Garrett. The girl gets too attached and starts to plan a future while I'm thinking we're just casual fun. I'm not looking to fall in love and make a huge commitment. Carrie is the marrying kind."

He'd be alone. Because while Max didn't trust Carrie to tell him the truth about the role there was one person he trusted even less. Himself.

# CHAPTER
## Forty-One

PAIGE WAS MORE upset than Carrie was. The author was pacing back and forth, her face red against her blonde hair, muttering about horrible medieval torture methods she'd learned about doing research for a book. If Max had had the bad luck to be in the same room with Paige right now Carrie had little doubt he'd be singing soprano.

"Next time I see him, I'm going to knee him right in the balls," Paige declared, her eyes narrowed and her lips pursed. She stopped and nudged Carrie, who had draped herself over the leather recliner in the impersonal LA condo. "Why aren't you mad? He broke your heart."

More than a few times in the last twenty-four hours, Carrie had asked herself that very question and each time the answer varied slightly. Mostly it was because she was too fucking exhausted to be angry. She'd been traveling round the clock since yesterday and she'd arrived at Paige's condo needing a shower, a decent meal, and twelve hours of solid sack time. So far she'd had two out of three.

"I'm not sure it's truly hit me yet," Carrie replied, her brow scrunched up as thoughts of the last time she'd seen Max raced through her head. "But even if it has, how do I benefit from being mad? It just prolongs the hurt and I don't want to hurt anymore."

"I want him to hurt," Paige said heatedly. "Just as much as he's hurt you."

Funny about that...

"I think he is hurting. That last night he appeared to be in great pain. You could see it in his eyes and the trembling of his hands. Even his voice didn't sound like his own. Of course he thought I was fucking around with Tyler Gaylord so that was probably it." Carrie sat up and tucked her legs under her. "Frankly I never thought I'd have enough power in Max's life to make him feel that way. I didn't walk away because he doesn't care about me, Paige. I walked away because he doesn't have a clue what to do about that. I think he was so scared he grabbed onto the first excuse to push me away even if it didn't make any sense."

Paige fell back into the couch cushions and huffed out a breath. "It's no excuse."

"No, it isn't. That's why I left. I think he would eventually figure it out but I can't be around while he stumbles in the dark, taking a baseball bat to everyone around him. It's not fair to me."

Paige's brows pulled down in a frown. "Why on earth would he think you were having an affair with Tyler?"

Another problem Carrie had turned over in her brain until it hurt. "I did run into Tyler at the movie studio after our meeting and we did go have coffee. Maybe a pap caught us?"

"It didn't make the papers," Paige reasoned. "If there was a photo you'd think we would have all seen it."

Nate strolled into the living room and plopped down next to his wife. "Unless the pap brought it to Garrett and offered to sell it for a price."

Carrie wasn't sure why a photographer would do that. "I'm not following."

Stretching out his incredibly long legs, Nate propped them on the coffee table. "Sometimes a pap can make more money offering an incriminating photo to the celebrity rather than selling it to a tabloid, depending on how dirty it is. I've got a call in to Garrett to find out. If Max never saw a picture of you and Tyler, why on earth is he accusing you of sleeping with him? That's just daft."

Nate was much calmer than Carrie had imagined. "Thank you for not flying off the handle, by the way. He's your best friend and I don't want to come between you two. This mess is mine and I'll deal with it."

Laughing heartily, Nate shook his head. "Darling, I am going to kill Max next time I see him. I've left several messages with him but he's - not surprisingly - avoiding my calls. I warned him and he didn't listen. He never listens."

There was one more thing that was worrying Carrie. "Technically by leaving early I'm in breach of contract. You don't think he'll sue me, do you? Or throw me under the bus in some way? If he thinks I cheated on him with Tyler would he give the story to the tabloids? Because that's all I need is to have my friends and family see something like that. The breakup photos were bad enough. I had to talk my brother out of catching a plane to London and beating the shit out of Max."

"He'll have to stand in line," Nate said, his jaw tightening. "As for suing you? He better fucking not if he wants to look at this side of the grass. Honestly, if there was a story about you and Tyler it would already be in the papers. That's what has me so confused. There's no evidence that you cheated."

Paige elbowed her husband. "Carrie thinks that Max was looking for a reason to end things."

Nate exhaled slowly, his expression pensive. "That's a real possibility. Max has, historically, had lousy taste in women so he doesn't trust his own judgment. He's skittish and jumpy when it comes to love. Then he finally gets a good one and he doubts himself. Thinks it can't be this smooth sailing so he looks for reasons to run."

Now that was hilarious. Nothing had ever been *smooth sailing* with Max.

Paige's gaze darted from Nate to Carrie. "So where does this leave Carrie? What should she do?"

Carrie already knew exactly what she was going to do. She'd made her decision before her flight had landed at LAX. It turned out she had learned from her broken engagement with Mark.

"Nothing. I'm going to do nothing about Max. I'm going to move on with my life and be happy. Life is too short to be miserable because of love and romance. If Max wants to apologize and work things out he knows my phone number, my email address, my Skype handle, my Twitter handle, and he fucking follows me on Instagram. I think he can get me a message in this electronic age. If he's forgotten all of those he can catch me at the coffee shop or the park. He can call you or Nate. He can literally sit outside the yoga studio I go to every Tuesday night and wait for me there. If he's really desperate he could take out an ad in the London *Times*. He has no shortage of ways to contact me, but I will say that so far he hasn't tried."

Carrie didn't expect him to either.

"That was definite." Paige slapped the cushion she was sitting on. "I'm proud of you."

"Don't be. I have a feeling I'm not done crying over the asshole. I'm just too tired to muster up any more tears. Catch up with me tomorrow."

And the next day, and the next. Max wasn't someone Carrie was going to get over easily. This was going to take some time.

# CHAPTER
## Forty~Two

ALL MAX DID for the next few weeks was work, drink, and sleep. It wasn't so much sleep as an altered consciousness brought on by too much alcohol but it was mildly regenerative. Enough that he was able to function on some level without curling up in a corner and hiding from the world.

Ironically his pain from Carrie's betrayal and subsequent departure only served to make his performance in the play deeper and more complex. Every night he received a standing ovation, and later he'd leave the theatre and face a throng of gushing fans who wanted him to sign their programs and get a picture. He did it all with a fake smile as if on autopilot. This was his secret and shame.

So when his mother and father wanted to meet him after a performance and have dinner he desperately tried to come up with a viable pretext. He already had plans with an unopened bottle of whiskey. Max loved his parents very much but comforting him was not their forte. Their own relationship had always been volatile and Max had grown up with slamming doors and shouting matches, then all would return to normal for their friends and family. The cracks in the veneer were never to be seen. In the last several years, Karen and Tim seemed to mellow in their marriage and there wasn't much fussing and fighting. Strangely, the less the couple worked in the movie business, the less they argued. Maybe now that they were semi-retired there was simply less to get mad about. Or maybe they now weren't competing with each other to see who could become more famous.

But his mother wasn't having any of his lame excuses, which was how he ended up sitting across from them in his old friend Albert's restaurant near the South Bank, eating pasta and checking his watch every five minutes.

Karen dove into her rosemary chicken. "Your performance is a triumph, dear. We're so proud of you. You're a shoo-in for awards season."

He'd been hearing that quite a lot lately when people came close enough that he could speak to them. The wise ones gave him a wide berth.

"Thank you but who knows about the nominations. There are many wonderful performances this year."

"None as good as yours, son," Tim said with a shake of his fork. "This is your year."

This most assuredly was not Max's year. If it were, he wouldn't have been divorced and heartbroken all within months of each other. The work, the acting, wasn't the panacea it had been in the past. When this play was over he might just take off several months or even a year providing he could get out of the contracts he'd already committed to. Alcoholism should scare off the movie studios. He was bound to be a full-blown drunk by the end of the play's run.

"We'll see," Max replied, not wanting to get into an argument with his parents. A headache was beginning to make itself known right behind his eyes, pounding away with tiny hammers.

Albert sidled up to the table and slapped Max on the back. "How's everything tasting here? Is my staff treating you well?"

"Delicious as always," Max praised. "My dinner is perfect."

Karen frowned and lifted up her water goblet. "That waiter hasn't been by to refill my glass in forever. Can you find him? He seems to have disappeared."

Snapping his teeth together, Max reined in a nasty response to his mother. Knowing Albert, he wouldn't allow Max to pay for the meal.

"He was just here, Mother. You said you didn't want any water."

Max kept his tone as cool as possible but Karen wasn't having any of it.

"That was ages ago, and I haven't seen him since."

*One. Two. Three. Oh hell.*

"He's right there." Max pointed to the young waiter a few tables away. "He's been by several times."

Tim squinted at the server and shook his head. "That's not him. That's someone else."

"It is our waiter," Max said, his jaw aching and tight.

Albert grinned and made a wave with his hand. "No

problem, Mrs. Hayes. I'll take care of it." He noticed the empty chair beside Max. "Where's your pretty girl tonight, my friend? She looked like she was a keeper."

Just the mention of Carrie even without hearing her name felt like a knife in the heart. Obviously Albert didn't read the tabloids. "I'm afraid she and I..."

Few people had had the bravery to ask Max that question. He didn't yet have an answer. He might say that he'd been taken in or he might say that he'd been idiot to let her go. Either or both might be correct.

Nodding his head, Albert signaled to the waiter. "Sorry to hear about that. Here's your water, Mrs. Hayes. Let me know if there's anything else we can do."

Albert drifted over to another table and the server came to refill Karen's glass. Just the mention of Carrie's name was enough to set his parents on edge.

"I think you're well rid of that girl," Max's mother sniffed. "She knew nothing about acting or the business. What you need is someone who understands your creative side. Someone who can be supportive of your career."

Max knew exactly what his mother was talking about. She'd said it before in more vague terms but she wasn't fooling anyone.

"What you mean is that I should be with a woman who can help my career."

Shifting in his chair, Tim coughed. "That's not what we're saying, son. What I think your mother means is that someone outside of the business cannot possibly understand the time and dedication this career takes."

Quirking a brow in question, Max took a hefty gulp of his wine. "Is that what you meant, Mum? That everyone outside of the industry is too stupid to learn about the movie business and too selfish to allow me to be an actor?"

"No," his mother exclaimed. "Not at all. We just...want to see you with someone that is your equal. Not a glorified assistant. If they can help your career, all the better. There's nothing wrong with using one's connections to get roles. If your father and I hadn't done that you would have grown up in a one-room cold water flat."

Nothing wrong with it. Perhaps his parents were right. Carrie had only been using the time-honored Hollywood tradition of "who you knew". It didn't make her a horrible person. In fact, some might argue it made her smart.

"First of all," he began, thoroughly fed up with their prattle about creatives and everyone else. He'd heard if before and he was tired of it. "Carrie has a Masters in Business Administration from a prestigious American university. She heads up Paige's entire business and directs a staff. Her title is Chief Operating Officer, not Chief Gopher. She is a brilliant and savvy businesswoman, something she should be incredibly proud of. As for understanding my career, that was never an issue between us. She was supportive and always eager to learn about the business. Carrie Johnson is a wonderful woman and much too good for me. I was an idiot to let her go."

Max hadn't planned on the last two statements but he'd been on a roll and they'd come tumbling out. But they were true. He shouldn't have pushed her out of his life. He should have held on for dear life. It was just a stupid little part in a movie. If he truly loved her - and he did - he ought to be fighting tooth and nail to give her what she wanted. Isn't that what he'd told Nate almost a year ago?

Never take a woman's dreams. Make them happen for her instead. He hadn't followed his own advice.

"I'm sure she's very accomplished," Tim said, holding up his hands in surrender. "But when you're gone for months on location is she going to understand? When rumors go around about you and your female co-star will she get upset? I think these are important questions."

Max leaned forward, his palms flat on the table. He wanted to be sure his parents heard him clearly. "You mean how understanding you were when Mum went to Rome for six weeks to make that movie with that handsome Italian actor? Like that? Because I don't think the two of spoke a civil word to one another for months."

Karen gasped and raised the napkin to her mouth as if to hide. "You don't know anything about that, Max."

"I don't? I heard you yelling at each other for weeks before you left and then the ominous silence and passive-aggressive bullshit when you returned. 'Max, tell your father it's time for dinner' when he was sitting three feet away from you. Then Dad flirting with every female between here and Suffolk to make you jealous. I'll say this for Carrie. If she was pissed at me she'd just tell me, we'd argue, and then settle it. Like adults."

Karen suddenly found the tablecloth fascinating. "You weren't meant to hear any of those arguments."

"But I did. Now we're going to have a nice dinner, but first I need you to understand that I will date and fall in love with whomever I choose. Next time I bring a girl to meet you I expect you to be nice and polite. You're actors. Pretend."

Silence fell over the table and Max dug back into his

meal. His parents might be a pain but they'd helped him frame his issues.

He still loved Carrie.

He wanted Carrie back.

He didn't care about the movie part anymore. Being without her was torture.

In fact, Max had a movie coming up as well. There might be a tiny part in it for Carrie. As soon as he returned home from dinner he'd pull out the script and give it a re-read. He'd prove to her that he could be supportive of her dreams. Then they could have a second chance.

There was only one small problem with that plan. She hated him, and he only had himself to blame.

# CHAPTER
## Forty-Three

THE LONDON SKIES were gray the day Carrie's plane touched down at Heathrow as if in sympathy for her heartbreak. Nate was done filming so he, Paige, and Carrie were coming back to the UK. She had spent three weeks in LA trying to get over Max and she wasn't sure she'd done such a great job. She'd found herself thinking about him far more than she should. She'd tried to keep busy with business but at night when she was lying in bed all the memories would come rushing back and keep her awake until the wee hours of the morning. Now she was tired, cranky, and generally bitchy.

She had only been back a few days when Tyler Gaylord called and invited her to dinner. Sick of feeling sorry for herself, she'd immediately said yes and set about putting together the perfect outfit to wear to give her confidence a boost. The weather was much cooler than LA so she chose a suede pencil skirt in red, a white lace blouse, and black knee-high boots. Taking a little extra time with her hair and makeup, she finished off the look with a swipe of crimson lipstick that matched the polish on her nails. She felt confident and put together, a far cry from her usual attire.

She'd spent way too much time in LA wearing sweat-pants and t-shirts while working at her laptop. Moping around wasn't going to change anything. In fact it, was beginning to make it worse. She needed a desperate dose of *get out of the damn house and live.*

When she entered the swanky restaurant, the maitre'd greeted her politely but reservedly. The mere mention of Tyler's name seemed to immediately perk him up though and she was quickly led to the corner table where her dinner companion was waiting. Tyler stood and grinned, pulling her in for a hug and a chaste kiss on the cheek. He'd become a good and undemanding friend.

"Thank you for having dinner with me." Pulling out her chair, he handed her jacket off to the maitre'd for safe-keeping and then returned to his own seat.

"Did you think I would cancel?"

"It was a possibility."

Carrie was glad she'd said yes for many reasons. One of them was the view from their table. It was absolutely breathtaking. With an entire wall of windows, it appeared that London was laid out before them like a feast. Opening the menu, she nodded to a table behind Tyler about ten feet away.

"Is that the Prime Minister?"

Chuckling, Tyler shot a glance over his shoulder. "Even politicians have to eat and the food here is as spectacular as the view. I promise."

Tyler's word was as good as gold. The meal was superb, one of the best she'd ever had, and they spent the next few hours talking, laughing, and catching up. She told him about all the things she was learning about the movie business while in LA and he told her about the press tour for his latest picture. The one subject they avoided was Max but it was there like the proverbial elephant in the room just waiting for one of them to bring it up. She swore it wouldn't be her. She wanted just one night of peace.

One crème brûlée - to share - and two cappuccinos were placed in front of them by the efficient but unsmiling waiter. Carrie savored the first bite of her dessert with its smooth as silk custard and sweet, crunchy topping.

"I think we should have ordered two of these," she groaned, her taste buds in heaven. "One for here and one to take home."

"I'll have the management pack you a doggy bag," Tyler teased, clicking their spoons together. "So do you want to talk about it, Red? I'm a good listener."

She didn't have to ask what "it" was.

"Not particularly. I'm trying to forget the last four months ever happened."

Tyler's smile dimmed as he nodded toward the entrance to the bar area. "Sadly, sweetheart, today is not the day you're going to be able to do that."

Twisting in her seat, Carrie's heart plummeted to her stomach and she had to fight for breath. Max, a drink in hand, was with two other men she didn't recognize and being led to an empty table far too near the one she was currently seated at. Her broken and battered heart decided at that moment to come to life again and it raced so fast it made the room spin.

Running through a dozen curse words in her head, she turned back to her dessert, effectively shutting out Max. Knowing his stiff upper lip with a dash of stick-up-the-rear-end, he'd never in a million years come over here. Too conspicuous. Too rude. It would ruin his British gentleman ruse that he had going on the world.

"Over eight million people in London and he had to walk in here and be seated right next to us," she marveled, taking another bite. "What were the odds? I must have the worst luck in the world."

She wouldn't allow herself to fidget in her chair no matter how much she felt Max staring at her back. It was like two lasers boring into her scapulas. His physical presence was palpable in the room. If she concentrated hard she could smell the citrus in his body wash.

"Do you want to leave? I can call the car service and we can be out of here in no time."

Of course she wanted to leave. But that wasn't the point. Max was friends with her friends. She couldn't run for cover every time they were in the same room. There was no time like the present to get used to this.

"Maxwell Hayes isn't going to ruin this amazing dessert. I'm going to sit here and eat every bite."

Even if it was killing her inside. Max may have broken her heart but he wasn't going to break her spirit. She still had some pride and she was going to cling to every shred of it like a life preserver in the days and weeks to come.

# CHAPTER
## Forty-Four

NATE'S EXPRESSION was grim when he opened the front door to his home and saw his best friend Max. "I ought to punch you right in the face, mate. You broke our Carrie's heart. We warned you."

Still not completely sober, Max grabbed onto the door frame for support as the ground swelled underneath him. He had to convince Nate to let him in. He needed to talk to Carrie. Desperately. He wasn't leaving until he did.

"It's not like you think," Max defended himself. Nate didn't have all of the facts. "But I need to speak with Carrie. Please let me in."

His friend's brows flew up in surprise. "She's not here. She has her own flat now. You didn't know?"

Max wasn't sure about anything anymore. All he knew is that he'd seen Carrie tonight having dinner with Tyler and it had been like taking a bullet to the heart. He was still bleeding from seeing her smile at a man that wasn't him. Frankly he didn't give a fuck what she'd done. She could shoot a man in the street and he wouldn't care. He needed her back in his life.

"I haven't seen or talked to her in awhile."

Stepping back, Nate ushered Max into the house. "You'd better come in and tell me what's going on. You look like hell. Are you...drunk?"

It was good to be out of the chilly rain. Max hung his wet jacket on one of the pegs next to the door and rubbed at his arms. Alcohol hadn't kept him warm. Or perhaps it had but it was beginning to wear off. "I'm sobering up now. I don't suppose I could trouble you for some coffee?"

"Sure, I'll make a pot. Have a seat and relax."

Nate disappeared into the kitchen leaving Max in the living room. He didn't sit down though, instead studying the framed wedding photo above the fireplace. Nate and Paige looked so happy and in love. They were truly the lucky ones.

"I can't believe you have the nerve to show your face here."

*Paige.* It was time to face her wrath and he'd known it was coming. Might as well get it over with.

"I can explain."

For a petite woman she packed a punch. She was right in his personal space, her finger poking at his chest and her expression fiery. "Explain? You want to explain why you broke Carrie's heart? Because I don't think you can justify that, you sniveling rat-faced git. I told her you were a good guy. I defended your pompous ass and then you go and do this. I can't believe you, Max."

She was the second person that said that he'd broken Carrie's heart. In his eyes, she was the one that had broken his but clearly that message hadn't been conveyed to his friends.

"Sniveling rat-faced git? I can tell you've been spending time with Nate."

"Fuck you."

Sighing, he lowered himself into a chair, exhausted and wrung out with all the emotions he'd been dealing with since seeing Carrie. "You don't want to hear my side of the story then? Because I'm not the villain here."

Nate returned to the living room, a coffee cup in hand. "If you're saying Carrie is the villain then you can just get the fuck out, mate. She didn't turn into the world's biggest horse's arse."

"I am not saying anyone is at fault. Can I please have that coffee and explain? I could use a few paracetamols too if you have them. I have a splitting headache."

"Suffer," Paige replied with relish, sitting on the couch to his left and leaning against the arm. "Now start talking before I change my mind and throw your ass back on the London streets."

With fits and starts and a second cup of coffee, Max told his story. How he and Carrie had a rough start but things had become good - very good - between them. He'd been happy and in love. When he'd mentioned the "L" word, Paige had rolled her eyes but he'd insisted that he was genuinely in love with Carrie. He'd been thinking about a future with her.

"If you *love* her so much then why did you act like a cold bastard when she returned from LA?" Paige asked in an exasperated tone. "Because I can tell you right now she didn't sleep with Tyler."

Maybe she hadn't then, but now? They'd looked happy at dinner tonight and Tyler had held her hand across the table. Max had wanted to rip his friend's arm from its socket.

"Because I was angry." Max hopped up from his seat and paced the space in front of the fireplace. "Because she used me to get a role in Tyler's movie. I'm tired of being used by women to get ahead in their careers, but I do love her."

Paige and Nate glanced at each other and shook their heads. Nate's brow was furrowed and he briefly dropped his head in his hands before replying.

"This is the first I'm hearing about Carrie taking a role in Tyler's movie. Why on earth do you think she's done that?"

"Because she was in LA when she was supposed to be in Florida. She told me she was going to her brother's party but then she was seen at a movie studio with Tyler."

Groaning, Paige's expression turned anguished. "Max, she was in Florida. I'm the one that called her in the middle of her brother's party and asked her to come to LA for a meeting with the studio. Me. Not Tyler. He just happened to be there—why I do not know. You'll have to ask him. I think they had coffee or something. That's it."

Pausing, Max regarded Paige closely for any signs of deception. She looked like she was telling the truth but he wouldn't put it past her to cover for Carrie. "Why did you want her in LA?"

Nate stood and clapped a hand on Max's shoulder. "We haven't made a big, huge announcement yet but Carrie is going to be a producer for the Flynn movie. That's why she needed to be at the studio. She'd been working on the production schedule and the budget and she was needed to make the presentation to the executives. Frankly, we thought you were already aware of this development."

*Producer? It would explain all the questions about moviemaking that she'd asked him.*

"Wait...no."

Max's sluggish brain couldn't seem to comprehend Nate's words.

Paige nodded. "Carrie is a producer. As for a role in Tyler's movie, I've talked to her every single day and she's never mentioned it so I doubt that's a real thing. I know he asked her but she was pretty adamant that she didn't want it." Throwing her arms wide in frustration, Paige gave him a pitying look. "Why did you think she'd taken a role? Did Tyler tell you?"

"Better yet," Nate interjected. "Why would you be all upset thinking she was using you to get a part in a movie? If anything, she would be using me or Paige, not that we'd care. We're the ones that introduced her to Tyler and everyone else. This didn't have a goddamn thing to do with you."

*Fuck. Just...fuck.*

It was beginning to dawn on Max exactly what he'd done. The consequences of his actions were horrific. He'd ruined his relationship with Carrie based on lies and innuendo. He'd been taken in. Again. But if Nate and Paige were telling the truth, not by her.

And he had no reason to think that his good friends were lying to him.

"Alana."

Nate shook his head, his eyes wide with shock. "No, tell me no. You didn't."

"She said..." Max couldn't speak through the lump in his throat. His stomach churned and he had an overwhelming urge to purge his very expensive dinner. This could not be happening. This could simply not be happening. "There were pictures of them together. Before. In London."

Tears were sliding down Paige's cheeks. "Max, you idiot. Yes, there were pictures but so what? You of all people know how the tabloids twist things to make them look like something completely different than the reality. You trusted that bitch? Over Carrie? How could you? Do you have any idea how much you've hurt Carrie? Do you?"

Somehow this couldn't all be his fault. "Why didn't Carrie tell me about the producing job?"

If she'd just said something, none of this would have happened. None of it.

"She said she tried when she got back to London but you said you already knew," Paige replied thickly, dashing at her wet face with the back of her hand. "But you're saying now that you didn't already know."

Replaying the conversation in his head, Max could see where it had all gone wrong. Carrie had tried to tell him her good news but he'd been so intent on the thought that she'd betrayed him he'd assumed he already knew what she was going to tell him. He hadn't wanted her to say anything so he'd interrupted her at every turn.

Because he was stupid and clearly didn't deserve her.

A fresh spate of tears ran down Paige's face. "She

couldn't do one thing right in your eyes. You were just waiting for her to screw up so you could end things. Then you could tell everyone that you were right. You knew all along that women only want you for one thing. That you have lousy taste in females. Well, this time you got it right, you fucker, but you screwed it up. So now you're not only wrong but you're alone. I hope you're happy because you deserve this. You deserve to rot in hell for what you did to her."

With that, Paige turned and fled up the stairs leaving Max and Nate alone. Swallowing hard, Max tried to formulate the words that would somehow make this less awful but he couldn't think of one single solitary thing. It was devastating. He'd lost the love of his life through his own massive stupidity.

"You fucked up, mate." Nate's accent was heavier than usual. "You're lucky Paige is letting you walk out of here with your manhood. I, on the other hand, don't have that kind of self-control."

"Listen, I know I–"

Max didn't get any further. Nate's fist connected with Max's cheekbone, sending him flying backward and into the wall with a thud and a curse. Stumbling to remain standing, he groaned and had to grab onto an end table to keep steady on his now wobbly legs. His face throbbed with every pump of his heart and it reminded him of the night he'd goaded Carrie to slap him. A little hurt to ease the big one of losing her. This pain might not be enough though. He might need to ask Nate to punch him again.

"That was for Carrie," Nate said through clenched teeth. "Paige might let you walk out of here unhurt but I can't. You need to open your fucking eyes or you're going to miss the best parts of life."

Rubbing the abused side of his face, Max grimaced. "I'll give you that one. I know I fucked up but I don't know how to fix this. What do I do? You messed up and got Paige back. What do I do now? I came here tonight to offer Carrie whatever she wanted as long as she came back to me. But my eyes are well and truly open. Now I realize I am the bad guy in this relationship but I can't think of anything that could make this right. But I love her, Nate. I really do love her."

"Balls," Nate muttered under his breath. "I can't believe I'm going to help you. You don't deserve it. Sit down and let's talk about this. There has to be something you can do. Groveling is probably your best option, but I doubt even that will work. You've fucked up well and proper this time."

Max feared his friend was right. He'd lost Carrie forever. He hated himself more than she ever could. He'd done this with his own arrogance and stupidity.

His fear of not being enough.

He'd pushed her away and he doubted she'd ever give him a second chance. But if there was even an ounce of hope he'd take it. He'd beg, plead, and grovel.

It was time to do some housecleaning in his life.

# CHAPTER
## Forty~Five

IT HAD BEEN two days since Carrie had seen Max at that restaurant. Two days of thinking about him. No, make that obsessing about him. How terrible he'd looked as if he was being tortured by demons. At first she'd been sort of evil and glad he was suffering but the more she thought about it, the sadder she became. Neither one of them was happy and this wasn't healthy. They both needed closure and to move on, otherwise this was going to eat at both of them until they were mere shadows of their previous selves.

She didn't want to feel anything for him but she was in love and to pretend otherwise would be a waste of time. Until she was over the jerk, she was going to worry about him.

Speaking of getting over a man...

Paige had called and tried to push Carrie into a blind date with some actor friend of Nate's. She hadn't admitted who it actually was but from the hints she was dropping it was going to be another famous man with too many female admirers. Carrie had had enough of those types to last her a lifetime. She'd rather be alone right now so she could heal.

Ice cream. That's what she needed. Wandering into the kitchen of her new flat, Carrie opened the freezer and contemplated her choices. Mint chocolate chip. Chocolate marshmallow. Caramel cookie swirl.

It was a mint chocolate chip kind of day so she grabbed the carton and a spoon, settling on her brand new couch. The television was on but the volume was low, more background noise than anything else. Everything in the flat was new since she still had her condo in Florida. It should have been fun picking out furnishings but instead it had been as depressing as hell. It had felt as if she was decorating a home where she would die alone.

Carrie was a third of the way through the carton when she heard a knock at the door. Few people knew she had moved from Paige and Nate's house so it was probably someone lost or maybe trying to sell her something she didn't need. She wanted to ignore the persistent and now impatient knocking but she was simply one of those people that had to answer whether it was a door or a phone. Even emails didn't sit in her inbox for long.

With an exasperated groan, she pushed herself up off the couch and set her ice cream on the table. She'd be back to it just as soon as she could dispatch her visitor.

"I'm coming. Hold your horses," she muttered under her breath, hurrying to the door.

The air in her lungs whooshed out and her knees almost buckled when she saw who was on the other side.

*Max.*

"What are you doing here?"

Carrie sounded almost normal which was an accomplishment, considering her heart was no longer beating and she couldn't seem to catch her breath.

He didn't answer her question, posing one of his own instead. "May I come in?"

*Get with the program, girl. Think. Use your head this time.*

"I can't imagine one good thing that would come from that."

His gaze dropped to the floor and then back up, those blue eyes beseeching. Jesus, she was such a fucking wimp. He gave her the puppy-dog look and she was all gooey.

"Please."

If he'd gone on and on pleading his case on her doorstep she would have said no. But it was the simple way he asked. Just one word. Quietly spoken but with so much emotion behind it. She found herself stepping back so he could enter.

But showing weakness was a terrible, awful, really bad idea. She had to stiffen her spine even when all she wanted to do was throw herself into his arms.

"You have five minutes and then you need to go."

Max didn't make a move to sit down, instead standing in the middle of her living room looking thoroughly ashamed. Good.

Like the other night, she noticed again that it appeared he'd lost weight. His cheekbones looked sharper and his eyes had a sunken appearance to go along with the dark circles underneath. His hands were shoved into his pockets and when he pulled them out they had a slight tremor.

Seeing him so emotional was doing things to her heart. That stupid organ that she'd let make far too many decisions lately. That piece of her was screaming in one ear to drag him into the bedroom but there was another voice just as loud in the other telling her to be careful.

*Don't listen to the bad man.*

Finally his eyes met hers and he nervously licked his lips. "May I have a glass of water?"

That piece of her - the part that couldn't forget what he meant to her - wanted to say yes, but she stomped on it with a virtual booted heel. No mercy. He'd given her none before.

"You won't be here that long. Now what did you want to say?"

His throat worked and then he cleared his throat. "I've done you a great injustice and in the process possibly inflicted irreparable harm to our relationship."

This was just like Max. Fifty words where a few would have done it.

"Is that the pompous ass way of saying you fucked up? By the way, there's no *possibly* about it. It's definite."

Sighing, Max shifted on his feet. "May I sit down and explain?"

Waving her hand toward the armchair, she took a seat on the couch only to find that he sat next to her, something she hadn't been prepared for. His delicious scent blindsided her and she had to dig her fingers into the flesh of her thighs to keep a lid on her tumultuous emotions.

"You've got three minutes left."

His hands rested on his knees, his palms rubbing against the material of his jeans. "I heard about you becoming the producer of the Flynn movie. I want to give you my sincere congratulations."

They'd already had this conversation and it hadn't gone well. "Thank you but you knew about that before, and if I remember correctly you said you weren't sure if I would do a good job."

That still stung. His approval shouldn't be that important to her but it was. Still. Max was at the top of his field and she wanted his respect.

"About that... I just found out yesterday actually when I visited Nate and Paige. That day I thought you were talking about something else."

Carrie frowned, her brows pinched together. "Something else? What did you think I was talking about?"

More silence. She didn't prompt him as he seemed to be trying to figure out how to answer her question. It wasn't a tough one so it shouldn't be that hard but for some reason it was. A terrible dread began to build in her abdomen. What had he done?

"I thought–I thought that you came back to tell me that you were taking a role in Tyler's next movie."

That made absolutely no sense. She'd already said a big, fat no. "Why would you think that? I know Tyler wouldn't tell you that."

Jumping to his feet, he paced the small space between the couch and television. "Look at this from my point of view, please. You were supposed to be in Florida and then someone tells me that you're in LA at the studio with Tyler. Think about how that looks."

"I was in Florida," she replied slowly, her temper beginning to simmer. "Then Paige called and asked me to come to LA. I sent you a text that my plans were changing."

Max stopped and turned to her, his chest rising and falling rapidly. "You told me you had news."

Throwing out her arms in frustration, she nodded. "Yes, that I was made a producer of the movie. That was my news."

"But see it from my vantage point."

"Okay, I will. My girlfriend calls me from LA and says she has news. She comes home to tell me that news and I'm a dick. End of story."

Max exhaled loudly, rubbing his chin. "It looked very different from where I was standing. I feared you had lied to me about your trip to the States. Plus you were seen with Tyler at the movie studio."

She had fucking had enough. "We were getting coffee. Coffee, Max. You know, that caffeinated drink I'm addicted to? We weren't at City Hall getting a marriage license. We weren't caught in a sleazy motel shacked up for the weekend. I spent an hour in his company and suddenly that means I've abandoned my career and picked up a new one. How is this possible? What Olympian mental gymnastics did you have to do to jump to those conclusions? Because I don't see it." She buried her face in her hands. "And even if I did take that role...what business is it of yours? Why were such an asshole when I came home?"

His head dropped back so he was staring at the ceiling. "Alana said–"

*Hell to the no.*

Jumping up from her perch on the couch, Carrie couldn't hold off her temper any longer.

"Don't," she said sharply, interrupting his reply. "I swear, Max, if your answer as to why you believe this was because it was something Alana told you...well...I won't be responsible for my actions."

The silence was deafening. She had her answer.

"You son of a bitch," she ground out through gritted teeth. "You believed your skanky, lying, gold-digging ex-wife over me? Is that what you're telling me?"

Carrie hadn't thought it was possible to be angrier than she was that day but she certainly was now. She was furious at the man before her. He hadn't thought any of this through at all.

Scraping his fingers through his hair, Max moved restlessly. "I didn't at first. I told her she didn't know what she was talking about. Then I called you and you were in LA much to my shock and you hadn't told me about it."

"Because I didn't want to bother you at the theatre," she flung back. "Time difference, remember? I let you call me and you'd been busy."

"You could have sent me more of a text than you did. All you said was that your plans were changing."

"I was at the airport, then on a plane, and then at the studio. The whole time I was exchanging texts with Nate and Paige as we prepared to present the schedule and budget to the studio brass. It was a big fucking deal and I was beside myself with nerves. I was a little busy with, you know, my career. But I did take the time to send you a text, Max. I sent a text that there had been a change of plans and would tell you all about it when you called. Which I did. So please tell me what I did wrong in this scenario?"

"It seemed so real," he groaned. "You were in LA and then being seen with Tyler. The two days I waited for you to come back it just ate away at me."

"How did Alana even know about the offer Tyler made me? Did you say something to her?"

He shook his head. "My former assistant is now working for her and I think Gemma got the information from Tyler's stylist. They're friendly." Moving closer, he reached out for her but she stepped back, knowing if he touched her all bets were off. She'd smack the crap out of him.

Frankly, she was still pissed the hell off.

"I'm so sorry," he said, his expression earnest, his eyes bright with unshed tears. "I am so sorry, Carrie. I love you and I want us to have a second chance. Can you forgive me? Can we try again? Do you love me too?"

It was the first time he'd said the L-word. The bastard. That he'd chosen this moment to tell her made her sick to her stomach.

"Love?" The words came out choked as tears pricked the back of her eyes. It was such a waste. These months with him had done nothing but break her heart. "You don't know what love is, Max. You don't even trust me. How can you love me?"

Wringing his hands together, he took a step toward her but once again she backed away. She had to be strong even when there was a part of her that wanted to tell him she loved him too. That they could run away together and live their life on a deserted island, just the two of them. No paparazzi, no movie studios, no interfering exes. Just sun-soaked days on the beach.

Then she remembered that she easily sunburned and freckled.

"I do trust you, love. I made a mistake but I know better now. Can we start again? Put this all behind us."

"And pretend it never happened?" she finished for him. "Sorry. Even if I could forgive, I can't forget. You treated me like I was *nothing*. Like I was dust under your feet. No explanations or discussions. I was shuttled out of your life like a pesky fan wanting too many selfies. You were *looking* for an excuse to get rid of me. It was only a matter of time and you would have found another reason. It didn't matter to you what it was or if it even made sense. You say you love me but I don't get the feeling that you really want to be with me. I need a man who will believe in me, stand by me when the going gets tough. I want a man that loves me so much he wants to shout if from the rooftops. He's thrilled and happy to have me in his life. He finds joy in love. I don't see you in that role, Max."

His anguished expression appeared real but he was one of the greatest actors on the planet, paid to mimic every emotion. It was hard to trust him when it was clear he didn't even trust himself. That's what this all boiled down to.

"I can do that," he said, his tone urgent and pleading, a few silvery tears slipping down his cheeks. "I can be the man you need me to be. I love you, Carrie. More than I ever thought it possible."

That part of her that wanted to believe was yelling in her ear and squirming under her boot. She had to grind down on it to keep it in place. Listening to it would only lead to more pain.

"I know you believe what you're saying, but even if you trust me...can you trust yourself? That's what this is about. Your fears. When will they rear their ugly head again? Because I can't take this anymore and I damn well deserve better." Sighing, she fell back onto the couch, exhaling a shaky breath. She was wrung out and exhausted. "You don't even know what you want. Do you remember that day you made that list? The big thing was that you wanted someone who could make a Baked Alaska. That's not a partner in life, Max, that's a pastry chef. I just can't take any more chances on you. I'm scared and I've been hurt far too much."

Touching her cheek, Carrie was shocked to find them wet with tears. She'd thought she didn't have any more for this man but once again she'd been surprised by how he could bring out the strongest feelings inside of her, good and bad.

"I don't want to hurt you–"

"Then leave me in peace," she shot back. "You say you love me? Then act like it. If you really love me you'd want me to be happy. Do I look happy, Max? Answer me that."

Straightening, he drew in a ragged breath. "No. No, you do not."

Standing, she walked over to the door and pulled it open. "Then please go. Let us heal and move on."

Carrie thought he might argue but he did as she asked, pausing in the doorway.

"This isn't over, Carrie. I'll be back. I won't give up on the love of my life."

If only he'd thought of her that way before throwing her out of his home.

"There's nothing for you here," she said simply, her heart breaking into a million pieces as she spoke the words aloud. "We are the very definition of the word *over*. Please leave."

She heard his footsteps on the front steps as she closed the door and locked it behind him. Not to keep him out but to keep herself in. It took all the strength she had not to fling it open and run after him, throwing her arms around him and telling him she loved him. Ignore all the warning signs that were blinking right in front of her.

Her back against the door, she slid to the floor and curled up into a ball, rocking back and forth as painful sobs wracked her body. Hot tears slid down her face and she could taste the salt on her lips. Nothing had ever felt like this. It was as if someone had cracked open her ribs and took a mallet to her heart.

How would she ever get over Max?

# CHAPTER
## Forty-Six

MAX SLAMMED two beers down on the table and slid in the booth opposite Nate. It was men's night out at the pub and they were supposed to be relaxing but there was no way he could be calm when his entire future happiness was at stake.

"I need your help."

Taking his time, Nate didn't answer right away, instead taking a long drink of his beer first.

"Give me one good reason to help you."

"You're my friend," Max retorted. "And even though I fucked up royally, you are still my friend. I want to fix this, Nate. I don't want to hurt Carrie any more than I already have."

"Did you stop by her flat yesterday by any chance? Because Paige spent a couple of hours over there last night picking up the pieces of whatever you did and eating massive amounts of ice cream. She was sick to her stomach when she got home. I blame you."

"I did and I'm sorry. I'm trying to make everything right, but I need your help."

"What did you say to her?"

The last thing Max wanted was to rehash the most painful conversation of his entire life.

"I apologized and she said she couldn't forgive me. She said that I was looking for something to be wrong so I could end it."

Nate seemed to be thinking about his reply longer than usual. "Was she wrong?"

"No," Max answered honestly. "I was scared and I didn't have trust - in her or myself. But all of this has woken me up and I don't want to be alone for the rest of my life. I love Carrie and I want to make her happy. I'd do anything she asked if she'd only give me another chance. I know I don't deserve one."

"You don't but women tend to be more forgiving than we deserve."

Max leaned forward, almost knocking over his glass. "She's the one."

Scraping his fingers through his hair, Nate groaned. "Do not make me regret this because if you manage to upset Carrie again, then Paige is going to unhappy. I don't like it when Paige is sad. Am I clear?"

"Very. Now Carrie said that I don't know what I want but I do. I just have to convince her of that."

"Piece of cake," Nate snorted. "She's not inclined to believe a single word from your traitorous lips. We're actors and therefore people are often suspicious of the things we say."

"Absolutely right. I need to make this a grand gesture

so she sees I'm willing to go out on a limb to prove myself to her. I'm willing to allow her to make a fool of me while everyone watches."

"I'm afraid to ask. What grand gesture do you have in mind?"

Max smiled and lifted his glass as if for a toast. With Nate and Paige's cooperation, he might just be able to pull this off. This was the first positive thing to happen to him in weeks.

"I have a plan."

———

Carrie and Paige stood offstage as they waited for the talk show to begin. Nate was a guest and Paige had asked Carrie along to the taping. She said it would be educational to see the behind the scenes action of making a television show. It was interesting but Carrie couldn't help but feel like she was in the way. There were people buzzing all around them, seemingly in a huge hurry while she and Paige stood casually in the wings of the soundstage.

"What is Nate promoting?" Carrie asked. "It's too early for the movie he just shot. That won't be out for at least a year. The *Thunder* movie premieres in a few months but this appearance seems a bit early. Wait...is it that animated movie he did the voice work for?"

Paige shrugged and kept her gaze trained on the set. "It's just to keep his name out there in between projects. He can talk about the play, the movie, and getting married."

The host, dressed in a bright blue suit and orange tie that assaulted the senses, took his seat at the end of a long U-shaped couch. One hand held a stack of index cards while the other smoothed his hair back from his forehead. One of the crew spritzed the top of his head with hairspray and then removed the tissues that were tucked into his collar to keep it free of makeup. Carrie could hear Paige suck in a breath as one of the crew began a countdown to air time. Why would her boss be worried?

"Are you nervous? Nate's done this a million times."

Linking her arm in Carrie's, Paige held on tightly. "It's not Nate I'm worried about."

*That was rather cryptic.*

The set fell silent and the host gave a toothy grin to the camera, oozing charm. "Good evening, ladies and gentleman, and welcome to our show tonight. We have a terrific lineup of guests and you won't want to miss this, so let's get started. The two stars from the *Thunder* movie series, Nate Mason and Maxwell Hayes, are here tonight so let's give them a big round of applause."

The introduction kept echoing in Carrie's ears.

*Maxwell Hayes. Maxwell Hayes.* It was Max. He was here. Despite everything she'd said to him that day, she couldn't control the pleasure that flooded her veins when he was anywhere in the vicinity. It might always be this way.

Paige had known about this. That would explain why Carrie's boss had a death grip on her arm. She was holding Carrie here so she couldn't flee. Not that it was even an option. Her legs were immobile, firmly rooted in the concrete below her feet.

"I can't believe you did this."

Carrie had said the words so softly she wasn't sure Paige would be able to hear them.

"He begged and pleaded. First Nate and then me."

It was hard to be angry when she knew Paige was only doing this out of love and concern. But dammit...

"Did he cry?"

Paige turned her head so she was looking into Carrie's eyes. "Yes."

"Good."

That's all Carrie had been doing so it was only fair but it didn't make her feel any better. The fact that he had been just as miserable wasn't nearly as satisfying as she'd hoped.

Nate and Max had joined the boisterous host on the couch, everyone all smiles and charm.

"You can't go on like this," Paige whispered. "I'll give you the same advice you gave me. When are you going to forgive him? When will he be punished enough?"

Carrie felt a twinge in her chest where her heart was supposed to be solidly encased in ice and locked tight. She had thought it to be dead, no longer beating. A little like her appendix. It might have had a use at one time but now it just sat there useless.

"He didn't trust me."

It came out like a whine and Carrie inwardly winced. Of all moments in her life, this one called for maturity and grace. Too bad that was in short supply even on a good day.

"He didn't trust himself," Paige whispered back as the three men on the set bantered back and forth, about what Carrie had no idea. She wasn't listening. The blood roaring in her ears made it difficult to hear anything. "He wants to now. Are you saying you won't give him a second chance?"

"Are you saying I should?"

Paige's hold on Carrie's arm tightened. "Just ask yourself one question. Are you okay living the rest of your life without him?"

Carrie already knew the answer to that. *No.* Since the day she'd ordered him out of her home she'd been anguished, fighting to keep from picking up the phone and calling him or just showing up at his front door. Unlike when she and Mark ended their engagement, she couldn't begin to fathom how she was supposed to move on without him. She wanted a future with Max. Marriage. Children. Picket fences and Sunday dinners.

She wanted to fight with him and then make up afterward. She wanted to watch his hair turn gray and the lines around his eyes to grow. She wanted his face to be the first thing she saw in the morning and the last at night. She wanted to see his blue eyes and stubborn chin reflected in a tiny human being that might have one or two of her attributes as well.

How on earth was she supposed to *get over* a love like this?

"I'm mad at him. He hurt me."

"Then be mad. Yell and scream. Just don't ruin tomorrow because you're angry today." Paige nudged Carrie. "Now be quiet and listen. This is why we're here."

Too distracted to take offense and honestly curious as to why she'd been dragged to a talk show, Carrie did stop speaking, instead turning her attention to the three men in front of the cameras. Nate was grinning and rambling on and on - as he was known to do - about the joys of love and marriage. It was lovely and sweet and Nate would surely be getting laid later tonight after extolling Paige's virtues for millions of viewers, plus the studio audience.

When Nate finally shut up, the smiling host turned to Max who looked quite somber after listening to his friend speak of commitment in such an enthusiastic manner.

"So Max, what are you looking for in a woman? What would it take to get you to settle down for good?"

Nodding, Max frowned and then reached into the breast pocket of his designer jacket, pulling out a folded up piece of paper.

"Funny you should ask that because I actually have a list of what I'm looking for. I've been working on it for a long time and I think I finally have it just right. Would you like me to share it?"

The crowd watching burst into a fit of applause and screaming. It was Carrie's turn to grip her friend's arm as the legs that were holding her upright went numb.

What in the hell was Max doing? Was he going to talk about the stupid Baked Alaska again?

"She has to hate getting up in the morning. No early birds for me. Then when she is awake, she has to need caffeine immediately. Lots of it. That's a requirement. Oh, and she should take it with lots of cream and sugar. She should want it disgustingly sweet. It should be like candy."

With a jolt her heart resumed beating, an action so painful it made her softly gasp. She'd missed part of what he'd said because now he was standing on his feet and facing her instead of the camera.

"She has to keep half of the household in her giant

handbag. She should make lists and then check them off as she finishes them. Her hair should be like a curtain of fiery red silk and her eyes as soft as brown velvet."

The block of ice encasing her heart melted and fell away. She could hear the plea in his tone, the love that no actor in the world could fake.

"She should be willing to fly thousands of miles to help her brother celebrate and then again at a moment's notice to be there for a friend. She has to want to give me lectures about being a better boss to my assistants."

He pulled a paperback from his pocket and held it up. "Her favorite book has to be *Scruples* by Judith Krantz. I really read it, Carrie. Honest to God."

A sob caught in her throat and she pressed her hand to her lips as the lock that had kept her emotions hidden away surrendered. Her perfectly calm and controlled existence was completely upended and any instinct for survival was gone. Her legs must have found the ability to move at some point because to her horror she was walking across the set, straight toward Max. Her body wasn't listening to her mind anymore. Only her heart.

This drama would play out in front of the cameras and the studio audience.

*I've lost my mind. I'm insane.*

Stopping in front of him, Carrie looked up into his eyes. The heavenly blue eyes that were currently dark with emotion. His own hands were shaking, the paper fluttering as he struggled to read from it.

"She should be able to put me in my place when I have a big stick up my arse and not let me take myself too seriously."

"I can do that."

She hadn't known she was going to speak until the words were already out there, recorded for all of posterity. She couldn't deny them if she tried. In addition to the cameras, there were hundreds of witnesses and those audience members had finally realized something very important was happening here. They were on their feet, clapping and yelling for Max to kiss her or for her to kiss him. In the distance, she could hear a voice telling him to sweep her off her feet and carry her away. Little did that man know Max had done that a long time ago, just in his own subtle manner.

There were tears, both hers and Max's. Leaning down, he shoved the paper into his pocket and raised his hands to cup her face, so gentle and tender. Any barrier she'd built up against him these last weeks crumbled into dust at his mere touch.

"She's going to have to be able to put up with my moods, my career, the loss of privacy, and my interfering parents. Can she do that? Is she willing to give me a second chance even when I don't deserve it? I love her so much."

Placing her own hands over his, she nodded. "You just had to be a drama king, didn't you? You just had to have an audience."

His smile widened and leaned down to brush his lips over her aching mouth. "What is it you always say? Go big or go home? Would anything else have convinced you?"

"I never say that. But you might have a point." Glancing toward the cameras, she raised her eyebrows in question.

"Um...I don't suppose you have a plan as to how we're going to exit the stage?"

Grinning wickedly, he swept her up into his arms bridal style, taking what little breath she had away. She had a feeling he was going to make a habit of that. Lucky her. "Of course I do. I made a list and the next item is Nate taking over the rest of the interview."

Good thing because Max didn't waste any time, carrying her offstage and through the back area to where a car was waiting for them. When they had settled into their seats, he pulled her into his arms and kissed her until she sitting on his lap with her arms around his neck.

"How many more items are on that list?" Carrie asked when the kiss ended and the car was speeding through the streets of London. "Can I see it?"

Max reached into a different pocket and retrieved a small piece of paper. "Let me know if there is anything you object to."

It was an honest to God list and it all started with Paige convincing Carrie to come to the taping. It ended with...

*Oh my.*

"This list turned pretty graphic near the end. Were you planning for us to do any of this in the car or are we waiting until we get home?"

That evil smile told her he had all sorts of plans. Lovely plans. Deliciously delightful plans.

"When we get home. I don't want to scandalize the driver, love."

He leaned down to kiss her again and she placed her hands on his chest, holding him off for just a moment.

"I'm still kind of mad at you."

His smile fell and his fingers slowly traced her lips. "I know. I have a lot of making up to do. I know that I need to prove to you that I'm ready for this. For...forever. I love you."

Carrie realized he'd never heard the words from her, despite her thinking them for a long time.

"I love you too. More than I ever thought possible."

Slowly exhaling, Max's body immediately relaxed. He'd been worried and tense. There had been no taking her for granted here today. He truly hadn't been sure of what she was going to do. In his mind, it was possible she might simply turn and walk away.

Carrie consulted the list again. "Can we do number thirteen as soon as we get there?"

"We can do it twice, if you like."

At least. Maybe more.

# CHAPTER
## Forty-Seven

MAX WAS CERTAINLY TAKING his time tonight. While Carrie had been trying to keep herself from ripping his clothes off in the car, he'd been watching her closely, his gaze never leaving her face. Those expressive blue eyes took in everything but also managed to say a great deal. He was fighting his own baser instincts. He was simply better at hiding it. His intensity was one of the things that had attracted her to him and it was exciting when all of his attention was focused solely on her. He didn't take out his phone, he didn't talk to the driver, he didn't even glance out of the window.

They'd practically fallen out of the vehicle before it came to a complete stop and then raced into the house and up the stairs, leaving a trail of discarded clothing in their wake. Now Max had her naked underneath him and he seemed determined to savor every moment of it.

His lips roamed over her jaw and ear, then down to her shoulders in an unhurried manner. His warm mouth kissed a path between her breasts and down her belly, using his tongue to tickle the sensitive flesh over her ribs. He kept her guessing where he was heading, placing feathery kisses on her instep before creating a damp trail from her knee to her hip then circling around to the backs of her knees.

Giggling as he nibbled at a toe, she held out her arms, urging him to lie on top of her. Every sweep of his tongue, every caress of his nimble fingers, and every kiss from his lips had lit a fire deep inside of her. She needed him desperately more than she'd imagined possible. They had said the words but this was important as well. A physical joining to pair with their emotional one.

"I need you," she whispered urgently, beckoning to him. "I want you."

Kneeling on the bed, he pressed his mouth to the inside of her thigh, sending a lightning bolt of arousal straight to her clit. "I want you too."

She smiled at him, hoping it was her best come-hither look. "Then what are we waiting for?"

His hands slid up her legs, pushing her thighs apart. "You are mine to love and care for. I've never been able to say that before and I'm enjoying it."

A sobering thought. Neither one of them had experienced anything like this before. If he felt a fraction of the love and devotion that she did, they wouldn't have any problems with being together forever.

And it was nice to belong to someone. She *was* his to love.

But that meant that he was hers, and that gave her an idea. Sitting up on her elbows, she reached out and ran her fingers down his hard length, drawing a strangled moan from his lips. Flattening her palms against his chest, she pushed him back onto the mattress, determined to worship his body as sweetly as he'd just done to hers.

Mirroring his actions, Carrie's lips traveled from his stubble-covered jaw, across his ridged abs, and down to his hair-roughened thighs. She would have continued on her journey but Max was an impatient and dominant man. His fingers tangled in her long hair, gently tugging her where he wanted her the most. Instead of teasing him longer, she surrendered to his demands and ran her tongue up and down the length of his cock before engulfing the head in her more than willing mouth.

Groaning, his grip tightened and she allowed him to guide her actions until he was panting, his hips arching off the mattress. Pulling off with a pop, she giggled as she kissed her way back up to his lips, their tongues tangling together. His strong hands lifted her up so she was strad-dling his body and she slowly lowered herself back down, taking in every inch he had to give her. As always, it was tight but the stretch was delicious. Sparks were already going off in her belly and she leaned forward as he thrust up, bracing her hands on his chest.

Leisurely, Carrie began to move, swaying her hips back and forth, making her entire body shudder and quake with pleasure. Max's gaze was white-hot as he watched her rise and fall, moaning with each heavenly stroke. His hands gripped her hips and suddenly she found herself flat on her back with a grinning Max hovering above her, still snug inside of her.

"You just had to be in charge," she groaned as his

mouth captured an already taut nipple, rolling it between his lips and scraping the sides with his teeth until she was writhing and begging. "Are you going to fuck me or not?"

Max chuckled in her ear, the vibrations making her tremble with need. "Does my sweet want it soft and slow or hard and fast? Ladies' choice."

Wrapping her legs around his lean middle, she dug her fingers into his muscled shoulders. "You know what I want."

"I certainly do."

Pulling out almost all the way, he slammed back in, eliciting a moan from both of them. He rode her hard, just the way she liked it and she urged him on, whispering filthy suggestions in his ear while her nails raked the damp skin of his back. Finally a man who understood that she could be a lady outside of the bedroom but in it? She was a woman who needed her man to make her scream with pleasure.

The world spun and narrowed to the two of them as she moved closer to release. Reaching in between them, Max placed his thumb on her clit so that it rubbed against the sensitive button with every thrust. It didn't take much and she was flying into orbit, stars whirling around her. Eventually they both came back down to earth, tangled together and spent.

Max lay on his back and Carrie draped herself over him, her head on his chest as he idly stroked her back. She savored the closeness and didn't want to ruin the moment with chatter or questions. There would be time for all of that later. If anything, they'd talk until they were blue in the face. It was good to just...be. She had a feeling with their busy lives these moments of peace and quiet wouldn't be frequent enough.

"You're mine to love and care for," Max said a long time later. Carrie thought she might have even dozed off for a few minutes. "To adore and worship."

"I am," she confirmed even though she'd agreed to that same sentiment earlier. "And you're mine."

"I promise that I will not take this for granted, Carrie. I know that I've been given a precious second chance. You didn't have to do it and I won't mess this up."

She could feel the rumble in his chest under her ear as he spoke.

"I know you won't. Both of us have to be more aware of how the things we say and do affect the other. We need to be kinder and more giving. Both of us. Not just you."

"I will make sure that you don't regret this." He paused, seemingly searching for what he wanted to say. "I know that you're giving up a lot to be with me - namely your privacy. From now on you'll always have to worry about cameras and tabloids."

That part did kind of suck. She was going to have to wear makeup whenever she left the house. No more yoga pants and tank tops to the grocery store.

"You're worth it. They're really interested in you anyway."

He pushed a stray strand of hair back from her face. "Once we're married and have children they'll be as focused on you as me, especially as you make a name for yourself in Hollywood completely separate from my career. If the Flynn movie is as successful as I think it will be, your name could be big in the movie business."

Carrie knew she should have been concentrating on the part of his statement where he was talking about her career but all she could think about was his casual use of the words *married* and *children*.

"Do you know what you just said?"

She might as well give him an out right now. He might be delirious from too much carnal pleasure and he simply wasn't thinking straight.

Lifting up, he moved onto his side so they were looking into his each other's eyes. "I know exactly what I said. Do you not want to be married? Or do you not want children?"

"I want both." Her honest answer tumbled from her lips before she could even think about a less embarrassingly eager reply. "I've always wanted four or five kids, actually."

His smile was breathtaking and he leaned down to press a soft kiss to her lips. "Me too. I'd like to start trying right after the wedding, maybe even on our honeymoon."

"I'd like that too."

It was hard to believe that this was truly happening. He loved her, wanted to marry her, wanted them to be a family. It was all she'd ever dreamed of and now he was offering it to her. It was like being given the world on a silver platter.

"Big wedding or small?" He frowned and rubbed his chin. "We should check our schedules and see when we have our next break. I don't want to wait any longer than we have to, plus I know we'll want Paige and Nate to be there so we'll have to check their schedules as well. Should we start making a list?"

She'd created an organized, list-making monster. There was a time and place for that.

"Yes, but not now." Carrie ran a fingertip over his jaw and then down his chest. "I have other plans for you. I love you."

A brow lifted and a smile bloomed on his handsome face. "Plans? I am yours to love. Have at it, my sweet girl. I love you too."

They'd plan their wedding later. Right now, they'd practice the honeymoon.

*I hope you enjoyed Max and Carrie's happily ever after! Look for Tyler's story in Wild On The Red Carpet!*

*Thank you for reading Swinging On A Star!*

# About the Author

Olivia Jaymes is a wife, mother, lover of sexy romance and mystery, and caffeine addict. She lives with her husband, son, plus two spoiled dogs in central Florida, spending her days with handsome alpha males and spunky heroines.

Visit Olivia Jaymes at
www.OliviaJaymes.com